Henry First

A Story of Excess

Basil Lawrence

PELTA BOOKS

PELTA BOOKS
www.peltabooks.com

PELTA™ is a trademark of Furness Kindle & Flint Ltd

Published by Furness Kindle & Flint Ltd
London, United Kingdom

4 6 8 10 9 7 5 3

Read more at www.h1novel.com

PUBLISHER'S NOTE

This is a work of fiction. Names, characters, places and incidents either
are the product of the author's imagination or are used fictionally, and
any resemblance to actual persons, living or dead, business
establishments, events, or locales is entirely coincidental

All adaptations of the Work for film, theatre, television and radio are
strictly prohibited

The second half of Chapter 6 appeared in somewhat different form in
The Mechanics' Institute Review

British Library Cataloguing in Publication Data
A catalogue record for this book is available from the British Library

ISBN-13: 978-0-9574945-1-0

The text of this book is set in Garamond

Printed and bound by CreateSpace
Charleston SC, United States of America

'Basil Lawrence has a unique writing style, and a comedic flair that works wonders throughout this novel . . . A joy to read, a book that brings about plenty of laughs, and a well constructed story from beginning to end, *Henry First* is the kind of book that we'd like to discover more often.'

—*Red City Review* ★★★★★

'A restaurateur takes desperate measures in Lawrence's delectably dark debut novel . . . The show must go on and does, with deliciously droll scenes . . . wickedly comical moments . . . snappy dialogue . . . The tone is surprisingly light, like an airy soufflé.'

—*Kirkus Reviews*

'an entertaining, darkly satirical novel . . . readers will enjoy peeling the layers to get to the core of the author's witticisms'

—*BlueInk Review*

'Simultaneously funny, dark, and stomach-turning, *Henry First* is a captivating commentary on our fame-obsessed culture. Highly recommended for those who like their social commentary with a little bite' —*IndieReader* ★★★★½

'Laced with potent dark humor . . . [a] sardonic look at the competitive world of gourmet cooking. In this complex recipe for literary success, Basil Lawrence steeps myriad ingredients in a broth so rich that *Henry First* may require a second reading for hidden nuance.' —*Foreword Reviews* ★★★★★

'a great book for clubs and classes; there are plenty of questions to ponder when the novel ends'

—*San Francisco Book Review*

'a dark satirical commentary on the absurdities of contemporary first world society . . . *Henry First* places emphasis on societal observations and sophisticated humor'

—*Portland Book Review*

'Peppered with an exquisite cast of supporting characters . . . this novel is meticulously constructed and a seductive delight . . . [A] literary feast for the senses . . . highly recommended!'

—*Literary Fiction Book Review*

ALSO BY THE AUTHOR

Plays

Modern Eating Habits

To my parents

PART I

The Competition

CHAPTER 1

Down in the Kitchen

HENRY FIRST was dying in the kitchen. Today's competition was conspiring to kill him: it felt like his chest was about to implode.

He watched Xun's knife slicing carrots – *whut-whut-whut* on the board – and as those orange strips marched away from the vegetable chef's blade Henry was convinced that he was doomed. It was his only thought – his brow showed the lines – and, for the moment, contemplating death seemed to be the only way of surviving the competition.

'Two minutes, everyone,' Henry said, and his sous chef, Zhou, nodded. 'And get Xun to sort out these vegetables.' Henry picked one up. 'I need them thinner. I could nail someone to a cross with this carrot.'

'Yes, Chef.' Zhou peered over the fryer, his face still rough from that morning's hasty shave now basked in the oily steam, and he began shouting at the entremetier in Mandarin.

Henry caught sight of the juicer. He had been trying hard to ignore it all morning. His restaurant was failing but his wife had insisted on buying a juicing machine the size of Wyoming.

On top of this, his early start meant he'd skipped his run and now he could feel his muscles growing loose and unloved. He really should go for a jog when he got home that evening, or run twice the distance the following morning. Perhaps the pain in his chest meant that he wasn't strong enough to withstand the perseverance that success entailed. If only he'd already finished with this competition, and then he could thank everyone sincerely and get on with his life . . .

The juicer squatted on the shelf, taunting him. 'Chin, unplug that thing and put it back in its box.'

'Mrs Dolores –'

'*In* the box,' Henry said, unable to talk about his wife. 'I need you cutting meat.'

'Yes, Chef.'

Henry watched the man return the chrome monstrosity to its cardboard box and haul it to the delivery door which opened onto the alleyway. As Chin was about to return to his station, where he operated the meat slicer, Henry motioned to his sous chef. 'Zhou, get them together for a meeting *dun shi.*'

Zhou waved his arms about as though fanning flames or bringing an aircraft in to land, and most of the staff moved towards Henry.

'Where are the waiters?' Henry said. 'Do I have to think for everyone . . .'

Henry had arrived in the restaurant kitchen at 4 a.m., and already it felt as though he'd been there for years. The roast cook had been joking at the grill, but now he saw Henry watching him.

'Jiang, leave the sauce and get over here,' Henry said. 'Zhou, are we having this meeting or aren't we?'

Shoes then legs then torsos as the waiters ran down the stairs. Zhou herded everyone to the area in front of the cold store.

'As you know, we're on full staff today for a reason,' Henry told his employees. 'In one hour the judges arrive. They're our number one priority. Everything else waits – our success depends upon it. Ng and the others will keep them happy front-of-house. It's our job to make sure this kitchen produces something extraordinary. Ng, if the judges decide to tour the facilities, let Zhou and me know pronto. Understand?'

Nods all round and 'Yes, Chef,' in unison.

'Chef, it's only one course?' Ng, the head waiter, asked.

'Yes, lampreys with lemon. I'm preparing the fish with Kong. For everyone else it's business as usual. Questions? No? Let's get this show on the road. *Dong shou.*'

Zhou began shouting like a drill sergeant and soon everyone was back at their station. Kong, meanwhile, collected the fish from the cold store. Henry pressed his thumb into the flesh: ugly little mothers, but as fresh as can be. He sliced lemons for the sauce, his knife working faster than thought. Around him everyone settled and the earlier disarray was transformed into a professional kitchen with its noise and aromas and heat – elegant to watch. Smiling because he loved the harmonious machine that he was part of, he began working on the lampreys.

The printer made a short high-pitch noise before spitting out a piece of paper with an order from the dining room upstairs and soon these little white paper rectangles formed a neat queue on the steel shelf above the serving area.

'Two times lamb cutlets, one time sole *lasserre*,' Shui read out loud. 'One time winter salad table seventeen.' Someone acknowledged the order and repeated it.

Whut-whut-whut. Xun's knife sliced through acres of vegetables. Behind him Chin cut through the bone of a dead mammal with the meat slicer.

'Keep them fine, Xun,' Henry shouted, 'or you're back on the boat.'

'One tomato soup with garnish, partridge and olive starter, chestnut soup and stuffed marrow. All table thirteen. Where's salad for seventeen?' Another blip.

There was spluttering at the grill and flames leapt up at Huo.

'Bring more lemons,' Henry said to Kong as the kitchen filled with the smell of burnt hair.

'*Re huo shao shen*,' Zhou said and the others laughed. If you stir up the fire you burn your fingers.

'As long as it's you and not the customer's food, Huo,' Henry called, then wiped his knife on his apron before taking a quick tour of the kitchen, from station to station – quizzing, tasting, shouting.

'Two shrimps *mariette*, table eight. One asparagus *nordaise*, one winter salad and one crab starter, all table two.'

'Lim, we need those salads today. Keep it together, people.'

'Yes, Chef.'

Kong had fetched the lemons.

Ng ran down the stairs two at a time calling out, 'Table seventeen!'

'One gazpacho, one lamb cutlets, one stuffed marrow and two hollandaise soups, table five.'

'Table seventeen!'

'We need winter salad,' Zhou shouted. 'Anyone?'

Good man, Henry thought.

Earlier that morning he'd told Dolores that out of adversity came greatness. She'd told him not to get his hopes up yet, but today was his day – yes, he could feel it. A positive attitude conquers anything.

Whut-whut-whut.

'Table thirteen's clear,' Shui said and Lim grabbed the four plates and was up the stairs. He was replaced by two more waiters.

'Winter salad,' Ng shouted.

'You tell them, Ng.'

'Yes, Chef.'

Kong stirred the sauce and Xun worked the knife and Huo and his brothers used flame and the machine yelled as Chin cut through bone and flesh.

'This is all you do, Kong – you keep that spoon moving. I don't care if the restaurant burns down around you. I need this sauce as smooth as your mother's milk. I don't want to come back and find it's curdled and rancid.'

'Yes, Chef.'

The orders were coming quickly – the blips now a continuous bleep – and as he watched Zhou directing this orchestra an underground train screamed past in a nearby tunnel and Henry heard its carriages jumping and hopping along the pitted tracks. Kong worked the spoon, Xun the knife, Huo the flame, Chin the blade.

Ng ran down the stairs. 'Chef, a message from Mrs Dolores. The judges going to be here soon, Chef.'

Damn. 'When?'

'Next ten minutes, Chef. She's not so sure.'

'Kong, focus on the sauce.' The kitchen was noisier still, each station an industry of chopping and slicing and preparing; spoon, knife, flame, blade. 'Get Dolores down here,' Henry said as Ng went back up with eight steaming plates.

Kun beat the steak. Kong dared not look up from the sauce. Xun had gone AWOL. Huo had burnt his sleeve. Zhou was losing the plot. Still no Dolores.

'Mu,' Henry called over a waiter, 'get Ng back here pronto.'

'Yes, Chef.'

The man scampered up the stairs with three soups and a stuffed marrow starter.

'Chef, I need to talk to you,' said Zhou. Something about the washing-up area, about the reasons for Fang's behaviour yesterday: an imprisoned brother and an unwanted operation. Zhou's mouth chewing the difficult English words while around them the kitchen deciding between inefficiency and failure.

'Do you think now is the best time to have this conversation?' Henry said, but Zhou didn't stop talking. His glasses looked like two smudged discs hovering in front of his eyes; a cobweb of fingerprints covered their surface. Constant readjusting and lifting those plastic frames. The verbal onslaught continued. *Not today!*

'Kong, how is that sauce coming along?' Henry shouted.

Kong nodded. 'Fine, Chef.' Huo grilled. *Whut-whut-whut*. Xun was at his station. Zhou opened his mouth once more –

The air turned pink.

Afternoon light underground? Henry speculated. Or am I having a stroke?

There was another burst of warm light as the blade took a second bite of Chin's left hand. The engine yelped like a kicked dog and the slicer spun to a halt.

A fine spray of blood and bone settled on their white tunics.

Everyone stopped work. Meat was left burning on the grill.

An afternoon that had been quick and that lacked thought or spontaneity began to wobble. Everything around him lost balance. Henry lost control of his life. He looked at Chin then closed his eyes. Now he really was dying. He'd meant to speak to Dolores about the machine. And yet . . . He felt sick.

Chin stared at Henry. Flecks of red had arced across the tiles and the cement floor. Bao's podgy walk had been interrupted first by the slicer's short sharp cry and then by a half skid; his left arm slammed into the steel countertop to prevent himself from falling, the bang making them all jump. Eyes found Henry, eyes were on him, eyes waited for him to . . .

Henry ran past Bao, looking at the floor – the red dots had smeared into a long skid mark that ended in a shoe-print – careful not to slip. And as he ran he heard a siren – how the hell did they get here so fast? – but then he realised the sound was Chin screaming.

Chin held his left forearm snug against his chest. His armpit was wine red. Up close Henry could see the thick liquid moving from fibre to fibre in his white shirt.

'Get First Aid,' he called out to Zhou. 'And an ambulance.'

'Yes, Ch–'

'And Dolores. Someone get Dolores down here.'

Henry knelt before the man, uncertain what to do. He prayed that the blade hadn't eaten anything vital, and then he was amazed to see a pair of clean hands lifting Chin's meaty right arm and extracted his bloody left hand. His own hands. Chin was crying. Henry caught a glimpse of Chin's stubby hand. Only the little finger and thumb remained. He could make out only a few of the words the injured man screamed: *'Shou zhi! Shou zhi!'* Fingers.

Henry called again for Zhou to bring the First Aid box as he watched the blood ooze. Then he had the box. He threw back the plastic clips. Dolores was next to him, yelling and calming everyone at the same time. Henry's hands shuddered against the hard dimpled case as he searched for something – anything. Now Dolores was on the phone. Fang knelt down beside him. Tied a cloth around Chin's wrist. Staunched the dark flow. Henry kept searching the box for something to assist. Anything to ease the man's pain.

'Dolores,' he said softly as he felt himself calm down and start thinking about what to do next, 'tell them that we'll meet the ambulance at the delivery entrance. They can get in back there. No sirens.'

She nodded.

'And tell them to get here now.'

He asked Zhou to take the others away. Give Chin some air. Fang's knots were precise and methodical. He neatened the bunny-eared flaps of cloth before tying and pulling the fabric stiff and tight.

'Shou zhi,' Chin said. 'Chef, please help me find my fingers.' His cries had turned into a soft lament: my-fingers-my-fingers-my-fingers . . . Of course.

Henry, Dolores, Zhou, everyone searched frantically for the fingers. They peered down the gaps behind the counters and between the red-splattered pans.

There was a clatter of shoes running down the stairs and he heard Ng announce that the judges had arrived.

'Ng, stay up there,' Henry said. He watched Ng take in the scene and realise what everyone in the kitchen was looking for. 'Go up and let them in. No, don't come any closer.' They were all tainted with sprinkles of blood. 'Get back up there, keep the other waiters up there, and let the judges in. You need to stay calm. Mrs Dolores has called the ambulance. Ng, go!'

Ng ran back up.

'They'll be here soon.'

Chin shivered. 'I need something,' he said. 'Alcohol.'

'Let's wait for the ambulance.'

'Yes, Chef.'

Henry called Zhou who was helping the others with the search and told him to take control. 'Xun will look for the fingers. Get the others back to work. Dolores will close the restaurant after the judges leave.' Chin shook uncontrollably. 'Close your eyes and try and relax,' Henry told him.

'The ambulance will be here shortly to take you to City Hospital, Chin,' Dolores said.

The kitchen was quiet. Xun, searched for the fingers. Chin closed his eyes.

'They'll be here soon,' she said as she held him close, comforting him.

'I'll go with Chin to the hospital, Dolores,' Henry said. 'I'll need you to stay down here.'

Behind him he could hear Zhou beginning to fill the waiters' orders.

'Close shop when the judges leave,' he told Dolores. 'And please ask Zhou to prepare the lampreys. Until then, we need to pretend this isn't happening.'

The paramedics arrived and carried Chin on a stretcher up the back stairs and out to the old loading bay. Henry felt strangely deflated; there was no adrenalin rush, nothing punchy. Someone was injured and they were there to help.

He followed the men closely and watched them slide the stretcher into the ambulance as if they were shoving a roast into an oven. There was something televisual about that action – he had watched these scenes many times before, seen similar paramedics elevating arms and loading ambulances. The nightmare afternoon rumbled on.

'What happened?' the paramedics had asked when they first arrived. 'He's cut his hand?'

'He cut his hand on a machine,' Henry said.

As one emergency worker climbed into the ambulance he was still asking questions: 'He's cut off a few fingers?'

'What?' said the second paramedic.

'Fingers' – Henry nodded – 'and I'm coming along with you.'

He climbed into the ambulance and huddled on the empty stretcher beside Chin. The vehicle sped down the alleyway, sirens blaring, and turned into the nearest avenue where they were confronted by the lunchtime traffic jam.

Henry watched the paramedics working. One clasped the stiff white-bandaged hand and raised it slightly. An oxygen cuff masked Chin's face. The other located a strap and shimmied it up Chin's good arm, and then began prodding and inspecting the veins. Then the man tried puncturing the skin with a needle.

'I don't think I'll get a fourteen in him,' he said, and this was followed by a *pok* noise. 'Nope, I was wrong. There you go.'

The ambulance leapt forward. The medic strung up a plump bag of liquid with the word lactate printed on the side. They lurched back. The man neatened the cable and then fastened a tube to the needle and secured the tube to Chin's arm with an inch of white tape.

Around them the ambulance's plastic Lego interior vibrated. The windows were edged with thick black rubber and on a shelf between the biohazard container and medical appliances was a box of tissues – household and nonthreatening beneath the calibrating equipment and an old No Smoking plaque.

Henry peered through the back window. Behind him cars were being angled into the gaps between the rows of trucks and vans. They were turning the four-lane road into a seven- or eight-lane highway.

He jumped as the driver gave a blast of a loud, business-like siren. The people in the cars behind them looked away from the noisy ambulance.

'We were parked behind your place eating lunch,' the first paramedic was telling Henry.

'Let's go!' their driver shouted, her head slamming back against the seat as she hit the horn. 'Scoot! Move it!' An even louder siren cut through the van.

'We couldn't find my fingers,' Chin was saying.

'What did he say?' asked the paramedic.

'It's no use,' Henry said. 'We looked, but they could be anywhere in the kitchen.' He saw what he thought was a picture of an archangel stuck onto the oxygen canister; he shook his head.

The ambulance jerked forward, stopped suddenly, and then they were on the move again, pounding up the road.

Henry hit the side of the vehicle as it turned a corner into a slow-moving tributary that had been dammed by a bus at the next cross-street.

'How much longer?' he asked.

The paramedic beside him looked out the window. 'Who knows with the traffic? Twenty, thirty minutes.'

'Nah,' the driver shouted. 'It only takes about ten minutes to walk.'

'Uh-oh, he's going,' the paramedic said as Henry felt the cars and city soften around him, everything losing focus.

Cold air. The confusion inside the ambulance returned when he opened his eyes. Its back doors were open and snow had settled on his arms.

'Welcome back, Cook,' the paramedic said.

Outside the city blocks had given way to a squat hospital surrounded by white trees. More dots floated about the air and Henry leapt out of the vehicle unassisted. After the grinning paramedic had helped him up from the gravel he caught a glimpse of Chin being wheeled through an entrance marked Emergency.

Henry never thought about calling Dolores until the forms had been signed, the bills paid, and he'd spent three hours in a bar across the street, worrying about Chin. By then it was too late and Henry knew he was a dead man.

CHAPTER 2

The Critic

SNOW FELL on grey buildings. It brushed finials and gargoyles, drifted past office windows and then floated over the bands of brick and glass before resting on the concrete park. Winter scraped the city's walls, and soon faint chips of plaster were spun off by the cold until the late-afternoon air was dry with flakes of snow and stone. A man walked across the square – the roads were full of humming cars, the only constant in the city – while around him the buildings were turning white and soft: fading landmarks that circled Golden Square.

Grant Whant glanced up at the city, his pockmarked face red from the wind, and the comparisons came naturally to him. Icing. Frosting. Lard. Bone. Teeth. He was in his early forties, his fine hair and shiny scalp adding an extra decade, and his suit had grown tight. He kept walking, ruining his shoes.

Running across the top of a building on Golden Square's eastern side were large steel letters, each the size of a man preparing to jump: BROAD WAY BUILDING. Today's bad weather almost changed the words to DOOMSDAY BUILDING. In the alleyways around the square the rusting delivery bays provided shelter to vagrants. Nightclubs outnumbered the stores; the boards advertising vacant premises outnumbered the nightclubs; the empty stores outnumbered everything. This ghetto was waiting for small-time investors confident enough to believe that they had found a bargain. And at street level, in the centre of the building and in the direction that Grant was heading, was a restaurant.

On the roads feeding into the square cars side-winded across black ice, their tyres thrumming as the drivers spun the steering wheels. It was snowing heavily and by now Grant's eyes were wet from the cold and the traffic fumes. He watched two cabs colliding in slow-mo on the road to his left: the back end of one bounced onto the pavement and came to rest on rubbish bags while the other car was jettisoned into the centre of Golden Square, kicking up sparks and sludge.

When he reached the far end of the square he saw people at the tables in Firsts. Dolores's rent-a-tramps? While waiting to cross the road he looked for Dolores though the glass windows wet with condensation. The traffic lights blinked green then red, halting the cars, and he walked up to the glass doors.

Once inside the restaurant he noticed that the people occupying most of the tables were not as neat as they'd first appeared. Waiters held up trays with glasses of alcohol but not much food.

Standing there, Grant realised that he'd forgotten about the ducting and piping that hung just below the restaurant's ceiling, the once-elegant curves that crossed and grouped and sub-divided above the diners, like a throwback from a previous decade. The room was also much larger than he remembered from when he first reviewed the joint. 'These rough, cathedral walls,' would be a solid enough start to the article he'd write about this experience. Waiters ran down the stairs on his left. Such a racket. A dumb waiter discreetly built into a wall would be preferable. Never mind . . .

No one else paid much attention to the outsized paintings hanging on the far wall. He looked at the patrons, then at the staff, willing someone to come over and greet him, and perhaps even offer to lead him to a table. Dusty white certainly played a large role in the design palette, as though selected by Miss Havisham.

Then he chided himself because this place was preferable to the contrived restaurants that filled the city, and he felt himself warming to its naïvety. If anything, Firsts was a quaint, harmless hell – trying hard to impress – that would forever be stuck halfway between the grotesquely fabulous places uptown and the seedy unfabulous joints further south. What wasn't there to like? And still he waited for a table.

He knew the judges' type, the sort of people they would be. They didn't give a continental about the food, and instead they would be concerned about ambience and their own self-importance. They expected a spectacle.

Patrice Czarny – Sunday Magazine editor, Amazonian goddess and Grant Whant's manager – was in charge of Furness Kindle & Flint's food division, FK&F Food, and she also oversaw Furness Kindle & Flint's restaurants, FK&F Restaurants. The FK&F restaurants were direct competition to this naïve, non-corporate restaurant Grant stood in, and were successfully bankrupting such independent restaurants every day.

There had been a time when the independents thrived, but under Patrice's rule the FK&F restaurants had changed from airport canteens into establishments that almost resembled restaurants. And while she was no culinary role model she certainly knew how to give everyone a memorable time.

Although Grant was employed by FK&F, Patrice liked him to maintain the pretence of impartiality (this meant she refrained from flattering him – 'the city's best food writer,' etc. – in the weeks leading up to the launch of a new FK&F restaurant), and he was about as impartial as an employee could be.

Earlier that morning she had been trying to encourage him to turn his reviews into celebrity fests. 'Without food, no one survives,' she had assured him, 'but civilians love reading about famous people. Go on, blend the two.' Blend, mix, knead. He listened politely and was toying with the idea of featuring a recipe for bread in his next review. He would never do this, but it made him smile.

He remembered the looks on the faces at Patrice's last bash: everyone convinced that they were witnessing something spectacular, and yet for him that FK&F restaurant had been derivative and formulaic, designed to appeal to the reptilian parts of the brain – he felt the same way about the weekly magazines that traded in misery and disease. The judges would be expecting one of Patrice's modern freak shows where wealthy intellectuals could get drunk and allow themselves to gawp at the less fortunate because everything was so heavily ironic. Firsts was just too white.

At last he saw Dolores's slim figure. She appeared to be leading two tourists to a table. Both men carried cameras. She smiled at Grant after she'd pulled out a chair for one of the men.

The tables looked different from Grant's previous visit. Neater: a small vase with iris; salt and pepper; ashtray; wine glasses and the cutlery framing the little explosion of linen napkin in the centre of each plate.

He tried not to stare at any of the patrons for fear of starting a turf war. His memory of a confrontation earlier that morning was still sharp. 'Got a problem?' the crazy had shouted at him on the train. Thank you for your enquiry into the general state of my mental health. I'm happy to confirm that, apart from your paint-stripper breath, I am problem free. In fact, let's declare me a problem-free zone. The spat had meant that Grant was invisible to the other people in the carriage, and he heard himself apologising when it became clear that no one else would join him in battle.

A fat man was sitting at a table in the rear of the restaurant. Grant found it difficult not to stare – again, that morning's memory – but his eyes were drawn to the man. The man's hands looked like shrivelled appendages: propellers mounted on a zeppelin. He ate like a real fat person. In Grant's experience, the obese were very dainty eaters, treating food with great respect when they consumed it in public. The thin and mildly overweight were the real swines at the dinner table: galloping and gasping their way through their meals; wolfing down air; spluttering and farting as though each course was a race to dessert. Instead, this man was dissecting his meal with a toothpick knife and a toothpick fork – he worked like a very methodical, very large surgeon treating a very small, very sick animal. When he was happy with the quantity of salad he'd balanced on his fork he conveyed it to his almost reticent lips. It was like watching Miss Manners. Top marks for etiquette, only please don't eat the judges.

'You made it,' Dolores said as she swept over to Grant with outstretched arms. Her enthusiasm surprised him because they'd met only briefly in the past, and he was touched by how keen she was on winning this competition. He caught sight of her drab shoes – scuffed and plain, the colour of unripe apples. She wore a cocktail dress with a plastic armband in the shape of a serpent that dug into her bicep. He predicted the fare would be equally uninspiring and he'd compose his witty review for the Sunday Magazine before consuming a single aperitif. The place would not survive.

'This is me doing glamorous,' she said. 'And aren't these people fabulous? Best guests I've had all year. So well-behaved.'

'Why are you talking like that?'

'Oh, darling, it's all gone to my head.'

'With this lot,' he said softly, 'I wouldn't be surprised if the police find your blood-splattered corpse in the dumpster outside.'

'That comes later, I'm sure. Let's get this off you.' She helped him out of his coat and gloves. 'Are my guests making you nervous?'

'To be honest, they look more together than the perps I work with. And I see you've made friends with Tiny back there.'

'He's a paying customer, is Mr Jolly, a renowned plastic surgeon. And you're being very rude.' She led him to a table. 'Does this one suit you?' It was next to the judges' table.

He nodded – he was warming to Dolores. 'When are the gods expected?' he asked.

'Who?'

'The judges.'

'Oh, *those* gods. I've been on the phone with your magazine and still no one can tell me anything. Where does your company get those people from?'

He shook his head. 'Pissup . . . brewery . . . go with the flow, Dolores. Mañana, mañana. Perhaps later I get to help Henry clean your brains off the floor.'

'Ng,' she called one of the waiters. 'Get Mr Whant a drink. We have a fantastic new range of fresh juices. No? Fetch a menu.'

Grant ordered wine. 'Forget the menu,' he said. 'What are you feeding the judges? I'll have some of that.'

'For some reason, Henry's got a bee in his bonnet about lampreys. He reckons that because the other restaurants will be going over the top, he needs to give them something pure and simple.'

'That gets my vote,' Grant said. 'And I suggest you get this lot drunk. The atmosphere in here isn't very conducive to digestion. It feels like they're waiting for the Second Coming. Christians versus the rest.'

'Don't you need a pen and paper?'

'In my head, my dear, all in my head. Feel free to carry on with whatever you need to, you know, *do*.'

She left him at the table and he spent some time thinking about what he would change if he owned this restaurant. The fat man had stopped eating, his pig-eyes blinking in the harsh light. Still no judges. Grant was scrolling through the list of missed calls on his phone when Ng brought him the wine.

He preferred to think of himself as a writer, and not as a journalist or a food critic but a real writer. A creator. A wordsmith. This pretension hid a fear that he was becoming – had become – a faceless employee. A number cruncher. A sometime hack. However, despite these fears and the countless hardships that came with working for a multi-national corporation, his column was fluffy and bouncy and all meals were reduced to his ratings trinity: GOOD for the restaurateurs who chanced to assign him a smooth Nordic waiter for the evening (he frequently awarded top marks); FAIR to the middle band; POOR to all others. Today, Firsts would receive a FAIR – a high FAIR – because Henry First was six foot two with white-blond hair.

He could hear someone slurping soup. Then the main course arrived at the table on his left and he watched as the diners – a Boris and a Doris Karloff – peered down at the inch-thick piece of meat lying on their plates. Each piece of beef was the size of a hand, veined and seared a delicate brown, with a thin rind of gleaming fat.

The steak resisted cutting, and Grant was drawn to the swaying movement as the she-ogre see-sawed her knife back and forth through the flesh. He was mesmerised by the blade's pornographic, in-out-in-out rhythmic humming sound. Then the woman neatened the isosceles of meat she had hacked loose, gently patting the flat of her blade against its weeping edges, before stabbing it with her fork and thrusting the whole thing into her mouth.

He looked away, nauseated, because he felt as though he'd witnessed something inhuman.

The Doris took another bite of flesh, and she smiled at Grant when she caught him staring at her; as she grinned he saw the gnawed bolus resting on her tongue like a fresh turd.

Perhaps Patrice was right, he thought; perhaps food was the ultimate commodity. The topic was surrounded with sufficient fanaticism and fervour. Over the past few years he'd seen food stories escape from the review section of the magazines to the front covers: health scares, famine, you name it. Even the fashion pages had become a gentle commentary on food deprivation: where would they be without glam photographs of frantic celebrities who regularly stuck fingers down their bloodied throats? And now Patrice wanted him to add to this noise.

'Hot food can be the scene of some very Cold Wars!' she wrote in a recent email. No one who witnessed the foodplosion in the final decades of the last century (portly anchors introducing clips of skeletal children whose skin and hair and starving bodies auto-digested before pizza-guzzling viewers) could deny this. Of course he knew she wasn't interested in that type of war. She wanted minor skirmishes among mild-mannered socialites and not the mega-death atrocities committed by warlords. Millions starved, but the dinner parties made headlines, got news-flashes, sold FK&F magazines.

'Food is a most effective celebrity weapon!' her mail continued, warming to the topic. It would be easy to do what she wanted, to retreat into this dazed, sated self-absorption. He could compliment and fetishise new fads; he could be a reliable war correspondent:

> Only on rare occasions will the naïvest hostesses fail to detect the threat behind a whispered request for more salt. Victory can never be declared. Nothing is ever assured at the dinner table. Social guerrillas can snuff out a gourmet's triumph with feeble, whispered phone calls to the press revealing details of anguished, E. coli-induced sleepless nights. These are dangerous times in the city. This is the story of one of those wars.

*

Wine stewards began filling glasses with water. When one reached a nearby table Grant told him, 'Alcohol, not water. Get these people drunk. Where's Dolores?' The man shrugged and called Ng, watched as Grant repeated his request, and then Ng said something that Grant couldn't quite understand and all three nodded at one another. He tried again.

At the table beside his, the woman was still chewing her way through the steak. He imagined her grinding loose the striplets of meat from the chunk of beef. After a hard gulp, she took a swig of the fizzy water to force the meal into her gut.

Grant saw Dolores talking to Ng.

'Give me a sec,' she said to Grant and then took Ng a few paces away from his table.

'Problem?' he heard Ng say.

The woman was laughing and took another bite of meat. Dolores went down to the kitchen with Ng. At the front desk the phone rang and he heard Dolores's greeting on the answer machine. 'Hi, this is Stacey,' said a loud voice at the other end of the line, 'with the *judges*. We're *stuck* in traffic about a block away from your place. We expect to be there in five . . . ten . . . who knows. Anyways, I've been asked to call you to, you know, to tell you that we're going to be there like *imminently*. Look forward to seeing you when we see you or whatever.'

Still no sign of his wine or fish, and the restaurant could do with some music. Dolores came back up the stairs and it took her a while to see him waving at her.

He told her about the message. 'Dolores, are you OK?'

'Yes, sure.' She sent someone who looked Rohypnolled and perhaps a bit frightened to tell Chef. 'Go tell Chef!' She spent about a minute neatening the judges' table and then went down into the kitchen.

Ng, head-waiter, hovered at the top of the stairs in the way of the other waiters who were going down with plates.

Grant saw a flash outside as a limo door opened. No sign of Dolores. There was a whip of cold air as Ng stepped out of the restaurant. Movement in the limo. After a kerfuffle out stepped a young girl who was followed by the Marx brothers: a Harpo; a Chico; a Zeppo; a Gummo; a Groucho.

The judges had settled at their table. They all looked sleepy and a bit second-hand. Competition rules forbade the consumption of alcohol or stimulants and Ng directed the steward to pour some mineral water.

Stacey, their chaperone, was chatty; the judges looked bored: they wanted to eat and leave. The longer they waited the worse it would be for the Firsts. Grant watched as they looked at their fellow diners and then conferred. He called over a young waiter who was carrying two bowls of soup.

'Where's Dolores?' he asked the waiter. The man smiled. Does anyone speak English any more? he wondered. '*You* need to tell *Dolores* to bring *food*,' he said as quietly as he could. '*Judges.*' This was ridiculous. Aware that the judges were watching him, Grant leaned up close to the man's face. 'I need you to go back down. Kitchen.' He noticed tiny red polka dots across the front of the man's shirt. The waiter's face was a blank. Grant pointed at the bowls of soup. 'Go and drop those off downstairs and fetch Dolores or Ng.' The waiter nodded hesitantly. 'Good. *Go on.*'

Grant saw Ng come striding up the stairs carrying plates of fish. Behind him was another waiter with more fish. Great, he thought, curtain up.

'I've just been saying . . .' Grant started saying to Ng as the man approached the table, and he pointed at the young waiter he'd been speaking to. Ng followed his gaze . . . and then Grant saw that the young waiter was at the judges' table, placing a bowl of soup in front of each judge.

'Change of plan?' Ng asked Grant.

'I have no idea if this is a change of plan. I don't know what he's doing.'

Ng went across to the judges. The Harpo swallowed a mouthful of soup. Grant looked out the window. He looked at the square and at the many-eyed FK&F Publishing building staring back at him from across the concrete park, and he heard Ng saying, 'Excuse me, slight misunderstanding,' to the judges. 'This fish, lampreys, they're for you.' Grant continued staring out the window and pretended he was out in the snow. They would enjoy this. 'Sorry,' Ng said, 'I'll take these away . . .' Ng instructed the young waiter to remove the soup.

'He's already started,' one of the judges said. Grant turned and saw that it was the Groucho.

'Yes, I do apologise for that,' Ng said. 'Bit of mix-up, but if you don't mind I'll take them away and then we can serve you your course.'

'It's one course per restaurant,' the Chico said. The other judges nodded. 'That's the rule.'

There was a long pause, and Grant looked at them. Ng was staring at him, pleading with him, and Grant stood up. What had he done?

Ng tried again. 'I'm so sorry about this slip-up –'

'One of our number has started eating,' the Gummo said. 'We'll need a bowl for everyone.'

This would never have happened if Dolores had been there to oversee things, Grant thought. There was no way that anyone could be held responsible.

'I'd really like to help you with this,' Gummo continued, his tone indicating that nothing could be further from the truth, 'but we have rules to follow. We need more soup.' The other diners were becoming more and more interested. Grant shrugged his shoulders and sat down. Ng returned with four bowls of soup.

*

Something happened. Something happened in the restaurant on the pissy square. The Groucho slurped his soup; the Harpo's pupils dilated making him appear druggy and free. Something had definitely happened. Nothing at the judges' table other than the movement of spoon to mouth, spoon to mouth . . . Grant watched. The restaurant faded away. No dainty taste and ironic rolling of the eyes, not this time from the judges; instead they were eating the soup. It was as if they had been transported beyond the waiters with their white aprons and the smooth leather chairs and the white linen tablecloths. The soup swallowed the paintings and the soup swallowed the judges and there was nothing but the soup, so help me God.

When the soup was finished the judges looked around, dazed. Gummo raised a fat hand even though Ng was standing right beside him. 'What is this place called again?' he asked. They all wrote the name in their notebooks.

'Do you have more restaurants?' they asked. 'Are you the owner?' Ng told them. More writing. 'And this soup? What is it called?'

Ng stopped. 'Healthy Broth,' he said uncertainly. 'No, Hearty Broth.'

'Not much of a name,' the Zeppo commented.

Stacey's phone rang – 'Right, we've finished here,' she quacked – and the crew were on their feet, still glancing at the empty bowls, heading for the door. Grant spotted the Chico whispering something into the Harpo's ear, and the Harpo motioned to Ng and then Grant heard the judge whispering, 'Get me the recipe,' even though he knew this was impossible, wrong: *everyone* knows that Harpo is mute.

CHAPTER 3

Lolling About

WARM AND COSY. It was the best that Henry First had felt in weeks. Even his brother-in-law's grumbling was sounding suave. Dolores was looking good. Sexy even. What a disaster.

Man down in the kitchen! Casualty! And then *wee-pah, wee-pah* as they head off to the hospital. *Wee-pah, wee-pah, wee-pah.*

'Henry?'

'Dolores.'

'Henry?'

'Dolores . . .'

'Damn,' she said, and then he heard her talking to Felix. Talking to Felix about him.

Normally Henry wouldn't set foot in hospital bathrooms – especially not in his brother-in-law's hospital bathroom – but he needed to be somewhere cool. He had touched the radiator when they'd first walked into Felix's room but it was turned off. Cold. The warmth was emanating from Felix's body. The blast had hit Henry when he opened the door. Whoah: furnace, step back! But Dolores had shepherded her husband into the room, oblivious to the thermonuclear explosion. Henry could feel her nudging him forward, trying to get him to move. Speed up in front, sir.

The bathroom was Felix's torture chamber; his private room of horrors. Henry was holding out for as long as he could. He figured that if Dolores really wanted to get him out of the bathroom she'd tell him that her brother needed to use it. Until then he was staying put.

On the other side of the door Dolores had stopped talking loudly, but he could still hear indistinct sounds. Vowels: *oooo, eee, oooo, u, ah, ai*, and the *eh-ee* of his first name.

Earlier she had met him at the hospital; he was waiting outside Casualty, leaning on the glass, enjoying the city – the nurses had twice asked him to step away from the automatic doors because they kept opening whenever he moved – happy in the knowledge that Chin was alive. Chin was alive and he'd asked if he could go home. Henry was enjoying the city. And then huffy Dolores pulled up in the cab without a kiss but lots of silence and they tootled off to visit Cancer Man.

Now he couldn't get enough of looking at the toilet roll. It had been ripped with force. The paper has been wrenched to one side and the shredded, taut edge spoke of pain and suffering. It transfixed him. That pull had gone above and beyond the call of duty, Felix old boy. All it needed was a gentle tug: it came ready perforated. A soft pull. Fold or bunch. Wipe. And isn't Mother Nature a real doll? In order to take your mind off the cancer she blesses you with some 'roids, a crop of apoplectic pimples fighting for attention on your anus lip.

'Henry, the carer needs to see to Felix now,' his wife said from the other side of the door.

'In a minute, Dolores.'

'I can come back later,' he heard another woman's voice saying.

'No need for that,' Dolores said, her firm tone aimed at Henry.

'Yes, come back in a while,' Henry called. 'I may be some time.'

What sounded like hostage negotiations followed – the carer wanting to leave, Dolores saying she must stay – and then Dolores announced, 'Henry, I'm stepping out of the room.'

'Sure, baby,' his voice echoed around him.

There were new voices in Felix's room: muffled efficiency and strains of exertion as – what? – Felix's body was comforted then gently restrained – a whimper? – beneath the sheet? The murmuring continued while Henry monitored his reflection in the mirror. His unshaven cheeks were a trampy, homeless red against the hospital's flecked white walls. He knew he should avoid reflections. They contained memories like the one of a car sneaking up on him while he was in the bar . . . his face against the window . . .

Henry stood up – enough time in here – flushed and pulled open the door, glimpsing a nurse's white uniform as she exited. Felix was still breathing – a good sign – and Henry slipped out into the corridor where he saw an elderly patient clasping the handrail, wheezing as though he were making a horizontal ascent up a berg, just behind Dolores.

'Will you find out about microwaving this?' Dolores said when she saw Henry and handed him a tub of broth. 'Not too hot,' she called down the corridor after him, 'and don't spill any. And get them to remove the lid before –' but he'd already turned the corner.

He saw the nurse before she saw him. Florence Nightingale . . . *ish*. Sexy. Plump rosy cheeks kept red by the pressure of her support hose. She smiled and noise came out of his mouth that sounded like *warbla warbla warbla microwarbla*. He cleared his throat and tried again.

'It's for my bro . . . it's for Mr Stoll.' He said the name slowly. 'That's spelt l-l, not l-e.'

'Is that bowl microwaveable?' the nurse asked.

'Most positive it is.' He held the bowl above his head and tried reading the inscription on the base. 'Says it's made from the finest plastics. Child labourers, I'm guessing.'

'Drink some of our coffee and sober up,' she said, leading him into the kitchen where he popped open the little electronic door.

'Yes, I'm fine,' he said when he sensed that she was about to tell him how to work the machine. 'My occupa –. I do this for a living.'

'I think you've got a bit too much soup there,' she said. 'Why don't we freeze some for later?'

He removed the lid and poured some of the liquid into a square plastic container that she'd found in a cupboard. The nurse closed this container and wrote Felix's name on one side before putting it into a small freezer.

Once she'd left the kitchenette Henry set his bowl with the remainder of the soup onto the glass tray in the microwave and slammed the door shut. After some thought he opened the door and balanced the lid on the bowl. He shut it with another bang.

'You all right in there?' the nurse called from her desk.

'All fine.'

'Call me if you need any help.' The sexy minx.

1 and 0 were everyone's favourite numbers on the touch-pad; all the other numbers were covered with grime. The machine looked as if it had fallen off a Soviet rocket. 34 seconds remained on the clock from some previous horror-meal and he hit the CLEAR button but the Sputnik failed to respond. Double-CLEAR and the machine went into cardiac arrest – *dreeeeeeeeeeee* – which he silenced with a quick START and then STOP. That gave him 33 seconds on the clock, which he tried overtyping with 120. 33 glared back at him.

The string of buttons running down the side of the launch pad was equally unresponsive to his poking. CHICKEN. ROASTED VEG. VEG/FISH. CRISPY TOP. *No! No! No! No!* Any bigger and this thing would put him out of business.

'OK, you little mother.' He twisted the POWER dial as close to 100% as dirt would allow. He selected GRILL 1-2-3 and CONVECTION followed by TURBO-BAKE before tapping the START button. The glass turntable inside the machine did a feeble half-pirouette and then rocked back and forth as the oven began filling with steam. The smell reminded him of a hairdryer.

'What are you doing in here?' said another nurse who walked into the kitchenette.

Henry popped open the microwave door then pulled his hand back from the hot bowl. 'Warming up some soup,' he said to himself. 'Not hurting –'

'We can't have this,' she said shaking a mug at him. 'Tracy.' Tracy, the younger nurse, looked in.

'It's not her fault,' he said. 'Honestly, I slipped in here without anyone noticing.' The masculine one wasn't taking any bait. 'I'll grab it when it cools down, and then skedaddle.'

The nurse cleared her throat – a signal for Tracy to follow her back to the reception desk. He heard some talking and then the evil nurse walked down the passage, past the kitchenette, with a triumphant swagger.

He popped his head out of the room.

'Safe?'

Tracy was no longer happy to see him.

'Will she be back soon?' he asked.

'Probably.'

'I got you in it, didn't I?'

'Not to worry,' she said matter-of-factly.

'Are you allowed to fraternise with visitors?'

'I don't think I've ever fraternised with anyone,' she said.

'I haven't seen you here before.'

'That's me,' she said, 'I blend into backgrounds.' She continued writing into a large book.

'Are you busy?'

'You went somewhere before you came here,' she said and then met his eyes, 'didn't you? A bar, perhaps?'

'Why, do I look half-slewed?'

'Not *half*-slewed, no.'

'I could have you down for subordination to a visitor or something. I'm the customer.'

'You'd be doing me a favour. How's the soup?'

'Still too hot.'

'Did you buy it downstairs? Because I've heard some stories.'

'No, I made it myself. Did you start early this morning?'

'I spend a fortune on night cream. Even you're not that drunk. How's your soup doing?'

'Hold on,' he said and seemed to swim back into the kitchenette. The bowl allowed itself to be picked up and placed on a tray, although the liquid looked molten and dangerous. He scuttled about for a spoon. 'Where are the straws?'

She came into the kitchen and pulled one from a box.

'Taste this,' he said, dipping the spoon into the soup.

'No thanks.'

'Go on. Make a drunk happy.'

'I spend my life making people happy.'

'Me too. Open wide. Careful, it's hot.'

She took a sip.

'Now I can tell Felix that a pretty woman's eaten from this bowl. Should make his year.'

'Mind if I have some more?' she asked.

'My God, I've got a convert.' She looked up at him. He could see that it was very good. 'Better than the stuff they dish up here, I'm sure. Now let's be honest, you want my body, don't you?'

'If this doesn't get him eating then nothing will.'

'Flattery, my dear . . .'

'No, this is really very good,' she said.

'Would you like another sip?' She took two more slurps. 'If I'd known it was this easy to get women I'd have done this a long time ago.'

'You need to give me the recipe.'

'Vegetables, meat, water. All in the preparation.'

'You're welcome in this kitchen any time, Mr Chef.'

'I tell you what, I'll bring you some next time I'm here.'

'Deal. You are a chef, aren't you?'

Henry saw Dolores standing in the kitchen and wondered how long she'd been listening to him.

'Here I am.'

'Is my husband wasting your time?' she asked.

'I've been tempting the staff with some soup,' he said, immediately regretting the word tempting. 'Got her away from her figures' – regretting the word figures.

'Felix is awake,' Dolores said.

'Yes, I'm off, I'm off,' he said. 'And it was a pleasure to meet you properly, Tracy. You can pay me compliments anytime.'

'So you've found a new friend,' Dolores said as they walked back to Felix's room. He didn't look at her but could tell from her voice that she was smiling. 'Nurse Tracy, is it?'

'Nurse Tracy.' He nodded. 'Married with four children.' Why did he say that?

'Poor soul. You never quite lose the weight after a child. And she must have been heavy to begin with.'

'Rubenesque.'

'Well the important thing is that she seemed to like you.'

'Dolores, everyone likes me,' he said, and he almost added, Except for your brother.

Henry angled the tray into the room, and as he placed it on the bedside table Felix opened his eyes. He was facing the shaded window, his head turned away from Henry and Dolores.

'Felix,' Henry said to get his brother-in-law pointing in the right direction, and then they sat beside the bed and watched the man mountain breathing. 'You're awake. I've warmed up some soup for you.'

'And chatted up the nurses while you were at it,' Dolores added.

'Which ones?' Felix asked.

'Oh, I don't know.'

'The stout one down the hall,' Dolores said. 'Mousy hair and sagging chest.'

'Dolores, she was helping me with the microwave.'

'Ooooooh, your soup is so delicious, can I have some more?' Dolores did the nurse's voice.

'Good man, Chef,' Felix said. 'I'm thirsty.' Henry decanted some old water into a thick green tumbler and handed it to the dying man. 'My straw.' Henry knocked the straw off the tray and, after a tedious search, located the thick tube under a pile of dusty periodicals. He held out the glass of water over the bed with an awkward hand that touched Felix's humid neck.

'Enough,' Felix said after a few sips. He gave a theatrical gasp of satisfaction.

'Would you like some soup?' Dolores asked. 'It's very good, you know. Comes recommended by Nurse Tracy. You know, the chesty one.'

'Well in that case . . .'

'That's my man, Felix.' Henry fiddled with the bed's controls and soon it was on the move – a *grrrrlllll* as metal strained against the patient, the motor winning out against gravity – and they both watched as what looked like a sunburned cadaver began tilting forward. As the bed neared a 50-degree angle the motor began slipping. Man had beaten the machine. 'Comfy?' Henry asked.

The corpse nodded.

'I've been telling Felix about the competition,' Dolores said.

Henry sat and listened to her. It felt like the room was closing in on him. Right now he'd prefer it if everyone either shut up about the competition or if Felix said something obtuse and impolite so that they could argue, and this would leave Felix feeling zany and mad until the next visit.

'So one of them got hurt?' Felix said.

'Yes,' Henry said without giving Dolores a chance to respond, 'someone got hurt.'

'They can't handle sharp knives, Chef. Not in their culture.'

A look from Dolores. 'Would you like some of the soup I prepared for you?' he asked. Or perhaps we should sit here and discuss racial stereotypes.

'In a minute, Chef.'

They waited. Henry turned on the radio and spun the dial past screeching stations, missed, and then found one playing soft classical music.

His 'Is that OK?' got no response.

Dolores picked up a magazine and offered to read Felix an article, but her brother shook his head. Henry pulled open the top drawer in the metal cabinet next to the bed to look for something to read. Multiple tubes of lip balm rolled to the back of the drawer, out of sight. Dolores skimmed the magazine.

After a few minutes Henry said, 'You should have a sip.'

'I can only eat Dee's food,' Felix told Henry. 'That used to get rid of this pain. I've got pain again,' he said to Dolores.

Dolores offered to call the nurse and stepped out of the room.

Ich kann nicht anders, so help me God! Henry leaned up to Felix, careful to avoid the drainage pipes, closer to his volcanic body.

'The young nurse had this spoon in her mouth,' he told the red face. The eyes watched him. 'She licked this spoon.' Now those eyes looked at the spoon. Felix's mouth opened and a pink baby tongue ran across the teeth. Henry dunked the spoon in the soup and held it up to the mouth.

34

'You know you want some,' he said softly. The dying man gave a slight nod. 'Do you want the straw?' he asked.

'No, Chef. The spoon.'

Felix began to swallow some soup. After the third mouthful the slow start had been replaced by marathon eating. With each mouthful he sucked the spoon . . . held it with his lips . . . more . . .

'You'll bring me some mags?' he asked during another mouthful.

'Next visit.' Henry nodded.

'Can't you pop downstairs while I finish this?' he said between gulps.

'They're closed by now. I won't forget. Steady now' – Henry held back the spoon – 'don't want you getting sick.'

'Chef?'

'Slow down,' Henry said, attempting to take the spoon away.

'I need you to do me a favour. Man to man.'

'A man-to-man favour? Sure.'

'Take one of my credit cards.' He looked down at the soup and then Henry ladled more into his mouth. Felix swallowed quickly. 'I need your help.'

'You've lost me, Felix.'

'This place takes care of my health. You and Dee are family. I'm still a man.'

'Yes?'

'It's in the bottom drawer under my bedpan. Have a look.' Henry reached in and found a copy of Flossing, Kissing & Fellatio. Two mouthfuls. 'I've circled one of those bitches in the back. You understand? I've got the cash.'

'Sure.' Henry glanced at the magazine. Man to man.

'Every Sunday night this sweet nurse, pretty little thing, washes me down at five or so. She wipes around my old man and pretends like there's nothing there.' It took Henry a moment to realise that Felix was referring to his genitals and not some geezer down the hall. 'Make an appointment for me with one of these specialists' – he indicated the magazine – 'at seven o'clock this Sunday, after my wash. The hospital staff don't care who visits late on a Sunday.'

'More soup?'

'Yes, more.' A mouthful. 'You OK with that?'

Henry nodded.

Dolores and a nurse entered the room as Henry was slipping the curled magazine into his coat pocket. He was careful to hang the coat over the back of the chair.

'He's been a hungry boy,' Henry said, sealing the plastic soup bowl with a *snuff*.

'Well done,' said the nurse to no one in particular as she injected some painkiller into the drip. 'Leave some of the soup for later, Mr Stoll. This will calm him down. You should sleep now, Mr Stoll. He'll be off in a moment.' Dolores thanked the nurse who glanced at her watch and then looked at them both before leaving the room.

Dolores went over to her husband. 'I think he needs some rest,' she said.

'I need a moment,' Henry said, and went into the bathroom, locking the door behind him.

Silence. His reflection was back in the mirror. Thick white handles formed a mini scaffold around the toilet. The punished toilet roll was still there. He needed a moment.

'Dolores,' he called out.

'Yes.'

'Honey' – the fake-sounding word seemed to drop on the tiles –'how did the competition go?' The face in the mirror looked normal.

'Apart from the excitement?' she said.

'Yes, apart from the excitement.'

'Well Grant seemed pretty impressed.'

'Nothing impresses him.'

'Well, he said he was impressed.'

'Oh that's good.' He washed his hands, then his face. 'And honey . . .'

'Yes?'

He looked at the sealed bowl on the shelf beside the basin. 'How did they rate the lampreys?'

'Oh God, Henry, there was a mix-up. I haven't told you about it all, have I?'

'No,' he said and picked up the bowl.

'But it . . . it went as well as could be expected. Under the circumstances.'

He eased off the dimpled plastic lid again, pushing it up with his thumbs. 'So what did you feed them?' He took his eyes off his reflection and looked into the bowl.

'Soup.'

And in the bowl, lolling about in the warm soup, were Chin's three fingers.

PART II

Dito, Dito del Piede, Rene

CHAPTER 4

The Shirley Temples

WHENEVER PATRICE CZARNY emphasised a word, or whenever the cab driver gunned the vehicle down a side street, the creature clinging to her neck – a stole that looked like a soft, oversized bulrush – appeared to shiver with excitement. Patrice was talking on her phone. It sounded as though she was presenting an infomercial. Occasionally she glanced at Grant Whant sitting beside her, and her face looked beatific, pre-orgasmic, and plumped with full-on sales sexuality. The cab continued up the frozen avenue towards her new restaurant, Central.

Patrice paused, raised a blinged hand (flash of acrylic nails), and patted the back of her Afro. 'I'll cancel tonight's launch,' she said, threatening one of the judges on the phone, the Groucho or the Harpo. It had been a very long call: when she'd walked over to Grant's desk earlier that evening – he was typing his review of Firsts into the corporation's content management system – she'd held the phone away from her ear for a few seconds and indicated that he should follow her to a waiting taxi.

'The corporates are haemorrhaging cash' – the car surged through the evening traffic, and Patrice was shouting – 'and there'll be blood on the streets by the time we've slashed our numbers and I can't afford to be usurped in the competition I designed. It is so very unseemly for one of my judges to gush about a competitor. I've never even heard of Firsts. If *anyone* challenges me I'll crush them like a tick.' She ended the call, smiled at Grant, and they travelled in silence for some time. Eventually she rang her secretary and instructed the woman to invite Henry First to that evening's launch party at Central.

'I've been thinking,' Grant said, not quite sure what to say but nevertheless feeling tremendous pressure to say something, 'that it probably makes sense for me to tone down my review of Firsts.'

Patrice looked displeased. 'No, no, no, no. Our company appreciates our contributors' independence. Perhaps' – she glanced out of the window; they were travelling parallel to a stretch of river grown icy in the shadow of five monstrous bridges – 'you shouldn't tone it down, but rather increase your EE.'

'What?'

'Your empathic emphasis. EE.'

'My "empathic emphasis"?'

'Corporate allegiance,' she said by way of explanation, not taking her eyes off the stagnant waves in the distance. 'Employee patriotism. We have such wonderful corporate values and we all need to be super-careful about undermining, or doing anything harmful, at such a sensitive time. Blood on the streets . . .'

Soon he would have to think of something else to say, in spite of his growing feelings of uncertainty. There were times when he'd be staring out of his office window at the buildings across Golden Square, trying to wish away his career, when he experienced a similar emotion. When he looked down at Firsts and when he thought about Henry, he felt it too.

They travelled in silence again and he was beginning to feel twinges of paranoia, the faintest murmurs of paranoia joining the horror that he was about to be fired, when their cab skidded across two lanes of oncoming traffic and, misjudging a turn, almost landed in a YMCA's lobby. The driver spun the wheel but they continued to slip across the icy road until the man yanked it hard left – YMCA posters and wide-eyed men clutching bathing trunks and drawstring bags and Patrice yelling *'Slow down!'* as she slammed her hand against the partition – and then the vehicle nosed back onto the correct side of the road.

The driver yelled something back at her at the next intersection as they sped north. She hit the glass again.

'Don't distract the driver, lady,' the man shouted over his shoulder. He pumped the accelerator through Chinatown. Grant was having difficulty breathing.

'You look a bit green around the gills,' Patrice said. 'Nervous?'

He shook his head. He wanted to be able to say something witty and reassuring, but his mind was coming up with sentences like 'God forbid I should be more empathic but less emphatic,' and besides, he hadn't quite gained control of his breathing.

'Honey,' she said, 'you can imagine how unhappy I am with having to communicate with everyone like this. Between you and me, if this was how I wanted to treat people I would have taught kindergarten. But EE is here to stay, and I need you to think of it as a form of job protection. I've set up a steering committee to investigate the viability of outsourcing all of our copy from Eastern Europe or Asia. As a department we need to protect ourselves, and that is why I need positive references to the corporation in our copy. That way I stay in command.'

'So I write about how great it is?'

'Precisely. The corporate will be distributing an updated style sheet. And it's possible they may be introducing a point system for scoring all contributions.'

'A *point* system,' he said, unable to stop himself. 'Like in a beauty pageant?'

She smiled. 'I'm sure they'd argue that this is slightly more scientific.'

'We get to skip the swimsuit round?'

Just then he levitated a few inches off the back seat as the cab flew over a slushy mogul before diving under a railway bridge. As the set of traffic lights in front of them switched from amber to red he felt the cab surge.

'We're here, we're here!' Patrice shouted. 'He's passed it.'

The cabby swung left, slicing the kerb. 'OK, lady.'

Patrice paid ('I have *so* got his number,' she said) and they scrambled onto the street in front of her new restaurant. 'Have fun killing yourself tonight,' she shouted at the driver as she slammed the door.

There was a group of photographers, all corporate employees, facing Central's entrance and taking pictures of socialites.

'Can I assume you've polished all your best adjectives and superlatives for tonight?' she asked Grant.

'Patrice, dearest,' he replied, 'my adjectives and superlatives – and perhaps even a few expletives – are always at your command. I may even give my baton a twirl. In fact I guarantee it.'

'Ms Czarny!' someone shouted and the photographers turned and there were pops and flashes as they captured her arrival.

'Hello, girls and boys,' she said with another dab at her hair and she ushered the paparazzi past security. 'It's too darn cold out here. Come on in for something to eat and drink. I bet all the pretty people are inside already. And play nice.'

Patrice's newest restaurant, Central, was a series of subterranean domed warrens – Grant thought labyrinth; he thought Minotaur – and its foyer had tall concrete skyscraper walls and penitentiary windows snug against the ceiling. He sipped champagne and watched the young waiters carrying trays with oysters on ice. At the entrance to one of the warrens Patrice was flirting with the press, killing time until the judges arrived.

Only after employing a variety of ineffectual hand signals was Grant able to persuade a student waiter to pause long enough to offer him an oyster. It tasted metallic, like a large blood clot, and following an unsuccessful attempt at swallowing it Grant headed to a corner of the entrance hall where he entombed it in a napkin and laid it to rest on the floor.

Champagne, crowded medieval rooms, echoing chatter, half-recognised glances, and more students carrying trays of seafood. He could sense that the guests were trying to decide how this evening rated on the social scale.

Patrice circled back to where he was still attempting to wash away the oyster's haemoglobic aftertaste with a fresh glass of bubbly and hustled him into a side room for a quick pow-wow. He resisted the urge to wipe the whole length of his tongue on his sleeve and tried following her conversation instead. Something about the corporation.

'You remember what we were talking about in the car?' she said at one point.

'The blood on the avenue?' A guess.

'Yes. The judges are all on message, and the cleansing's about to begin. You don't seem very well.'

'I'll be fine,' he said. 'That journey was a killer.'

'He's here,' she said. Grant looked blank. 'Henry First is here. He got here shortly after the judges arrived – he introduced himself and shook my hand like a chump. He even said that he dropped everything to join us this evening.' She laughed. 'The little fool. I told him I've got a lot lined up for him. You and I really must do everything in our power to assist him – so much so that I want you to become his new best friend. Now let's go celebrate.'

They followed a pale-lipped student past four distracted photographers and into one of the warrens.

'Take a look over there.' Patrice pointed at a nearby wall. 'Just below that line of brick. You see the holes?'

On a row of glans-toned bricks he could see clusters of holes, and each hole was surrounded by a dirty nebula. 'Old decorations,' he suggested. 'Paintings or shelving.'

'Slings and manacles,' she said. 'This place used to be an S&M haven. Friends of mine met here, told me about it, and so I bought it. Let's get slammed on champagne and then I'll see what I can do about Henry First.' And here she pulled Grant into another room.

Grant would never be quite sure about what happened next, but without question it all turned a bit weird. Perhaps it was something he'd eaten? He was convinced that it must be the bloody oyster because he spent the next few days trying to force something – the news? the booze? the oyster? – out of his body, and at night his dreams were overrun by a troupe of pre-pubescent tots performing a full-length cabaret on his bedroom ceiling. Whenever he closed his eyes on his sickbed he could see them: the little sideshow in his cerebellum courtesy of the poison seeping through his body.

He recalled things becoming muddled at Central. At one point they had walked into the dining area and – this he *thought* he remembered – he caught sight of some rouged Shirley Temples sauntering across a makeshift stage. The evening's entertainment? he wondered. A few of these girls propped themselves against the bar counter (within rubbing distance of sweaty executives) and then the tots began performing love songs. One particularly mischievous Miss pelvic-thrusted her way through a Cole Porter number, her pink tap shoes working her little calves across the wooden countertop while her vampiric mother (stage left, an eyeliner as thick as a crayon in one hand) mouthed the lyrics and kept waving at her daughter, reminding her to smile.

Patrice was ecstatic; the crowd enchanted. And all this time the only thing Grant felt certain about was that he was ill, and when he tried attracting Patrice's attention, tried saying, 'I need a cab', the show surged on around him and swallowed his pleas for help.

In one routine all thirteen starlets gave a world-weary rendition of *I Just Wanna Be Loved By You* in which the five youngest girls shot centre stage where they began squirming and gyrating. They wore ruffled knickers with suspender belts – 'Patrice,' he said, 'I need a cab. I'm dying here.' – and onstage there was more faux petting and blinking of dewy eyes before they all lined up and began high-kicking, their frilly Pollyanna dresses shooting up in the air.

'*Patrice*,' he said again but the Lolitas were too loud, commanding everyone's attention. He felt himself weakening, he could feel . . .

The number ended and after a hasty costume change they were off again. They twirled around *(a one-two-three-four!)*, and executives applauded, mothers wept. Mayhem.

'Patrice . . .'

'Fabulous,' he heard Patrice saying from what seemed to be the other side of the room, 'front cover stuff!' And as he turned in the direction of her voice he saw her looking at him, really looking at his face. He stood there, mute. She continued talking and as he tried stepping towards her, to hear what she was saying, his legs misbehaved and folded beneath his body.

And that was how the cabaret kept him company, tap-dancing on his bedroom ceiling, while he tried to sleep.

He only woke when the cherubic chanteuses took a final bow and eventually disappeared, and for the first time since the launch party he no longer felt as though he was dying. His teeth were still tender, and yet he would be glad to be euthanased. He'd spent the past few days clasping the icy toilet bowl, the soft echo of his breath in his ears as he coaxed himself to move, kneel, sit, void – his body expelling enough fluid to fill a small sea – and he had memories of a hospital visit.

Then there was the sound of his neighbour walking about in the flat above, the footsteps directly over his bed. With each step Grant's room vibrated – the window rattled

– and for a moment it seemed as if the man would break through the plaster and come thrashing onto the floor below. What could he be doing up there?

After two more days the illness was no longer terrifying but had become rather boring and he tried reading the novels on his bedside table. He managed a few pages from each book before stopping: he couldn't bear having someone else chattering away inside his head, competing for space, wanting to tell him their story. He closed his eyes and thought for a while. Later he would be woken by the sound of Patrice leaving a message on the machine.

He returned to the novels but their words were dead on the page. After he discarded the books he picked up the dictionary from his bedside table and surprised himself by making it through the Introduction; then he turned to the letter P where he began reading the entries with ease. As a book it was a bit short on laughs, but the religious/sexual juxtapositions raised an occasional smile: he noted that *penis* came just before *penitent*. Biologists, zoologists and botanists appeared to have all the best words (plumbeous, pilose) and he hoped he'd be able to spot a catchy word for future reviews. The poetic and literary words didn't appear to add much to the language.

The next morning he found himself lying in a warm rectangle of sunlight. Sunlight in this weather? In the bathroom he caught sight of a leper in the mirror lurching toward the lavatory. Sure enough, there was also sunlight in the mirror's world. He gave his face a quick wash, avoiding the mirror, and went to the kitchen to find something to eat. After a furtive search he prised open a tin of soup and swallowed a few salty mouthfuls before returning to bed and switching on the radio. He shut his eyes and drifted off to sleep while meteorologists argued about the cause and duration of the winter storms.

*

It was late afternoon when Grant was finally awake; the fever had subsided and he was hungry and horny. He had a shower, dressed warmly, and then slipped out of his flat. In the hallway downstairs he sorted his mail into a neat pile, ready to collect when he returned from shopping.

Outside, the sun was trying hard to set while storm clouds moved across the pink sky. Walls of snow had been built on either side of the pathway; it was raining gently. He returned to his flat – collecting the mail on the way up – grabbed an umbrella, a heavier coat and some leather gloves before setting off again for the supermarket.

Dithering for a moment outside the store he turned away and crossed the road to walk down a familiar side street now made strange by the ice hedges. He navigated this winter maze and soon found himself trotting down the steps into a subterranean public toilet where the rain distorted the midwinter light filtering through glass ceiling tiles.

Men stood at a row of urinals – porcelain-grey curves built into a biscuit-red wall, chest high (no splashing, no straying eyes) with an elegantly tiled edge. On the opposite side of the low-lying wall were seven identical curves. Two were occupied.

Tar-stained doors hung on Grant's right, hiding the toilets. One was locked. He walked past the doors and around the wall.

The two men standing here were eager – cautious, but very eager. Yes, eagerness was in the air. He stood at the urinal between them. The arms belonging to the men on his left and right were frantic, blurred. Masturbatory zealots! Another man came round to Grant's side of the wall, the business side of the partition, and all eyes were on the chap on his left. If he pulled that thing out of you, Grant thought, you'd expect to find a skewered kidney hanging from its end.

Water splashed down the flight of steps leading up to the street. Outside there were flashes followed by thunder as the storm grew closer and just then a huffing man with rain-streaked glasses and dripping nose tottered down. The men on either side of Grant stopped the pumping action and embarked upon some serious – if imaginary – pissing, their heads bowed and their pelvises static. And as they all focused on this sudden, intense urination – pretend steam rising from jets of invisible water thundering in front of them – he could feel the newcomer looking at the row of stern, downcast faces around him. Monster Prick on Grant's left enquired with a quick glance to see if this was a welcome intruder – a member of the chorus who was late for curtain-up? The rest waited: the action would continue when this latecomer exited – or took a casual stroll around the dividing wall to join them . . . to join the ensemble.

As a child Grant Whant had been taken to the theatre each year to watch a Christmas musical: *Oklahoma!, My Fair Lady*, you name it. In one extraordinary theatre with a huge vaulted ceiling that had been painted to resemble the evening sky, a husband-and-wife team choreographed, directed, produced and starred in productions that always started in the same way: the first scene would take place before the curtain, a couple of minor characters and perhaps a prop, lit with follow spots. Once this scene was over the stage would light up behind the actors, and the flimsy gauze scrim turned transparent to reveal the rest of the company of actors frozen into position on a sumptuous set. It was mirth stuck for a millisecond: perhaps a garish, cavernous feast; or a noble green-felt hunting party; and once it was watercolour-dirty Covent Garden. And only after the scrim was fully raised would there be a sudden rush of movement, an over-animated din after a whispered cue. The audience always applauded this transition from nothing to movement, stasis to robust animation. Yet it was somehow clear to Grant from the way the actors watched each other – monitoring and maintaining the level of forced revelry – that they had been silent only moments earlier. It was as if the fear of lapsing back into the silence drove them on, and their frenzied whoops could only be subdued by the appearance of a main character with as yet unsaid lines . . .

The newcomer walked around the wall and it was as if the scrim had been raised because everyone around him was off, arms pumping frantically, eager for someone to do something outrageous. And outside the heavens applauded.

His work done, Grant washed his hands and then climbed the steps with his umbrella clacking against the black iron railings. Halfway up he stopped to grapple with the umbrella, setting its mechanism free.

The rain was heavier than before and at the end of the road a gust of wind ripped at the contraption, sluicing water onto an elderly woman whose scalp and hair were vacuum-packed into a cellophane bonnet. Before he was able to apologise to this hunched lilac creature impeding his way she looked up and swore. Such ferocious language! Then the hag forced him to wait while she wiped her face before brandishing her own umbrella – a tarpaulin monstrosity – in defiance and set off, scratching her way through the dripping city.

Unnerved by this turn of events – a twinge of emptiness might also be returning – he was about to cross the road when he saw someone running towards him. 'Is anything wrong?' she asked. It was Dolores First. He was surprised to see her standing there in front of him, inches away, looking concerned. 'I thought it was you,' she continued. 'I saw you standing in front of the supermarket a few minutes ago and I thought you looked disorientated. You were down there for an awfully long time – I almost went down to see if I could help you. Are you all right? I'd heard you've been ill.'

'Yes, I've been ill,' he echoed slowly.

She took his arm and walked him across the road. 'You're looking very red, quite feverish. I was watching you back then. You were almost run over.'

He ran a hand across his brow, wiping away the sweat from his recent subterranean activity.

'Yes, I think . . . I mean . . .' he said giving both of his hands a quick glance.

'Do you live nearby?' she asked.

'Yes. I was out for some essentials.'

'You're in no condition to be walking around in this weather,' she said. 'You're out of breath and I can see you're feverish. You feel very hot. There is no way you can cope with a supermarket in your condition.'

Uncertain about what to do, how to react, his forehead still feeling the touch of her own swiftly applied hand, he stood in front of the supermarket staring at her.

'I really appreciate –'

'You look as though you've just run a marathon. Are you sure you're well enough to be out of bed? I've got the car with me. Tell you what, I'm popping in for a few things anyway so it's no trouble buying you some essentials. You should be taking care of yourself.'

Uncertain whether he was feeling dizzy because of her exuberant generosity or his flushed reaction to his recent activity, he followed her meekly to her car. He gave her some money, she made a note of what he needed. 'I hope you don't mind, but I'll change a few of the items on your list. You can do without the caffeine. You should be building up your body. Right?'

'You're the nurse, Dolores.' He sat in her car feeling unworthy as he watched her walking into the supermarket.

The rain turned into sleet and then the sleet became snow.

On the seat beside him was a copy of the latest Sunday Magazine. The restaurant-review page did not feature one of his past articles, or even a collection of his best throw-away lines. Instead it was business as usual: there was his photograph above his review of Firsts. His 'FAIR' had been replaced by 'GOOD'. For some reason Patrice had hyped his review, and its style was now predictable and derivative: her gushing prose, her z-list names. There was even an emphatic reference to Central.

On the facing page was an advert for The Restaurant of the Year Competition: it was her declaration of war.

CHAPTER 5

Snowscape

OUTSIDE THE RESTAURANT, the city had frozen shut; inside the restaurant, Henry First contemplated an almost-empty plastic bowl.

He had thrown out the soup.

Dolores was cleaning the kitchen – she had been at it since they arrived that morning – and he could hear the sound of her working hard to rid them of their bad luck. He'd thrown out the soup – his shamanic peyote cactus, his gypsum weed – along with the whites everyone had been wearing one week ago and the cloths that had swaddled Chin's hands.

On the table beside the bowl lay an unopened envelope with a cerise border, together with a neat pile of cards, one from each of his employees, all containing the same brief letter of resignation. Bad news looking bad.

There was movement outside the restaurant, and after staring at the snow and then through the snow Henry saw two baffled explorers edging their way past the pawn and porn and the surgery emporium on the northern edge of Golden Square. He recognised the type: Hubble telescopes dangling from their necks, shoes more suited for a gymnasium. They looked up at the buildings on the square; he watched them attempt to locate street names or a distinguishing feature, and then one of the tourists unfurled a map and held it outstretched for a moment before it was ripped away by a blast of spray from a truck thundering north. The map floated up the avenue and he soon lost sight of it in the falling snow. That sums life up, he thought. It was directionless. He looked at the bowl and wondered why he hadn't thrown it away. The memory of Chin's fingers was still disturbing, yet part of him refused to believe what he'd seen, and even after he'd flushed the leftover soup down the hospital loo he still couldn't bring himself to believe that he had eventually found Chin's fingers.

The air in the bowl still held the smell of soup.

Henry continued watching the tourists' laborious shuffle along the square's perimeter before they fell into his restaurant and asked him, the near catatonic man sitting at a table, for directions back to civilisation.

When he had finished his detailed explanations they looked about, and, realising that they were in a restaurant, asked for something to eat. There were busloads of hungry tourists out there, he thought, shut up in their hotel rooms with mini-bars and trashy commercials while the city froze. He nodded and led them to a table and a few minutes later found himself downstairs in the kitchen making pasta; and for one of the bewildered visitors this dish might be irresistible, but for the other one not.

Once the diners had departed Henry returned to his favourite table and tore open the envelope. Inside was a brochure (Patrice had written her phone number on its cover): *Join our Family! Furness Kindle & Flint – Fellowship, Kinship & Fidelity.* Even though FK&F was all the way across the square and hidden by the snow they were making inroads into his restaurant.

He went to the bathroom where he found Dolores standing in front of the basin holding her hands curved up toward her face like a surgeon awaiting gloves. Water trickled down her arms and dripped from her elbows as she stared out the steam-streaked window into the morning. He wanted to ask how she was.

'Another quiet day,' she said without turning. Now she was tearing at her fingertips while behind him, in the restaurant, was nothing.

'We're open for business,' he said, trying hard to sound upbeat, and she nodded. 'I just served two customers.' Happy birthday to us, he thought, and wondered if Dolores had remembered that Firsts had launched exactly one year ago today.

Downstairs, the lights humming loudly, Henry walked into the kitchen with the bowl. It was hard to believe that a week ago, on the Friday, this humming noise had been drowned out by the noise of steel on steel and the chaos of preparation and cooking and bleeding. He felt ill. Dolores had done a good job cleaning up but he could smell the fear.

He washed the pans he'd dirtied while preparing the lunch for the tourists, and then began reviewing the state of the kitchen equipment, making notes as he went along. The blades on the bone-cutter were blunt and its metal safety guard needed tightening. All of the machines were due a service. He wondered if he should chuck everything away, along with the empty bowl, and start over again? When he had finished his inspection he began tidying the storerooms. Only once he was certain that the kitchen was clean did he throw the bowl away.

Later that afternoon he returned upstairs to his table. Outside he saw three people leaping out a new nightclub called The Military-Industrial Complex (FK&F Nightlife) on the southern side of the square, and then the solid doors shut behind them and killed the music.

By now the snow was heavy, the sky darker.

At one o'clock he made a quick lunch for the two of them and prepared more soup for his brother-in-law, and then they shut the restaurant and ventured out into the storm.

Snowdrifts filled most of the streets leading south and they were slowly feeding on what remained of Golden Square. Henry and Dolores trekked north through the uninhabited, snow-filled gorges, a new plastic container with Felix's soup in Henry's backpack growing heavier and icier as they fought through the weather. They eventually took refuge in Fellini's, a coffee shop situated just outside an underground railway station.

Dolores collected their drinks from the baristas. 'Those pastries were delivered by snowplough, no doubt,' he said. The coffee was sharp.

'Do you think our staff would have made it in to work today?' she asked. 'Our ex staff.'

'I'm sure they're out there as we speak, in that snowy tundra, looking for work. Falling into crevasses or puncturing the roofs of stalled cars with their crampons or being rescued by firemen.'

'We can't blame them,' she said.

'Yes, who needs loyalty?' Henry saw a slovenly figure shuffling in the white outside. 'Poor bastard.'

'That'll be us soon . . .'

'You know what the problem is?' he said, dipping his spoon into the froth. 'The people in the corporates didn't even bother trying to make it into work today. It's the blue-collar workers that keep this city going. Laziness is a by-product of a well-educated workforce. Instead of earning money and getting on with the job, they're too self-absorbed and self-interested to battle it out any more. And none of them enjoys their job.'

'*We* don't like our jobs.'

'We own our company,' he said.

'But still we don't want to be there.'

He finished his drink. 'Did you see the FK&F brochure?' he asked, and she nodded. 'They'll never buy us out, you know. They'll say that they'll buy us out, but they never will.'

'We might get a launch party out of the deal, though,' Dolores said. She had been teasing him about the Central launch party he'd attended earlier that week. 'Do you think

I'd be lucky enough to be invited to our own FK&F launch party?'

He was on a roll. 'You and I will become part of the corporation and before you know it they'll have taken control of everything but we'll never see their money. And we'll have to deal with highly educated but unmotivated bureaucrats who are indecisive and constipated by childhood trauma and first-world junk. And of course they use this nurturing bullshit as a cover for their cold hard capitalism. If we don't meet their targets then we're out. And it'll be like today – none of them will be working because of a bit of snow, but you and I will be expected to put in long hours in one of their food sweatshops. Central was a decent little restaurant before it sold out.'

'Let's talk about this later,' she said.

'I don't want to join a corporate crèche.'

'You sound like someone else I know.' She was talking about her brother.

'Would you do all this again?' he asked. 'The restaurant. *This*?'

'Of course.' She kissed him and took hold of his hands across the table. 'Why not? We should get moving if we want to visit Felix.'

'You'd do all of this again even if you knew then, even if we knew a year ago, what we know today?' He looked out the window. 'Felix isn't really an option in this weather. I'm half expecting to see a glacier come sliding past this window.'

'We should keep trying,' she said. It was her answer for everything.

The hospital was quiet. Weather had turned the building into a squat igloo sandwiched between a long biscuit-glass monstrosity and a prawn-and-coal brick affair.

Downstairs a porter gleefully informed them that the elevators would remain sealed by order of the city fire department until the roads were declared safe for travel.

The soup sloshed about in the plastic container in Henry's backpack as he followed Dolores up the emergency stairway.

'I'm guessing this is the sixteenth floor?' she said when they reached a landing with a large red 16 on the wall.

Henry's breath was white and hot on his chest.

Felix's room was empty, and the hospital sheets were stretched tight across the bed. There were no machines and no laboured breathing. Henry felt Dolores reach out for his hand as they stared at the vacant bed in the hard winter light.

He called a nurse, and they both sat together in the passage, his hand resting on her arm, while the nurse went off to make some tactful enquiries about Felix's whereabouts. His brother-in-law was eventually located but before Henry would follow the nurse down two flights of stairs to the new room he excused himself and went into the now-vacant bathroom where he looked deep into the toilet bowl, peering closely to examine its white ceramic surface, and then he flushed the toilet twice in quick succession.

The room was dark and muffled, Felix shivering beneath his blankets, while against the far wall the television was experiencing its own snowstorm as grainy images shuddered and tumbled.

Henry took out a brown paper bag from his backpack, which he placed in the bedside cabinet, trying hard not to disturb the large pile of newspapers and magazines on the top of it, and then sat next to Dolores in a chair beside the bed.

The man was dying. Henry saw the wrinkles, etched deep into the cheeks and neck, as well as the marks of secondary infection on the sides of his nose where the nostrils met his bristled cheeks. Dolores reached out to wipe away what she thought were traces of make-up deposited by her kiss. However, the purple shadow on her brother's skin merely darkened and remained on his face.

They let him sleep.

When a nurse wheeled a machine into the room Dolores gave a slight jump. Henry smiled because he remembered Dolores swatting away the smoke from one of her crushed cigarettes in the days when she thought no one knew she was a smoker. Felix lifted his head as the nurse connected him to the machine that began checking his vitals. They watched her update the chart at the end of the bed and then she opened the quilted curtains and the dusty pewter blinds.

'It's depressing enough being trapped inside here,' Henry whispered to Dolores, 'without him having to see the devastation and death outside.'

'Oh, those are very pretty flowers, Felix,' Dolores said, annoyed with her husband. She read the card. 'Who's Jessica, Felix? And why does her note say you owe her money?'

'I need to go potty,' Felix said. Everyone seemed to be pretending that they hadn't heard him.

'How on earth did you get here today with all that snow out there?' the nurse asked. 'They've given us emergency quarters in the hospital.'

'Well, you know, we made a special effort to see how Felix was doing,' Henry said. 'You're looking good.'

'I said I need to visit the sand box,' Felix said.

Henry had a theory that Felix's happiness was dependent upon his slow visits to the toilet. Once, Henry and Dolores had caught him fresh from the bathroom, his hospital gown transparent against his wet chest and back, as three nurses settled him into bed. It was not a sight Henry wanted to see again. He stood up.

'Mr Stoll stopped eating again.' The nurse adopted the tone of someone speaking to a naughty child. 'I'm not sure if he's told you?'

'We've brought some more soup,' Dolores said to be helpful.

'Well, if he keeps this up,' the nurse said, 'we're all going to be in big trouble. Isn't that right, Mr Stoll?'

'He's not eating at all?' asked Dolores.

'I tell you what,' the nurse said, taking the container from Henry, 'home-cooked food makes everyone feel better, doesn't it, so this should do the trick. Now let's all give Mr Stoll some privacy so that we can get him to the restroom.'

*

Felix was propped up in bed, a backrest holding his head forward at what looked like an uncomfortable angle, sipping diluted cola from a plastic cup. There was no sign of the flowers.

'They moved everyone down to this floor because everyone was dying from an infection on the 16th,' he said. 'Their excuse for the move was that the sewerage pipes were blocked.'

Henry felt a cold prickle on his scalp, and he became conscious of the sound of his own heartbeat. He focused on Felix's grey sheet lifting and falling in time with his brother-in-law's breathing.

'And of course you know why they bothered, don't you?' Felix continued. 'The longer I'm kept alive the more insurance money this place gets. These new nurses have stolen some of my magazines.'

They all seemed to be thinking about this for some time. Henry noticed that the bedside lamp focused a weak trickle of light onto the wall behind the bed.

'Are you going skiing this year, Chef?' Felix asked.

'No,' Henry said, bracing himself for Felix's reminiscences. The skiing trip was their only shared family holiday. 'Perhaps another year.'

'If you want we could organise something for when you're better,' Dolores said.

'My only memory of that holiday is of the pain,' Felix said abruptly. 'I've always had problems, as you know. Our uncle studied to be a doctor. There is no shame in speaking about the body in Dolores's and my family. I've had severe bowel complaints since that trip. I think all those falls ruptured my insides.'

'I don't think that's necessarily true,' she said. 'You did well . . .'

Henry had never seen anyone more incompetent on the snow than Felix Stoll. Felix clinging to the instructor's yellow canvas jacket, his self-congratulatory roars when he made it onto the chairlift, and the detailed advice he would dispense at every supper lecturing everyone in the lodge about the nuances of skiing and snowboarding, convinced that he had taught his instructor. He always delayed dessert by having the waiters line up and demonstrate his techniques for surviving avalanches. (Henry recalled some hokum about doggy paddle as the great wave of ice-rock-flora terror rushed at your body.) 'You see these?' he would say as he pointed at his second-hand skiing jacket to fifth-generation Austrian skiers eating pig and stewed vegetables at the tables around him. 'These metal blocks help locate you after an avalanche. Swim away!' Here Felix's lengthy demonstration – arm movements bringing on a bout of unintended wheezing – started afresh. 'Swim *away* from the noise. Easy.'

On the fourth day Felix never came down to breakfast. Henry loped upstairs at Dolores's insistence and gave a polite rap on his brother-in-law's bedroom door. Receiving no response he tried the door – open – and entered.

When he passed the bathroom for a second time he heard someone muttering inside. Henry stopped outside the door and waited. He heard Felix whispering comforting devotions – 'Oh Christ. Oh Jesus. Oh Christ, Lord, Baby Christ.' – as, Henry assumed, the man's straining innards felt like they were tearing apart. When Henry closed the bedroom door after him he heard a shout: 'Dolores? Are you there? Get help!'

'I remember the pain,' Felix said with what appeared to be nostalgia, grasping Dolores's hand and pushing himself up toward her face. Henry heard the man's nails scratching the raised gentian letters on the hospital sheets – * PROPERTY OF FK&F HEALTHCARE * DO NOT REMOVE * – as he shifted his bulk. Henry had felt those nails brushing against the back of his own hand whenever Felix dispensed his paterfamilias greetings and farewells, and now he saw them pressing into Dolores's cheeks when she leaned in to kiss him. He thought again of Chin's fingers and he was relieved that they had changed rooms, and were away from where he'd disposed of the evidence. From where he sat Henry could smell the medicine on Felix's breath.

'Count yourself lucky for having such a caring wife, Chef. The world has no use for good people any more.'

'Yes, Felix,' Henry said, bracing himself for a lecture about the government's foreign policy gleaned from the angled paper mountain threatening to spill off the bedside table. On the top of the papers Henry could see architectural and news magazines. He was familiar enough with Felix's soliloquies to know that he must pay attention because if his brother-in-law felt that he had not quite grasped the subtlety of his sermon he would stop and ask questions. Hesitation meant that the lecture started from the beginning again. He tried hard to look alert and interested.

Felix emphasised the events signalling the end of the world ('We're living through one of the bleakest periods of history') and he identified signs of moral decay from the middle-class journalists whose work would one day engulf his bed. Felix's panic list: Good v. Evil ('The filth they broadcast from that thing has seeped into our society, into our thoughts. They've got us paying for it, wanting it,

which is the con of the century! We're subsidising humanity's downfall.'); lawyers ('Psh. Filter feeders. No,
they're a *membrane* separating the rich from the poor.'); and
on it went. Then he threw Henry off-guard by
momentarily segueing into an aside about the sins, or more
precisely the temptations, of the barnyard. Later he would
provide an update about wilful killing ('You know you're
in trouble when killers can afford million-buck shaves paid
for by the sordid photographs of the floozies whose
throats they've slit, ear to ear.'); the evils associated with
displaying excessive drives ('Swearing and drinking and
drugging away their lives. I've seen them, their faces heavy.
Sexual meat.'), but there was never any mention of obesity.
Felix ended with a rant about drug-fuelled displays; re-
ligious persecution ('modern-day Huguenots'); the effects
of poverty and homelessness – his point being that the
indigent were failures who were ruining things for
everyone else.

A porter walked into the room carrying the soup,
interrupting Felix's diatribe.

'Put it at the end of his bed,' Dolores told the man.

'He's new here,' Felix said once the porter had left.
'Eastern European. What is that?' He sniffed in the
direction of the soup. Ah, the real Felix, Henry thought,
the fussy Felix who would soon be pulling back from
Dolores when she raised the spoon up to his mouth.

'Broth,' Henry said. 'Water, stock, vegetables . . .'

After some convincing Felix took a sip of the hot
liquid. It ran down his chin as he pretended to swallow.

'Chef, were you at the opening of the new restaurant?'

'Which one? It's a big city out there . . .'

Dolores gave Henry a look. She retrieved the magazine
Felix was reaching for and handed it to Henry. On the
front page was an airbrushed photograph of Patrice
Czarny standing outside Central.

'You sold out and entered their competition, didn't
you?' he said as Henry pretended to read the article.

'I entered it for the publicity,' Henry said.

'For the *publicity*? Who enters competitions for the publicity?'

'Henry doesn't like competitions,' Dolores said, still trying to feed her brother.

'It's not that Henry doesn't like competitions,' Henry said, 'but rather that Henry thinks that it's not really a competition when there's no chance of winning. So that's why Henry's decided to focus on the publicity instead.'

'But you must win. If I can give you some constructive criticism, Chef: you're not going to win serving them soup that tastes like this. Hell, you can forget the publicity. And don't worry about repeating your father's mistakes.'

'Shut up, Felix,' Dolores said quickly. 'Just shut up.' She held out the spoon for him but by now her brother had collapsed back onto his headrest, and his body seemed to sink slightly into the mattress while his shoulders curved up against his cheeks. She put the spoon down and turned to her husband. 'We should get going.'

CHAPTER 6

THE HOT 100!

GRANT WHANT was flanked by a line of bored Furness Kindle & Flint executives at the long table on the far side of the Metropolitan Room. Earlier he had caught sight of them all tiptoeing up the steps of Obsidian House, the FK&F Publishing building (their bonsai prances taking them over the thimblefuls of water that had collected in the grooves of each step, such dainty and sprightly little people), and now their faces were hidden behind the flower displays that wilted on the main table. In front of Grant four stunted ice buckets were sweating into the cloth.

Patrice Czarny was standing behind the podium to the left of the main table, speaking to the audience of restaurateurs and Sunday Magazine employees. On the wall behind her was a rectangular outline of dirt – all that remained of the old 'NO' signs ripped from city building in the wake of the recent Relaxatory Proclamation. The sign had been 'NO SMOKING'. In front of Grant grey smoke blanketed the audience of restaurateurs who were puffing away, making up for lost time.

Henry and Dolores First were in the third row and he had a somewhat hazy view of the right side of Henry's face. A good, strong face.

FK&F Advertising (based in Islamabad? Turkmenistan?) had organised the launch party, and they were responsible for the card the size of a bedsheet – 'GOOD APPETITE!' – hanging a few inches above Grant's head.

Earlier, Patrice had pulled a cord to unveil the competition's logo: a heavy-duty knife, fork, spoon and chopstick radiating from a single point on a red background. He appreciated the slogan's simplicity, but he felt somewhat uncomfortable with its faintly Teutonic echoes. The *Nazi* Restaurant of the Year Competition? Beneath the logo was the magazine's new slogan: SLOW DOWN, PLEASURE UP: SUNDAY MAGAZINE!

Applause.

'Thank you,' Patrice said, now that she had finished her introduction. 'Thank you all for your *wonderful* energy. Our four chief judges.' She nodded at the four men sitting on Grant's right. Each judge grew animated as his name was called, and then he slipped back into a semi-vegetative state.

It wasn't so much Grant's reluctance to relinquish control of the competition, the magazine's competition, but rather the horror of seeing it turned into a common little monster that offended him. He had hoped that the competition would be a catalyst: it would get the public eating and talking about great food. It was meant to be a gourmet feast. It would find the best of the best. He remembered how, that morning, he had spent time sobbing over the dictionary in his bathroom. There seemed to be an increasing number of unexpected moments of sadness in his life recently, and this morning, just like this evening, was one of them: *chrisom* was one of the saddest words he'd ever read.

Patrice held up a hand that stopped the applause. She mentioned their *marvellous* sponsors: FK&F Healthcare, FK&F Banking, FK&F Publishing . . . The list went on. Grant used the time to review his plans for that evening: a quick drink here, something to eat at the after-speech buffet, and then out to play. He wondered whether anyone was taking Patrice seriously. It must be tough for her in the world of mere civilians, he thought.

He looked at his fellow executives and wondered if he'd ever be invited to their little elfin world to play with all their expensive corporate toys. They sat beside him with their fond memories, no doubt, of their carefree lives skipping through their boardroom bowers. The giggles and smirks as they discovered money hidden under tuffets in the shade of cool glens . . . He despised these usurping, wedge-heeled gnomes.

Patrice's speech continued as a large razzmatazzy banner was unfurled above the Nazi-like logo. This one had a picture of a large funnel:

1,000,000

100,000

10,000

1,000

THE HOT 100!

10

1

'*You* are the Hot 100,' she said while jabbing a finger at the crowd who responded with claps and cheers. '*You* are the Hot 100! Over the next month, your restaurants in this great city that we are privileged and proud and *truly honoured* to call our own, yes, this *great* city, will have the chance to compete for the prize because *you* are the Hot 100, and we'll continue until we find *the* restaurant of the year, ladies and gentlemen, *the* restaurant of the year!'

There was a rumour that Patrice had initially wanted the deciding vote, but she relented when it was pointed out to her that she had entered all of her restaurants in the competition.

Grant glanced at his watch. Eat, drink, fun. Heavy flakes fell outside.

'We'll pay your *Hot! 100!* restaurants a visit *in person*, with full media coverage, of course, and you will have another chance to impress the judges, then the top ten will be selected, again in extraordinarily difficult and challenging conditions, and the *Top! 10!* will compete for the title of *the* restaurant of the year. *Yes!*

Applause. He had once enjoyed discovering new restaurants and watch them flourish following his recommendations – once, it had all been real. Now he had a position and pension to protect.

He covered a yawn – one of Patrice's restaurants would win – and continued staring at Henry and Dolores, but mainly Henry. That face. They looked like the perfect couple; he was the perfect man.

And now they were drinking perfect champagne.

Grant was with the wonderful Henry First.

'You're officially one of the elect,' Grant told him.

'We're not sure about all this,' Henry said.

'It's too corporate for my husband.'

'It'll get your name in the papers.'

'Along with Patricia Czarny,' Henry said.

'Patrice,' Dolores corrected him.

'Don't let her hear you calling her Patricia,' Grant said. 'She hates Patricia – it's a verboten word. She thinks she's a man-eater, so lock up your husbands and Ketamine your horses – that sort of thing. I'm thirsty. You thirsty?' The champagne was going down well.

Henry offered to take their empty glasses and they watched him walk past the table laden with sweetmeats in the centre of the room under the large chandelier, and on to the bar. Grant observed a few starving middle-aged women also looking at Henry.

'Do they know what caused your illness?' Dolores asked.

'Food poisoning. No, don't worry – not your place.'

'I got the flowers,' she said. 'Thank you. It was very sweet but unnecessary. Henry called you my secret admirer for a day.'

'Yes, well' – he laughed – 'I'm not sure if he's aware, but he's on very safe ground as far as that is concerned.'

'I think your fan club may be approaching at ten o'clock.'

'Roger that,' he said and then glanced to his left. Two women wearing black cocktail dresses (clones of the many other starving middle-aged women in the room) bared their teeth at him. 'Hmm, I know the type . . .'

'They're deciding whether they should come over,' she said.

'You don't, by any chance, have a gun on you?'

The women sidled up, smiling cautiously. The room was filled with identical women: svelte, sexless creatures armed with alcohol (never food) who appeared to be listening intently; who appeared charming in a manufac-tured, charmless sort of way. The men in the room were cast from a similar mould: self-obsessed and concerned with their bodies and faces.

'You're Grant Whant, the food reviewer,' announced the woman, her face drawn and unhealthy, on his left.

'Yes. Good to meet you.'

'I'm representing television,' she told him without further introduction. 'Lucilla's with the PR company here at the Metropolitan Room. For the moment.'

'Well it's been a pleasure meeting you –'

'Do you only work in print or do you also do tele-vision?'

'I have done some television' – her saw her eyes light up – 'but I'm mainly confined to print these days.'

'Well, anyway, I'm Janique. And you' – Janique was addressing Dolores now – 'do you work for Mr Whant?'

'Before you go any further,' Dolores said, 'I must ask if you both go to the same stylist?'

The question confused the women and it looked as if Janique was about to ask her clone if they did in fact share stylists.

'No, I don't think so,' Janique said.

'But we're both wearing Armani,' the second woman said, 'which probably explains it. Lucilla. I'm her life coach. Janique's going to work in television.'

'So she was telling us,' Dolores said. She turned to Grant. 'You don't have a PA do you?' He shook his head. 'Then I guess I don't work for Grant. It's been lovely chatting to you both and good luck with your career.'

'It's a calling, really,' Lucilla said, and then Henry arrived with the drinks and Janique asked if he 'did' television. He denied all responsibility and they walked away, mid-sentence, to another group.

'Tell you what,' Henry said and he nodded in the direction of the windows on the east side of the room. 'How about we move over there?'

The city stretched out beneath them, Golden Square and Firsts in the foreground, while in the distance lights reflecting in the water.

The buildings looked soft in the afternoon sun. It was no longer snowing and summer air blew across the city. There would be a few days of warm, indifferent weather before the buildings sealed themselves (their windows, their doors, their vents) against the killing heat. On the radio that morning they had forecast storms for the two weeks leading up to Easter: weather trumping God.

'I thought I was going to be stuck at the bar for ever,' Henry said. 'Who were those two women? And had the one been caught in a fire?'

'A fire?'

'He's talking about her face, Grant. No, my sweet naïve husband, she's had some work done.'

'Extensive work, judging by her permanent smile,' Grant said. 'I'm guessing that Lucilla is a cocktail dress away from finding a surgeon who'll give her another touch-up, while the other's a cock away from a job on the box.'

Dolores laughed. 'That seems to be their agenda,' she said.

They sipped champagne.

'It must cost a fortune to clean these windows, don't you think?' Henry touched the glass. 'The protective bars used to run across here. With the Relax-Proc these places get to remove safety barriers if they interfere with the view.'

'Let's not talk politics,' Dolores said. 'And anyway this place has enough bars already. It looks like an Art Deco prison.'

'Now that you've had a good look at the competition,' Grant said, 'and the other restaurateurs, do you think you have a chance?'

'Of winning? Probably not.'

'Why is this such a big thing for you, Henry?' she said. 'It's still a chance.'

'My life consists of chances, Dolores, but they never seem to take you where you think they will. Don't you agree, Grant?'

'You're both in a different league.'

Dolores smiled. 'Are you saying we're better . . . or worse than this lot? Don't answer that. The truth is that Henry doesn't want to consider the possibility of winning because he didn't think of entering the competition in the first place. It's a boy thing.'

'Nonsense,' Henry protested.

'You're sulking because Felix spotted the competition before you did. And you know he'll ride your case about it if we get through to the next round.'

Grant's phone rang. 'I'm sorry,' he said to them and answered the phone.

'You horny bastard,' a male voice said in his ear.

'Hello?' Grant replied, uncertain whether he had mis-heard. 'Who is this?'

'You horny –'

'Yes, I got that.' He stepped away from the Firsts and into the path of an oncoming waiter. 'I'm sorry. Sorry.' Once Grant had helped the waiter to his feet the man be-gan picking up broken glass from the carpet.

'Who are you?' Grant said into the phone, but the connection was dead. It rang again as he was about to return to the Firsts.

'Hello,' the voice said firmly. 'Let's get one thing straight: you left me a message. You responded to my profile.'

Oh God. Yes. He felt a wave of intense embarrassment and panic, lost his grip on the phone, and almost cut off the caller.

'Yes, hello.' He remembered the websites he'd visited last night.

'Sounds like you're having fun there. I'm Andy. So are you gay or bi?'

'Um . . . yes . . . the former . . . and you?'

'Me, I'm into men. What about you?'

'This isn't really the best time. Could you perhaps, well, could you call me back later? Hello?'

The man swore and ended the call. Grant muttered some-thing into the dead phone and then said a cheerful goodbye – for the sake of the Firsts – before switching it off and then slipping it into his pocket.

'I'm giving you a hard time, aren't I?' Dolores was saying to her husband. She kissed him quickly. 'Another boy thing.'

'I suppose that if we don't win I can always blame Felix, hold it against him. I'm going to slip out to see how things are shaping up for tonight at the restaurant. I'll be back shortly.' Henry said his goodbyes.

'I don't think I've met your brother,' Grant said when they were alone.

'No,' Dolores said, still looking out the window. 'He's ill.'

'I haven't met him,' he said again for some reason, and then cut himself off because it sounded wrong.

'Do you have any brothers or sisters?' she asked. Her voice sounded calm, as if they were talking about the weather.

73

'I'm an only child.' He avoided intimate conversations because they tended to embarrass him, but he knew they were a necessary part of getting people to trust you. 'That sounded a bit like a confession, didn't it?'

She smiled. 'A lonely boy.'

He wondered whether she could tell that he didn't fit in with the rest of the FK&F crowd, or whether she thought that this was his scene. It was all puff, PR, self-serving bumf, everyone pandering to the corporation. Of course this was why they had changed his initial competition idea, getting the public excited about real food . . .

'You work with real food,' he said suddenly.

'I'm sorry?'

'I spend my days staring at a computer screen – so much for creativity – while you get to work with real food.'

'My husband does.'

'Exactly.'

She looked at him and shook her head, uncertain what he was getting at.

'Would you like some booze?' he asked, and before she could answer he had returned with two full glasses. 'You work with food. You make something.'

'We own a restaurant but I can't even feed my own brother,' she told him. He waited. 'The treatment's affecting him so badly that he's stopped eating.'

'I'm sorry to hear that.'

'I'm trying to find something he'll like,' she continued. 'With the drugs and treatment and everything else that's going on, he's lost his appetite. He's getting weaker and it's so frustrating. I thought we may have been on to something a week or so ago. We all have our own set of problems.' She gulped her drink.

'Slow down.'

'No, you finish yours. I need another.' She went to find some more.

He looked out the window, half-expecting to see the season change in front of him, and he remembered his first summer in the city – it had been so unexpected. When he arrived, the aeroplane doors opening to admit the tangy heat and then the journey to the run-down hotel where he unpacked his belongings into the far side of a cupboard. He had strolled around the local area and come across a midsummer park. Here he gawped at the flowers that were somehow beyond full bloom, astonished by the decadence rising from the beds, the colours humming and vibrating the afternoon air. Drugged, he wandered around the city gardens, working hard to avoid the wilting bridal parties who were posing for wedding portraits – the bride and groom looking staid and Plain Janey against the furnaces that raged in the swaying beds behind them. That day he crisscrossed his path again and again, retracing his steps through the park. It was then, during that astonished walk, that he understood for the first time this hemisphere's obsession with the height of summer. It was an epiphany: his moment in the rose garden. As he stood among the shocking flowers – volcanic eruptions and bullet-time lava floes – the books and poems and plays and musicals about midsummer moments made perfect sense. And now he remembered the city's summer welcome, and each subsequent summer was more intense.

Dolores returned with two more full glasses.

'Does your brother have difficulty swallowing?' he asked.

'He says that everything tastes like nothing to him.'

'You should go for a meat soup. He'll need the protein.'

They drank in silence.

'I've decided,' she said, 'that we'll get as much mileage out of this competition as possible. Free advertising never hurt anyone. We might even win.'

'You won't.'

'But if we did?'

'Your name's not Patrice Czarny.' He looked at her. She really was quite pretty.

'Cynic!'

'This whole thing is rigged, Dolores. Bottom line: if you win this competition, I'll give you my . . .' He stopped himself and laughed.

'What?'

'Nothing.'

'No, go on, you were going to give me your what?'

'Friendship. You have to realise that everything, everyone, is up for sale.'

A sheet of ice fell off a building and shattered on the northern part of the square. He swore.

'These women do all sorts of things to their bodies, don't they? The whole not-eating thing. It's self-hatred, don't you think?'

'I suppose they're happily unhappy in their own little non-eating clubs.'

'Do you think they enjoy punishing themselves? As a restaurateur it's difficult for me to stop thinking about food, let alone stop eating it. We shouldn't be too hard on anorexics, though, should we? They're hard enough on themselves.'

'Dolores, honey, everyone, including the anorexics, is the enemy. You do see that, don't you?' He had drunk far too much. 'You're in the business of food, I'm in the business of food. And this place – this competition – is anti-food. "Nothing tastes as good as thin feels."'

'What?'

'"Nothing tastes as good as thin feels." Patrice Czarny's mantra.'

Henry joined them. 'What on earth are you two talking about?'

'Food,' Grant answered. 'Is there anything else?'

They were standing close to the taut window.

'Fab view,' Dolores said. 'Did you see the sheet of ice hitting the square?'

Henry nodded. 'Feel the glass. Touch there,' he said.

Grant placed his hand on the glass. It felt like cold metal.

'It's so cold it feels hot,' he said.

'It is hot,' Henry said. 'You can feel the warm wind outside. It picked up that ice and dumped it in the square like a sheet of paper.'

The window thudded against Grant's palm. Wind carried sound from the grey suburbs to the skyscrapers where it hit this glass and the hundreds of thousands of panes just like it. Dolores put a hand beside his. On the wall on either side of this Olympic-sized pane were three metal studs – the remains of the protective metal barrier.

'Have you finished networking?' Henry asked his wife. 'We should get back to the restaurant. I suppose this lot have managers looking after their places.'

'Grab my coat, will you?' Grant said. 'I need to have a word with Patrice and then I'll catch up with you downstairs.'

They said their farewells where, a few hours earlier, there had been snow, and Grant was watching the beautiful Henry First slide an arm around Dolores's waist as they walked back to their restaurant when a taxi pulled up alongside him.

'Go south,' Grant told the neck and thinning hair, and they were off. They rollercoastered down the avenue, the seat coughing as the cab bounced over the cross-streets.

Half an hour later he had the driver circle the block twice before he stepped onto the street. He walked up to, and then past, the entrance, having decided on a brisk stroll around the city block past the faded lettering of forgotten pubs, their windows smeared with torn posters and mud. The employees of a cab company watched him pass, their faces yellow then soapy white as the sign on their wall glared TAXIS & CAB CARS. As he hurried by he heard the dull clicks of the cerise neon tube spelling out OPEN 24 – 7.

Before long he was back at the entrance, staring. He checked the note in his pocket and then his watch. By the time he located the door in the shadows – a dull studded affair – he was ready to stop the expedition and continue home. The door slammed shut behind him, and he was inside, looking around, trying to appear nonchalant.

The lobby was worn (damp magazines, wicker table) and a man – the gatekeeper – sat snug behind a scratched plastic barrier; his long hair stuck to his forehead like a lacquered wig.

'Name,' the man demanded. His fingers scuffed the page of an exercise book with four inked columns as he waited for a response.

'Henry First,' came out of Grant's mouth, which struck him as mildly humorous, and he had to suppress his smile. He watched the man hesitate then misspell the words, his pen continuing erratically beyond the final letter and finishing with a dismal paraph.

'Thirty-five,' he said pointing an elbow to the rate-sheet taped on the wall.

30 SINGLE ENTRANCE + 5 DEPOSIT (REFUND WHEN KEY
IS RETURNED!!!)
NO KEY = NO DEPOSIT.
COME ON GUYS LET'S WORK TOGETHER!!!!

'Here's an extra twenty for the special,' Grant said as he dropped some notes into the large cage drawer.

The man shunted back two warm towels and a key bound with a loop of elastic.

Grant felt himself kick into autopilot and soon he was watching himself removing his clothes in a corridor lined with gym lockers that smelled of damp bread (no, musty cucumber). His hand grabbed a towel, locked the door and snapped the jangling key to his left wrist.

Beyond the locker area was an empty gym, the equipment old and incomplete. He walked past the forgotten weights and trudged up a flight of wooden stairs into a busy pool area. All the men wore white towels around their waists. As he watched he saw an occasional hand reaching down to secure a moist knot.

He glanced at his watch again and then sat on the plastic ribs of a deckchair, waiting, his toes growing fluffy and wet on the cool tiles. There were hazy images on a squat television bolted high above the row of men lounging against the opposite wall; his closest companion had a large hairless rectangular head – his skin florid with rash and heat. This man removed his glasses and gave them a brisk rub with the corner of his towel. Nestling behind each ear was a thin imprint of a spectacle arm and some bristles that had missed the last shave.

Three things: there appeared to be a holding pattern around the pool, men circled and passed through an archway painted with too-ripe grapes into what must be the steam rooms and showers; most of the men were in their late twenties; none of them looked at him. He could sense that the man on his left was eager to begin a conversation and because of this he focused his attention on the reds and greens on the television screen. A hand touched his.

'No.' Grant stood up, and looked at his surprised companion and saw that the man was merely rearranging himself on his chair.

'Are you prepared to die for love?' the man said. He had an accent. 'Are you prepared –'

'Yes, I heard you the first time. What is this, Medieval Europe? I mean, how on earth am I meant to respond to that?'

'Well if you're not interested, just say so. No need to get all defensive.' Grant was uncertain whether he should sit back down again because he felt embarrassed by having to stand.

'If you don't mind,' Grant said, 'I'd rather not continue this conversation.'

'What are you here for? What are you here for? *Exactly*.'

'Yeah, sure, whatever.' Grant walked away, past the un-wholesome pool and through the archway and down a wide passage lined with dripping doors. An elderly man stepped out of a sauna on his right, his broiled skin hanging from his back and legs. The skin on his face hung away from his eyes, exposing flesh that looked tender and steaky. Disorientated, the man stepped towards him with a bald calf, and then turned towards the showers at the end of the passage and stumbled away, his heavy towel slapping against his legs as he walked. Grant followed the man to the noise of the showers and watched him man-oeuvre past the younger occupants. The man secured a dripping nozzle and hit out at the two pressure valves.

All the thinking he'd done about this place was sexier than actually being there, he thought. He'd noticed the ads in the city's gay mags, groups of Adonises fresh from the gym, flash smiles, welcoming eyes. These places thrived on youth and rejection, and here it was . . . all around him. The promise of youth made him feel unsexy and fat. Rejected, unsexy, *old* and fat.

It took a while for his eyes to acclimatise to the steam room's medicinal haze. He could make out shapes of men sitting against the walls, their legs snug against each other. Most of the towels were still firmly bound about waists. The atmosphere was of restrained primness: decadent convent girls waiting for their turn on the dance floor. They were all watching one another – at first there had been a few glances in his direction but his boring search for a place to sit soon lost him his audience. With a few apologetic grunts he managed to encourage someone to make space for him beside the door that had been propped open by a party of whispering teenagers.

There were a few people speaking very softly, but the main activity appeared to be sitting and waiting. Nothing happened. He thought gay men were fabulous, horny bastards. More nothing happened. The smallest bit of movement created excitement – and even though nothing was happening – everyone was on the lookout for some wrist movement or some extravagant rearranging of a towel. The amount of activity appeared to be inversely proportional to the age and beauty of the mover: the young and pretty remained motionless, bored with all the attention; the older trolls were spry and willing to flash and fondle.

He was shivering in the draft. For a moment he considered saying something to the teenagers holding open the door, but when he took a quick look at the group he realised that they would probably ignore him and then delight in victimising him for the remainder of the evening. The place was hell. Lichen stains grew across the grouting and nothing was happening and there was still nothing to see. The vent pumped out a dull cloud of steam and hot water; his throat burned; his left side was cold. After a few minutes the red-faced man from the pool walked in and insisted on squeezing beside him.

Grant thought about Henry and his wife, and he wondered what Patrice was planning for them. He had spoken to her just before leaving the party and told her that he was becoming best friends with the Firsts, which was halfway true, and she had replied with nothing more than a smile. They were becoming friends – Dolores and him, he could feel it. It didn't bother him that he was cultivating the friendship because he liked Dolores and her husband and would ideally have wanted to be close to them, and it also gave him a chance to prove his loyalty to Patrice.

The man sitting next to Grant was pressing against his thigh. Then a severed hand floated into view, all slippery fingers and strong ivory nails tripping on the ceramic tiles. It was *something*, Grant acknowledged; something was happening and it would lead to something else, but now he longed for the earlier nothing. The man held his hand above the tips of his fingers, making it appear like a little person walking across the tiles, index and middle fingers taking a stroll. The fingers continued to march the hand beside Grant's leg before one pointed to the steam-room door, towards that pruinose barrier. Grant shook his head. The hand twisted and the thumb revealed a thickly foiled condom lying in the centre of his palm.

Action in the corner! A young man was crouching before an even younger man! Observers scrummed around and after a few minutes of trying to look through this circle of men Grant gave up and turned to head for the door.

'Stay and watch,' he said to the bald man who was standing just beside him. 'More fun than me.'

'Are you still pissed off with me?'

'Number one, I'm not angry with anyone, I just happen to think that you're not for me. Number two, I'm not sure I'm in to dying just yet. At least not with you.'

'So that's a "no", then?'

'We're sitting in a roomful of naked men. Go wild. Just leave me alone.'

'You can be fun.'

'Are you a masochist or just stupid?'

The showers were not much warmer, and after a quick visit to the remaining steam rooms he spent a few minutes in a sauna watching a dusky child sleeping in the dry heat. The towel clung to Grant's legs and his eyes burned. It felt as though he had been there hours. Even the pretty boys with their feet dangling in the pool were looking bored. This place was in a holding pattern like the city around him. Everyone waiting.

He returned to the stairs and walked up to the next floor . . . away from the lockers . . . further away from the exit.

At the top of the landing was a dark corridor with more doors, perhaps a dozen or so all leading to the rooms of infinite delectation.

He glanced into one of the rooms and saw a dusty light bulb and plastic sheeting over a worn foam mattress. Most of the others were occupied, and despite himself he felt an adrenal kick thinking about the possibilities: the flaccid bodies, the chests thick with hair, legs, arms scarred by the marks left by the Kevlar sheeting's seams. He looked at his watch again – he had more important things to do. From behind the closed doors he was able to make out the noise of standard, buff Hollywood porn. There were a few men in the corridor – too serious, too focused, all waiting.

And in the middle of the sexual fantasies   God, it would be starting in less than five minutes! – he heard the sound of a glass smashing on the tiles in the pool area. He looked down at his bare feet – his small and vulnerable toes – and he felt his heart beating in his ears. That would be just great, he thought, cutting himself on broken glass.

He left the passage with its wooden doors and headed back for the stairway to the first landing, and there he caught sight of a man stranded in the centre of a mis-shapen pool of blood – homosexual *en meurette*. The man lifted his foot and Grant saw that the underside had been sliced open. At the edge of the inky pool of blood an attendant was motioning for the man to remain still, waving both hands as if shooing away chickens.

He walked around the tableau – giving it the widest possible berth – and headed for a red door.

Later he hurried down the stairs to the lockers where he changed quickly, his legs and crotch difficult as he pulled up his trousers. Twice he stepped on the saturated towel with his sock.

He perspired in the early-morning air as he headed for the cab-hire company; the office was open but unable to supply any cars. The streets were empty and the snow had melted away.

'Yes,' he said as he stepped back onto the street, 'next time I'll reserve a cab.'

He walked south to the station – passing a church – towards the arched lights reflecting off the river. Is anyone still prepared to die for love? In his dictionary the word *penis* came before *penitent*; *chastity belt* and *chasuble* were bedfellows.

CHAPTER 7

WombWell

DOLORES FIRST'S HAND reached beneath the duvet and slid across the sheet until her fingers found Henry's empty pillow.

She got out of bed, switched on the light and opened the cupboard with care, slowing the door's arc with her hand to prevent any noise. As a child, the extra pillows and blankets had always been hidden on the top shelf of her bedroom cupboard, but now she kept them within easy reach. They were all there.

The spare room was unoccupied, and in the lounge the sofa was empty.

She called out for Henry and heard the sound of her own voice in the dark, but no response. Dolores called again from the kitchen. Where was he? Dead . . . dying somewhere? *Dao mei*. She tried to remember what had planted those words in her mind. After drinking some water she wiped her mouth on the dishcloth that had dried to a crust over the kitchen taps, and then she stared out the window. *Dao mei*, again. It was still night but the city was awake, and somewhere in that noise was Henry First. Of course, and this was another thought, he was out jogging.

She returned to the bedroom and opened the cupboard door, and saw that his running shoes were gone. How simple. She would wait on the sofa.

*

She woke up when Henry was carrying her to their bed.

'I'm sorry,' he whispered, 'go back to sleep.'

'You've been out for a long time,' she said. She stopped herself from adding, You had me worried sick.

'I needed to clear my mind,' he said. 'I went for a run.'

She saw his watch. 'Henry, it's just before 4 a.m.' He smelled of cigarettes and his face looked worn. He put her on the bed and was covering her with blankets. 'We should be at the market,' she said. 'We should be there together.'

'I couldn't sleep.'

She rehearsed the sentence: Perhaps, next time, you'll leave me a note. If you have time . . . 'Leave me a note next time, will you?'

'Sure.' He ran his right hand across her forehead; his fingers were damp.

'You'll be fine.' She kissed him. 'Somehow we'll both survive all of this. I should get up now.' She followed him down the passage, where he grabbed the towel hanging over the bathroom door. 'How about some breakfast?'

He touched the tip of her nose with a thumb; a quick flick, a soft dab. 'That would be *purr*-fect.'

'You were restless last night,' she said, looking at him.

'Dolores, does this look like the face of someone who ever gets his beauty sleep?' He was in the bathroom. 'I need to . . .' He smiled and began closing the door. 'I need to, you know . . . ablute.'

In the kitchen she stared into one of the cupboards for a while before deciding to brew some coffee and set the table. By the time she was frying some bacon and eggs, Henry had emerged from the bathroom wearing the bathrobe that he had insisted on buying himself – she called it his gigolo robe – his hair towelled dry and his skin smooth from the shave.

'Help yourself,' she said and he poured two coffees, both black, and then he dropped a cube of sugar into his cup.

'A lot of people out there?' she asked.

'The usual suspects: insomniac dog-walkers, twenty-four hour shoppers, bus drivers getting their hair cut before their shifts . . .'

'Next time I'll join you.' She grabbed four slices of bread from the sealed plastic bag on the counter, and then stopped to look at him. '*I* jog,' she said emphatically as the slices dropped into the toaster. She thumbed down the lever and the toaster began to click.

'It's just that I've never seen you exercise in your life.'

'Drink your coffee.'

'Right,' he said, beaming. 'Great coffee, as always.'

She served the bacon and eggs with a halved tomato, set the plates on the table, and sat opposite him.

'Let's run away,' he said after a few mouthfuls. 'Now.'

'This might not be the best timing in the world.'

'It would be great timing. Screw the competition. Just you and me. If we hurry we could catch a flight by mid-day.'

She let him eat. There was a clatter as the toast leapt from the toaster: Surprise! 'I'll book something for us at the end of the month.' For the second time that morning she glanced at his watch. 'I really should be in the bath by now, shouldn't I?'

'We've got time,' he said. 'Speak to me.'

'How are you feeling about today?'

'Let's talk about something other than the competition.' He asked her about a spiritual workshop she had recently attended. Dolores had booked her place and then ignored his request that she cancel, even though it had eaten up the weekend and the first three days of that week. 'It's my time,' she had told him, so he knew not to press her.

'Much nudity?' he asked.

She smiled. 'They asked us not to talk about that.'

'Ms Hard-To-Get.'

'There can never be enough nudity, if I'm honest,' she joked.

She finished her breakfast and went to the bathroom. He followed and watched her preparing the room – now she was grabbing a fresh towel from the cupboard, now she was filling the tub with water.

'How are you feeling about today?' she tried again.

'It can happen, you know. One minute you're handing out lotus flowers in the airport and the next you find yourself in a mass wedding.'

'And we're *still* talking about the course . . .'

'How about we go back to the bedroom?'

They looked at one another. It had been a while.

She shook her head, turned on the cold water, the hard jet drowning his words. Then she slipped off the T-shirt and pants she had slept in and, after testing the water with her hand, turned off the tap and eased herself into the tub.

'I think I'm ready for today,' he said, sitting on the lip of the bath while she washed, her skin looking soft and vulnerable in the warm water. When she sat up to reach for the soap he dipped his hand into the water and drew a line on her stomach with a finger. 'On Saturday afternoon I saw one of our new guys showing off a scar over here,' he said as he touched her skin again.

'That's romantic.'

His finger ran across the small curves of her ribs towards her armpit. 'The sous chef, Rams.'

'Ramanuja?'

'That's him. He'd unbuttoned his top and was showing the others a long scar on his waist, a kidney scar, I'm guessing. When he saw me watching he became embarrassed, as if I'd caught his hand in the cookie jar.' The price of a ticket to the First World. He shuddered at the thought.

'You never really know about other people's lives, do you?' She pulled the plug, stood up and he handed her the towel. 'Something I've been meaning to say to you' – she dried herself – 'don't you think Felix is looking so much better?'

He nodded.

'Where's the time going this morning?' She tied the towel around her.

'Your brother drives me up the wall when I visit him,' he said as he stood back to give her space to get out of the bath, 'so that must be a good sign.'

'When *you* visit him?'

'Sure.'

'*You* visit my brother. Without me?'

He nodded. 'I stop by after work when I get the chance. I even saw him while you were being rebirthed.'

'Come on.' They went to the bedroom where she finished drying and slipped on the new dress she'd bought for today. He put on his chef's whites. She thought about Henry's visits to Felix and smiled.

'Why the hell does that producer want me to dress up?' he said. 'They must think I wear my uniform on the train each morning. They're bound to be upset when they realise that I don't wear a toque.'

'It'll make good television,' she said. 'Do you want me to go with you to the market next Friday morning?'

'You hate the market.'

'What can I say? This course has made me into a kinder, gentler person.'

'I'll be fine. I'm getting deliveries next Friday.'

She looked at him. He always told her that delivered food tasted of carbon monoxide.

'I'm trying deliveries for a week,' he said when he saw her face.

'Next week?'

She was brushing her hair and he addressed her reflection in the mirror. 'Sure.'

'You think the week of the competition is a good time to try this out?'

'So, no sex, but there's time for a discussion about produce deliveries? Mornings were our time for sex. Sex in the kitchen, sex in our first apartment, touching in the last train back home –'

The security phone at the end of the hallway buzzed and she couldn't hear his words for the second time that morning.

'I'm happier,' she said to his reflection in the mirror.

'I know,' he said softly, kissing the back of her neck. The buzzer, again.

'There isn't really a good time to say this sort of thing, but I feel better.' The buzzer sounded again. 'You should answer it.'

She could hear him saying, 'Sex on the sofa, sex in the bathroom . . .' as he walked down the passage.

'It's that horrible woman,' he said when he returned to the bedroom, 'and she needs us to "hurry on down".'

*

A truck idled on the eastern side of Golden Square. Thick cables led out of the vehicle, through Firsts' front doors, and into the kitchen where Henry stood waiting. He was down below in the kitchen but also up in the restaurant where Dolores watched his image repeated on the small television monitors around her.

Henry looked into the camera, unaware that he was looking directly at his wife, his face uncertain. Everyone was waiting for Janique, the presenter, who was in Make-up. Standing around Dolores's table were some technicians and crew and restaurant staff.

When Janique eventually emerged from the hair and make-up truck she threw open the restaurant doors before striding past Dolores down to the kitchen. A few minutes later an order came up for some of the restaurant staff to join Janique downstairs.

'Are we ready, then?' the man on Dolores's right asked no one in particular before heading off to another one of the vans. 'On my way.'

*

The image on the screens shifted and lost focus; zoomed out until it found Janique and Henry, and then zoomed back in again. It pulled tight onto Janique's eyes, embarrassingly close, the image twitching as it lost and then regained focus. They were talking, Janique telling Henry where to look.

'We're shooting?' she asked the screen. She nodded at him. 'Always at the camera during pauses, Henry, never away. Look at me when you're talking. Ignore the monitors – just pretend they're not there. Oh, we're going. Just have fun, baby. Where are your staff?' There was movement off-camera, and then Akhilesh, Ishwar, Chandresh, Ramanuja and Vasudev were positioned in the back of the shot before being told to ignore the cameras and the demonstration. 'Right, we're going.' Her voice changed as she stared into the camera. 'You're with Janique and *this –*' Pause, overlong pause, and then quickly: 'is *WombWell*.'

Henry spoke about his life, the restaurant, the competition. He ran through his preparations for the competition.

'*Next* Friday,' Janique said, stopping him. 'I thought this would be screened on Easter Monday?' She addressed the camera. 'Hold it. This *will* be screened on Easter Monday? So we're doing this in the past tense? Are you sure about that, Phillip? You're not? Oh, *we're* not. Phillip, park that thought. Present. Tense. On camera it's already Good Friday? Right.'

Another woman had emerged from one of the trucks and made her way into the restaurant and sat beside Dolores.

'This part is more fun for them than it is for us,' she said. 'You're Dolores First, right?' Dolores nodded. 'I'm Lucilla.' She handed Dolores a card that had the words LIFE COACH and SPEED COUNSELLOR printed in vermilion. Dolores recognised Lucilla from the Hot 100 party. 'Janique's looking fabulous, don't you think? Had her eyes and neck done right here.' Her hand waved vaguely towards Golden Square.

Dolores looked back at the screens and concentrated on the demonstration.

Henry had just run through the recipe's ingredients.

'I'm mushroom intolerant,' Janique said as she peered nervously into the bowl of morilles. She poked them with her finger. 'What is that *smell*?'

The mushrooms were Dolores's idea, farmed in the disused limestone caves in the troglodytic Loire valley. When Henry unsealed the container earlier that morning they had smelled smooth, nutty, velvety. Dolores imagined their soft, buttery taste.

'And this?' Janique said, finger hovering.

'This is the lamb.'

'You mean mutton?'

'No, it's actually called lamb,' he said, smiling. Dolores heard the sliver of control in his voice, and she smiled to herself. '*Young* mutton.'

'But while they are alive we call them sheep and lambs but when we eat them we call the meat mutton,' Janique said. 'Don't we? Think about it, we talk about cows in the field, but we eat beef. And yet they're the same thing.'

There followed a socio-tabloid-linguistic discussion about the intricacies of naming meat, where Janique's assertion was that mutton, pork and beef were always differently named from their animal source in the English language, while Henry countered with the example of fish and lamb. Things turned French (her name was not just for show, it transpired) and her *porc* and *boef* were countered by Henry's *agneau, sanglier, chèvre, grenouille, lapin, lièvre, dinde, canard, poulet* and *biche*.

Cutting-room floor, Dolores thought as Janique wordlessly tilted the plate of meat to the camera. The Karakul lamb had been reared and then butchered by a German whose Bavarian-style farmhouse overlooked the Namib dunes rich with diamonds. It had arrived that morning.

'I was expecting some fish,' Janique announced, 'today being Good Friday.' Henry didn't respond.

His increasingly tense review of ingredients continued on the monitors around Dolores, and then this was followed by a close-up of Henry hacking at the mushrooms.

'Look at him go,' Lucilla said. 'You're safe with her, as far as your husband's concerned. She's a bit of a minx while they're shooting, but she would never cheat on anyone after her experience of her own husband's latest affair. So no need to worry. Do you?'

Puzzled by the question, Dolores looked at Lucilla to see that she was offering a cigarette.

'No thanks,' Dolores said.

The mushrooms were now frying in a pan.

'Everyone can do this at home?' Janique said on-screen. Henry nodded.

Close-up of Janique's face and she glanced to her left. 'Look, we need to stop this for a moment. I'm glowing in this heat. Sorry, Henry. Make-up! I'm not sure why I have to be the one monitoring everything, Phillip. It's difficult enough interviewing without . . .' A make-up artist began padding Janique's face with a small sponge. 'Thank *you*!'

'Janique thinks she caught her husband having an affair,' Lucilla said. 'It's not like she walked in on them; though walking in on them would at least have given her some decent closure. No, she hasn't caught them . . . rutting. Not yet, anyway. She loaded software onto his laptop and left it recording for a week. You should see what he's been up to with some floozy. We're waiting for the right moment to confront him.'

'I see,' Dolores said.

On-screen the make-up artist had stepped out of shot and they continued the interview. Soon Henry was preparing the fruit, small and round and as yet unnamed, harvested from the canopy of a Madagascan rainforest by a pair of chatty French botanists who had been suspended from a dirigible. It had a sweet, vaguely citrus smell. They were also Dolores's idea, and expensive enough for neither her nor Henry to be able to read the invoice.

'The secret to any chef's success lies in the spice,' Henry was saying as he dipped his fingers into a small white bowl filled with hard black peppercorns, 'and this is pepper from the spice market in Cochin. It arrived less than an hour ago. Here, smell this.'

Janique looked blank. 'Pepper?'

'Cochin is in India.'

'Sure. And what's in that big pot thingy over there?'

'Stock. It's the base flavour that all dishes start with, a bit like the first layer of paint on an artist's canvas –'

'*Shut up!*' Lucilla said to the monitor. 'Isn't he just fabulous? For now we're satisfied with punishing her husband. Take a look at that chunk of carbon on her finger. Armondo gave that to her last week. He knows that she knows that he knows. She's doing really well though.' She leaned over to Dolores, burnt cigarettes on her breath. 'Janique's real breakthrough was when she started talking to me about her *shmundie*.' Dolores watched Lucilla fanning her face with her hands, her eyes reddening. Although Dolores hadn't heard the word before she had a pretty good idea what it meant. She looked around to see if anyone had overheard the word.

'Then I knew,' Lucilla continued. 'Girlfriend, you're on the path to salvation! The little things are the giveaway, aren't they? Can we get *something*?'

Dolores called one of the wine stewards and Vyomesh returned with mineral water and glasses. Lucilla wrinkled her nose at him and said, 'Vodka, honey,' and he brought a bottle with ice.

Around them there were close-ups of Henry preparing the lamb, his fingers running across the surface of the meat – soft and vulnerable.

'Janique's twelve-year-old wants a facelift. Frankly, I can't blame him. If he has just the right amount of work done he'll look like a toddler again. Trouble is finding the *right* surgeon. The medical equivalent of your husband, honey – an *artist* with a scalpel is worth his bodyweight in silicone. Henry's got the touch, all right. Janique tells me that if this goes well with her series of Hot 100 interviews there are plans for a WombWell series. So what do you do? I mean, apart from working for your husband. What *else* do you do?'

'This is it.'

'Dolores, honey, speaking professionally now, you need to *make the time*. You're so *funny*. All work and no play. You can't always be pushing yourself. You need to make time for Dolores. And that way your body will be given a chance to stop looking so worn and grumpy.

'I should warn you not to go on about Janique's husband if you get to talk to her after this shoot. God, I've got a *verkakte* headache. Never slept a wink. What's *that*?'

Dolores had taken out a small plastic tube from her bag. 'They're for your headache. Homeopathic.'

Lucilla accepted two little white pills, and, after gulping them down with a mouthful of vodka, she continued. 'Now, about Armondo's affair. I have a feeling that he's a happy shopper.' Dolores looked a little puzzled. 'Christ, he shops on both sides of the street, honey. Armando is sleeping with another *man*. Frankly I think this is the best thing that could have happened to him. Sad for Janique, I admit. But you're with me on this, aren't you? I can tell. Life is too short to hide behind formality.'

Whenever Henry offered Janique an ingredient to smell or taste, she would turn away from him to pull a face or grimace at the camera, and then smile when she looked back at him. At first Dolores assumed that he was playing along with Janique, but watching her on-air retching when he passed the fruit under her nose, Dolores wondered if her husband had seen the presenter's gurning.

'Let's just say I know from personal experience that Armando has a habit of changing lanes without indicating. One moment he's working away your front door, and then you lose concentration for a second and you've been taken by surprise because he's gained entry via the servant's entrance, so to speak. Not that I'm a prude, but a girl appreciates some warning, don't you agree? Here, take this.' She pulled out a large, well-thumbed yellow book from her bag – *Anal Needn't be a Stab in the Dark* – and handed it to Dolores, who placed it on the table in front of her, and then moved it to the empty chair on her right. 'You change your position,' Lucilla was informing her, 'and it'll change your life. But praise God Armando finds himself. Let the man be happy! Let him be true to himself. And you, hold on to what you've got, honey. Your marriage . . . your lovely, plain, uncomplicated, *uncompromising* nature . . . the good things in your life. And if you agree to have work done, call me. I recommend Janique's surgeon. Well, he's her husband's, actually. He lipos fat out of her thighs, and I know what you're thinking, that she doesn't have any fat on her, well believe me, good clothing covers a multitude of sins. She is *loaded* with cellulite. So he extracts, makes a paste from the collagen which she applies to her face twice a day, and the results are just fabulous. She booked this surgeon after he had successfully bleached Armondo's *tukhus*.'

Henry had finished crushing the fruit. He picked up a small glass cup containing a fine brown substance, a sweet nugget of sand from the inner core of a termite mound, and angled it towards the camera.

'Have you had anything done yet?' Lucilla asked.

Dolores shook her head, not taking her eyes off the demonstration. Janique handed the sand back to Henry, smiled, and then turned to the camera and rolled her eyes.

'It's us hags that go in for repairs,' Lucilla was saying. 'A life lived too close to the flame.'

A life spent avoiding the fridge, Dolores thought. She considered telling Lucilla about how dangerous operations were, and how easily things could go wrong. The power could fail, and then you're relying on the hospital's backup. An untimely blackout and the patient lies dying with her face peeled over her chest while the surgeon attempts to summon an electrician. But nothing could shut Lucilla up.

Henry poured some red wine into the cup containing the sand. He held the cup up to the camera and then poured the contents onto a piece of muslin cloth stretched across a bowl.

'We've decided to punish Armondo,' Lucilla said abruptly. 'When he's been out to see this *person*, Janique has a slap-up meal waiting for him at home.' Lucilla stared at Dolores.

'And this is punishment?' Dolores eventually asked. Henry had mixed the fruit and the mushrooms: earthy red with honey brown.

'She comes on to him. She makes like she's horny, and they end up having sex. Last Thursday they went for it twice in a row. He could hardly walk the next morning. Look, I'm so bored with this conversation. Let's talk about *you*. You're both all over the place. You're both *ridiculous*. I can't open a magazine without seeing a First. You're the couple of the moment, honey, so tell me about you and your husband.'

'What's to say?'

'Subject change,' Lucilla announced. 'We need a table for next Friday. You can get someone to action that?'

'Of course.'

'If I'm honest with you, this is the most unflattering lighting I've ever seen in a restaurant. Porn lighting. I'm saying this from a place of love, you realise that. Any chance you can get it seen to – *professionally* – before Friday? Just a thought. Janique's got a wardrobe change scheduled. Come on, she's dying to meet you.'

Despite her protestations, Lucilla dragged Dolores into one of the trucks. She wanted to see Henry, but she couldn't extract herself from Lucilla's grip or her company.

Janique arrived and kissed them both. '*You* are?' she said at Dolores.

'Dolores First.'

'Right,' she said, grabbing Lucilla's hand and leading her into the adjoining room. 'Take a seat, honey.'

Dolores sat on the edge of the sofa, waiting. She could hear them talking in the room alongside hers. Her head hurt. The perfume in the trailer was making her eyes water and she covered them with the palms of her hands for a while and waited, listening to the muffled voices.

'I think I should go,' she said out loud after a few minutes.

'No, wait for us, honey,' Lucilla called out.

When Janique emerged from the dressing room she was wearing an organza shawl that appeared to be floating a few inches away from her shoulders.

'What do you think?' Janique said, giving the shawl a twirl. Lucilla stood beside her.

'You look angelic,' Dolores offered.

'Yes, angelic's good,' Janique said. 'We like angelic. I don't know if I have the right shoes, though. And that's not angelic in a mutton-dressed-as-lamb kind of way – is it, Dolores? But then you're not the sort of person to tell me if it was. Am I right?'

'Janique, she said you look angelic. Give the woman a break.'

'Lucilla, that depends whether this is giving you a Christmas-fairy feel, or if it's more like angel-appearing-before-Our-Lady Annunciation chic?'

'Or the angel accompanying Adam and Eve out of the garden,' Lucilla said. 'Me, I think the whole ensemble makes your bum look massive.'

'Thank you,' Janique said firmly. 'Now that's the sort of feedback I'm looking for, Dolores. My bum looks too big, so this goes back on the hanger for some other poor cow who doesn't pay for Lucilla's honesty.'

A phone rang and Janique retrieved something the size of a tube of lipstick from her bag.

'*Pronto!*' she screamed. 'Baby! Sure, baby. It's going so good, money well spent. They want you? No, away you go.

Yes, honestly. Phone me later. Thanks for the call, *ciao ciao*. That bastard.' Then she stared at Dolores. 'So this makes me look hippy?'

Dolores watched the wardrobe assistant zip Janique up in a second dress; she saw how he had to pull the fabric away from her back to avoid knocking the zipper against the bumps of her spine.

'I look huge in this thing, don't I?'

'It suits you,' Lucilla told her.

'But I look like a –'

'Janique,' Lucilla said, 'remember what we spoke about earlier? Well you're doing it now. It's so embarrassing.'

'I didn't know it extended to all areas of my life.'

'Well it does. You're fine in that outfit. Phillip needs to get this shoot wrapped.'

*

Henry was preparing a red-wine sauce on-screen. No one would allow Dolores to go down to speak to her husband.

'Next Friday's the big day, Dolores,' Lucilla said. 'Nervous?'

'A bit.'

'It's an abundant universe. We are graced with an abundant universe.'

They watched the screen in silence. Janique had upped her quota of eye rolling and gut retching.

'She'll be wearing that outfit to taste the food.'

'I see. Would you mind if we watch this section?' Dolores asked.

Henry had finished grilling the lamb, which he held up for inspection. Janique gave the camera a sly look, then there was a wide shot where she was still staring into the camera, now bug-eyed, but Henry was glancing to one side – at a monitor, perhaps?

He placed two lamb cutlets on a plate and drizzled them with the red sauce before garnishing the dish with mushrooms and fruit.

Close-ups of the dish. By now Dolores could smell the food from upstairs, and she closed her eyes, savouring the aroma.

Henry sliced the lamb into five thin strips.

Janique's face. Dolores knew that once she tasted the food, she would pretend to retch. She might even drop the pretence.

Henry placed a hand on Janique's arm. Plate in hand, he turned to a small purple saucepan that stood alongside the large saucepan containing the stock.

'Don't do it,' Dolores said in a soft voice. This woman was about to throw up on television and make a fool of her husband. It would make the news.

Henry scooped a tablespoon of liquid from the smaller saucepan and drizzled it over the lamb and set the plate in front of Janique. Dolores was on her feet.

Close-up of Janique. Dolores ran down the stairs. Janique lifted the fork to her lips and bit.

It was in her mouth. Dolores was in the kitchen, aware that her husband was looking at her. Janique looked down at the plate. Now she chewed. She looked up at Henry, all the while chewing, and then, about to swallow. Dolores grabbed the camera and the image on the screen tilted violently. And as Janique looked up, she half-reluctantly vomited. Dolores remembered where she had heard *dao mei* for the first time. It was after Chin's accident. The look on Janique's face said it.

'I think it's a wrap,' Dolores said as she pulled the camera away from the cameraman.

CHAPTER 8

After the Storm

ENRY FIRST dreamt of a car in the days following Janique's near-success and his near-failure.

That car was a familiar but unwelcome presence in his dreams. It was there when the flicker of late-night television woke him. It was there when he gave in to involuntary, public-transport slumber on the evening train back to the suburbs. He would wake up doped and feel panic if he couldn't read the station names whipping past the carriage windows. He never dreamt about anything else. What he wouldn't give for an honest-to-God nightmare that would prove that *this* was reality and *it* was fantasy, and that the confused man he saw in the mirror still had a peaceful inner life. No one sleeps in bed any more, he realised, and he could hear people moving about the city at night. He was less afraid of real dreams than he was of these casual glimpses into his past: he was forever seeing the car reflected in showroom windows or shop-fronts; he was forever hearing it in the city sounds.

On the following Wednesday, as their early-morning train made its way into the city, trundling past the flat-roofed industrial estate buried under snow, he saw four pedestrians ambling down a deserted road, one of the men clasping his coat against the pepper wind. The train sped past unwelcome visions: a car being towed out of a ditch; his father's car with someone slumped at the wheel; what remained of cars in a scrapyard.

Henry had few early memories and he preferred his past to remain coyly well-hidden. Dolores, sleeping in the seat beside his, insisted on excavating her memory and would attend rebirthing seminars and self-discovery workshops with gurus and gym mats and disposable paper cups. 'If we had a dog we could take it for walks in the park,' she announced one Monday morning fresh from a weekend of mind expansion.

Where did that come from? he wondered.

He glanced at the grey-lined notepad in Dolores's lap. CHICKPEA SOUP. She'd been threatening to change their menu for the past month. CHICKPEA SOUP. And so it should remain. Or perhaps the heading should be SOUP and below it a simple, elegant word: CHICKPEA. He could see she had given the dish a tag line but he failed to decipher it.

In an ideal world adjectives would be banned from menus. No nestling or drizzling or basking allowed.

AROMATIC IRISH SIRLOIN RESTING ON A BED OF COARSELY CHOPPED ROCKET. Pseudo. IRISH SIRLOIN. Phoney. SERVED WITH DOUBLE-FRIED NEW POTATOES. Blah.

He looked at Dolores. There were times when he wanted to run away from her – he suspected she felt the same way about him – and he wondered if them both wanting the same thing meant they were made for one another.

He remembered that Felix had requested another package, and he reminded himself that he would need to visit the hospital's newsagent. Can't deny a dying man some fun, he thought, though lately he noticed the fun was being left unread in the bedside cabinet. Felix's ideal woman looked like a dark-haired teenage boy. Henry would page through a couple of magazines until he found images of women sexless enough for his brother-in-law.

And afterwards . . . And afterwards he would listen to Dolores in Fellini's while they drank coffee. They often stopped by Fellini's after their bedside pleasantries with Felix, and this way he had come to associate the smell of bitter Italian coffee with the stench of dying.

A memory was keeping Henry company lately. He must have been about seventeen at the time, though in his mind he felt like a child of nine or ten. It started abruptly with his father asking about his college plans, his voice so loud and clear that Henry looked up, looked around for his father in the train. Dolores was asleep with her head resting on his shoulder.

'I've been giving it some thought,' his father said, while from behind the closed door at the end of the hall they could hear his mother cleaning. He sat on the train waiting for his father to continue. In the other room he heard his mother talking to herself. His father asked to see the travel book that Henry had been reading.

The memory continued with his mother speaking to him in the family kitchen later that night. 'What did he promise you, Henry?' 'He'll help me with my trip.' 'Did he promise you money?' 'No.' 'No?' 'He said he'd double whatever I saved.'

Henry remembered how his family could operate without a father for days at a time – they were professionals. And when the man eventually returned from one of his trips it would either be with the excitement and extravaganza of a marching band or else he would walk resolutely to the bedroom and close the door behind him without a word. In the days that followed there were phone calls, and after school Henry would find that pieces of their lives had been repossessed. No one answered the phone and after a while it stopped ringing. And when the stranger who looked nothing like his father – though this *was* his real father, he was sure of it – emerged from his parents' bedroom, his family appeared to be unaffected by the echoing rooms.

They would wait for his father to build himself up again and within weeks he'd be boisterous and thrilled to be alive, determined to beat the system. The family would sit down to another pre-victory meal and his mother would try and remember how to smile. And near the end of the memory where he felt nine but was about seventeen, at the end of this childhood memory when winter began turning into spring, he handed his father the money.

The train pursued the city, travelling west. Henry stared at the sunlight on the distant buildings, while trying hard to forget the past. The scene looked fictitious, almost CGI. They passed squalid tenement suburbs with dappled walls and children with streaming eyes, and then the train swung sharply to the right, pushing Henry against Dolores, while beneath their shoes and the briefcases of their fellow travellers the train's wheels negotiated the confusion of pitted tracks and decaying points before it darted into an ancient tunnel. The engine whined on the incline as it pulled the carriages into the late winter light.

On either side of the tracks, surrounded by rusting shopping carts, were the icy landfills providing shelter to the ecosystem of plastics and carcinogens; beyond these ecological disasters were empty shops and a boarded casino, and somewhere in the distance lay the sea.

A boy and a girl sat on the seats opposite Henry and Dolores. They had been out drinking the night before and they both looked tickled and comforted by their alcoholic heat. Henry closed his eyes. His father had once walked beneath slick neon palm trees and holographic ferns swaying in a casino's electronic breeze, his mind on cigarettes and the long drive home. He may have crossed the Bo Peep bridge and the Plexiglas tributary before continuing past the islets of slot machines and through the doors out into the cool evening air. It had rained that night. The water must have felt real in comparison to the casino's digitised shouts and hoots, real enough to soak him before he found his car. He imagined one of his father's awkward prodding reverses – he could see him almost sailing through the parking boom before the sudden stop – and soon he would be on the road. Music and heat.

Henry stared at the young travellers sobering up before looking out the window at the no-man's land lying between the sprawling, self-replicating suburbs and uncertain careers. And then the train stopped between stations, and its carriage-lights flickered off. There were no announcements as they sat waiting in the shadows for the jerk when the wheels would begin turning.

In front of him the girl was kissing the boy and the noise woke Dolores.

Henry pressed his forehead against the glass – he could feel his skin against the cold dirt – and looked at the bleak landscape until he saw the train's reflection, like a lone ferry, in a large rectangular showroom window in the distance. He saw his own silhouette in the window and behind it the outline of a car waiting patiently.

His father had not been thinking about the money he had just lost – his son's money; instead he would have been shouting insults at the world and revising his strategy. He doubted his father thought about the boy lying in bed waiting for him to arrive, waiting for him to make good his promise.

Henry felt a dip in his stomach as the train started moving. There was a second pull and he felt the leap of his father's car as the tyres shot off the gravel and spun freely before they hit the ground and rolled to a halt. He felt the wet metal pressing against his father's head and he remembered the sound of his mother talking to herself as she switched off the outside light. Elsewhere his father's body began its patient wait, head lying against the broken windshield, feet propped up on the passenger seat, and the soles of the shoes speckled with gum and a few irregular pebbles.

They were on the move again. On the seat in front of him the young lovers were still at it. Outside the wasteland gave way to brown low rises and traffic. He knew he should return his father to the casino where his face was still lit by neon primaries, the dot-matrix prize-money spelled out on the boards above him, and the gamblers' awkward curtsies around the table as they dug their elbows into the green baize while they played to win. He needed to think about the man before the casino staff stopped serving him; the man whose table was still fringed with spectators as the thin discs of money towered before him.

*

Henry was attempting to leverage his brother-in-law's wheelchair over the raised threshold of the room that housed the MRI unit – it was like trying to push a loaded wardrobe across carpet – when a large nurse with red hair and a freckled face said, 'Leave that chair outside. We don't allow metal in this room.'

She grabbed Felix by the arm and eased him from the wheelchair, past the stencilled warnings on the door, towards the hulking equipment – the hollowed leviathan that hummed with waves and particles. Felix's tumours were once again elbowing their way through his brain, nudging aside the bits of matter that governed his appetites, and it was time for another peek inside.

After much effort – three nurses sweating like a team of stevedores – Felix sat on the edge of the MRI scanner's raised bed, his shoulders lifting and falling as his chest battled gravity while his podgy right hand rubbed a bruised knee. For someone without an appetite he hadn't lost much weight.

'Mr Stoll,' the wheezing red-haired nurse said, 'you're not wearing anything metal, or jewellery, are you?'

'All stolen in this place.'

She raised her eyebrows. 'We're going to need you to relax so that we can lie you down.'

'In *there*?' Felix was staring into the machine. 'You can't fit a human being in there. A python, yes.'

'You'll be fine,' Henry said. The duty nurse walked towards him – this was something *she* could handle – and ushered him out of the room before shutting the door.

Henry returned to a nearby changing room where he sat on a sofa and glanced through a magazine: sexy-diet wealthy-diet Grant-Whant's-Establishments-Extraordinaire famous-diet dieter's-diet.

If Henry had known earlier that morning when they entered Felix's room – Dolores carrying a bowl of recently microwaved soup – that he would be playing chaperone to Felix's visit to the MRI unit, he would have made his excuses and left. This was not the day for it, especially now that his life seemed to be interfering with his nightmares.

He remembered seeing Dolores sitting beside her brother and then she lifted the plastic lid, releasing a cloud of steam that ballooned up and was swallowed by the air.

'Vegetable,' she'd announced, triumphant. 'Nothing fancy.' She held the bowl close to her brother, giving him a chance to smell the meal, all the while stirring it with a spoon. Perfect consistency. Felix opened his mouth and accepted. As he was about to swallow she tilted the spoon to make it easier for him, as one does with a child. Felix had smiled. 'Good.' She dipped the spoon back into the soup, skimmed and then held it towards him for another gulp.

While Dolores fed her brother Henry had walked over to the windows and looked at the buildings opposite: each a life, and each housing a set of mortal questions. After a few mouthfuls Felix lay back, exhausted. Henry looked at them and gave the soup a quick glance, yet when Dolores caught his eye he turned back to face the city and its other lives.

'You're pacing yourself?' he'd heard her ask Felix.

'Give me a moment,' Felix said.

'He's a champion soup eater, Dolores,' Henry had said. 'I think I can see the river from up here, Felix. We're high enough. How tall do you reckon that building over there is?'

They waited for a response.

'Must be about fifty, sixty storeys,' Dolores said. Her brother's eyes were now shut. 'Don't you think, Felix?'

Henry looked at her.

'Felix.' She ran a hand over his cheek. 'Come on, sit up and have some more. Did they give you something to eat earlier today?' She scooped another spoonful and held it in front of him. 'Come on, one more tiny mouthful.' He refused to cooperate: his lips remained closed and then he pulled his head to one side like a surly toddler. She wiped her eyes – not tears, only a headache. 'Do you need to sleep? We'll be here tomorrow.' She saw that the television was switched on. 'Mind if I turn that up?' They were showing a cookery demonstration.

'Big changes in the food industry, Chef,' Felix said, eyes now open. Henry nodded. 'You haven't been following the news?'

'Not on this one, Felix,' he said. They watched the programme – it nauseated Henry.

'Work eat work sleep work. Yes, I know all about your lives. Me: sometimes I eat, but mostly I sleep.'

'They mentioned our place?' Henry asked. 'The restaurant?'

'All of last night they were showing excerpts of that piece where Dolores tackles the cameraman,' he said, smiling.

She held up another spoonful, hopeful. He shook his head. No. They watched television in silence while Henry thought through the arguments. If you can't do it for your own flesh and blood, who can you do it for? Some greedy socialites who puke up what you've fed them, hating you for making them fat, purging before a snort-up in the bathroom? Henry's answer was No. Don't even think it, he told himself. No.

A woman shuffled past the MRI's changing rooms, her hair held tight against her skull with overlapping clips and the skin dark around her eyes like shaded pools. Behind her, from the direction of the unit, came a muffled scream. This was followed by the sound of a trapped animal thrashing about. Felix.

Henry looked at the woman's drugged face, her plump skin, perhaps trying to find a hint of beauty now lost, but she turned to find the source of the commotion and caught him staring at her, and there was one of those moments – a caught-looking moment – and he felt as though he'd intruded and looked back down at his magazine. The woman shut the door of the adjoining changing room and elsewhere a large mass, an inhumanly large mass, bulky and unforgiving, threw itself onto the floor. Henry got up and closed the door to his changing room, and tried to focus on the magazine: sexy-diet establishment-diet transubstantiation-diet extraordinary-diet antidisestablishment-diet famous-diet dieter's-diet.

Now he could hear yelling followed by a variety of distant alarms. What does one say to one's brother-in-law as he lies stinking up hospital's death row? he wondered.

Dear Felix . . .

'You're looking much better today,' was once Dolores's standard opening line whenever they arrived at his hospital room, but there came a point where reality began trumping fiction. They danced around the truth, filling time with compliments and small talk, until Felix would feel compelled to give Henry an update of local and world events.

'I insist you read Benjamin Sterling,' he'd once said from his deathbed, 'Harvard professor, and his review of Fourierism.' Sometimes Felix would try and lever himself up a few inches – he never succeeded – before glancing helplessly at the lopsided array of journals and magazines on the metal table at his right elbow.

'No, Felix, no!' Dolores would yelp.

'Felix,' Henry would say with less enthusiasm, 'don't worry. Don't strain yourself.' Something along those lines. Once, Henry attempted to pacify him and brushed against the pearl-grey pipe draining his abdomen. Felix's body appeared to seize up – and then Henry stepped back when he realised that the man was wincing in pain. Now Felix would settle down well before Henry had a chance to approach the bed or come anywhere near his overheating body.

'Well, it's in there,' Felix would continue, pointing at the journals, 'you can see it some other time.' Yes, Henry would be sure to have a quick look when he was clearing out that crap while Felix's body was cooling in the morgue.

The lectures almost always ended with a question: 'And so, Henry' – he would stretch out a hand to reinforce the seriousness of the topic – 'how is the business faring?' Henry didn't know anyone else who still used the word 'faring'.

'We're hoping things will pick up.'

'You should expand the premises,' Felix would bellow. 'Have you spoken to my friend's husband, the architect?'

This was also well-trodden ground. Felix was delighted when he thought he was ahead of Henry – Felix at the front of the race forever glancing over his shoulder at the runners behind him to dispense advice and tips. Godfather Felix. But Henry knew better than to piss off the dying (or their relatives), so he would settle into a chair to listen to a treatise on architecture or interior design or Rawls's veil of ignorance.

'She's one of my *best* friends. I don't know why you don't just contact her husband, the architect.'

When Felix outlined his plans for Firsts' global dominance he never discussed money. Henry suspected that Dolores updated her brother on his failed attempts at re-financing – 'But Dolores, there's so much cash out there! People are literally falling over themselves. The money is *in their hands*. They're *dying* to invest!' – when he wasn't in the room. All this while Henry would be out performing errands: punching codes into the hull of a humming snack machine or heating up the food that Dolores insisted he bring from the restaurant but that Felix would never eat. When he returned with the contraband he could sometimes see that the latest revelations of his inadequacies had been well-received. And despite this – or because of it – Felix never offered financial assistance.

During some visits Henry suspected Felix of sliding in references to his own father. Innocent remarks, perhaps, but they estranged him further. When they were walking out of the hospital lobby Henry would sometimes turn to Dolores and say, 'What do you think he meant by all his talk of things going *through* my mind? According to Felix, everything I should have thought about today, every thought that should have occurred to me over the past year, all should have gone *through* my mind. And then the references to bullets . . .'

'Bullet *points*,' he recalled her saying afterwards. 'I specifically heard Felix saying bullet points.'

Bullets, nevertheless. He hoped that all the preparation for their visits didn't interfere with Felix's beauty sleep.

*

Felix clasped the wheelchair's armrests, two fists of pain, and grinned at Henry. The nurse who was wheeling him into the MRI changing room had dried arcs of blood on her uniform and shoes.

'I could feel their heavy poison crawling up my veins,' he said as he showed Henry the track marks from the nurse's unsuccessful injection attempts. 'I could feel the venom going for my head and heart.'

'What the hell happened in there?' Henry said, avoiding the nurse's glare.

Felix wore a new gown but his slippers were splattered with red drops. When they were alone he held up a bruised arm. 'They said they would count me down as the poison went into my arm. They started at fifty. *Fifty*! Back from fifty to zero – do you have any idea how long that takes? I mean, begin at twenty-five if you must and double your spaces. Do you have any idea what it does to the human brain when you have to wait that length of time? NASA gives ten counts and then it's lift-off or abort. Who are we to question NASA – they should know a thing or two about counting backwards. Instead, we have western medicine injecting death into my arm and the girl at the controls starts counting back from *fifty*. Women run things in this hospital, have you noticed? They resent men. I could see it in the red-haired one's eyes. Anything with a penis and they want to chop it off. God forbid you should ever get ill.' His voice a threatening whisper. 'God forbid you're hospitalised before your medical insurance is sorted out.'

The door to the adjoining changing room opened and a woman stepped out – Henry assumed it was the same woman he had seen earlier – except this time she was wearing a burka. A middle-aged man and a young girl in flared jeans and a T-shirt were walking in front of her. All three glanced at Henry and Felix.

'One of those was in the room next to mine when they had me on the sixteenth floor,' Felix said as the family walked towards the nurses' station, 'moaning, always moaning. I tell you, it's not very pleasant, being forced to lie there, listening to that. Dolores says you're making a name for yourself in my competition. Money streaming in. *Now* you must sell the business. Now. Take my advice while I'm still alive.'

Henry assured Felix that things were under control and then he made a point of looking at his watch. 'We're running late for your ultrasound appointment.' He had visions of technicians peering into the valves of Felix's grainy heart as he lay groaning on starched linen. 'Let's go.'

*

The image on the monitor was unlike anything Henry had expected: from the front the ventricles were well-behaved and appreciative, two sets of elegant hands resting together as though in prayer, and then they performed a sudden double-clap which was followed by the image of the gently praying hands again, then by another double-clap. Rest-*lub-dub*. Rest-*lub-dub*. Flesh and blood, Dolores would have said. He's her flesh and blood.

Henry's thoughts returned to that morning in Felix's room when they were watching television while he worried about their futures.

'They're going to re-record our WombWell interview,' he remembered Dolores telling her brother. No response. 'I was made to sit next to a loopy dame.'

'It wasn't much fun making it,' Henry had said.

Still nothing. 'I told them that I accidentally tripped into the cameraman.' Felix looked at her. 'So you *are* listening.'

'Thank God they cut Janique's theories about what we call meat when we eat it,' Henry said. 'She'd obviously never eaten lamb before.'

'I think I understood her point,' Dolores said.

'She did not have a point. She couldn't answer me. We call fish *fish*, lamb *lamb*.'

'But normally –' Dolores began.

'That is *normally*,' he said. 'We'll even talk about the type of fish. Have some *tuna*. Do you want some *tuna*? QED.'

'I think you're being unfair. She was saying that we use words to disguise what we're really eating.'

'No, *you're* saying that.' His voice was loud. 'I'm surprised you're defending the drug induced ravings of a loon.'

A knock at the door.

'I'm not defending her,' Dolores said quickly. 'It's just that she was making an interesting point.'

A nurse had opened the door.

'A wrong if mildly interesting point,' Henry said.

'I'm sorry?' the nurse said.

'Nothing,' he said. 'You caught the tail end of another conversation.'

The nurse was carrying a tray, and then stopped when she saw the bowl of soup on Felix's table. 'You read my mind,' she said to Dolores. 'I thought I'd surprise you with some of your own soup but I see that you've beaten me to it. I was defrosting our freezer and I found a little container of frozen soup with Felix's name on it.'

'My brother's not been eating,' Dolores said.

'I'll pop this on your table, anyway,' the nurse said to Felix. 'You should try feeding him again in a short while.' She left the room.

Felix, still propped up at the end of his bed like a Buddha, was eyeing the new bowl of soup. 'You're pissing off the hospital's catering staff,' he told Henry. 'We'll have industrial action if they find out that you're bringing food in for me.'

'Want to try a mouthful?' Henry said.

'He's not hungry, Henry.' Dolores was watching the cookery programme. 'Can you believe the things they get up to on these shows?'

'Let's give the soup another try,' Henry said to Felix. 'We can always ask them to refreeze it if you're not interested.'

Dolores was doing her best to concentrate on the programme. 'Henry,' she said, 'Felix needs some rest before this afternoon's tests.'

Henry dipped the spoon into the liquid, slid it over the bowl's lip before holding it out. 'Open wide.'

Still no movement from Felix. Henry had felt uncomfortable. The memory of this made him even more uncomfortable. Why was he doing this? he remembered thinking at the time. Why had he done that?

Felix pushed his head forward, perspiration on his cheeks, and Henry watched him stretching up towards the spoon. Now Felix opened his mouth. In went the liquid and his head fell back on the pillow. Henry stirred the soup, looking at it.

'More,' Felix whispered, leaning forward for a second mouthful.

And this was how Dolores found herself watching her ill brother, her brother who had half his stomach pickling in a sample bottle on a shelf, her brother whose brain was bursting out of the confines of his skull, her ill brother swallowing the soup. His appetite took hold of him; his body appeared to grow more robust with each mouthful. Each time Henry drew the spoon away to scoop up more soup Felix followed its path; perhaps wanting to take it from Henry's hand. Still more perspiration.

At one point Henry said, 'Do you want to feed yourself?' He handed over the spoon. His brother-in-law finished the soup, unassisted, and at the end of the meal he looked at them both. Old Felix. Alert Felix.

'Sorry,' Henry said, 'no more soup.'

'There's some in the other bowl,' Dolores said.

'It's cold,' Henry said.

'More tomorrow?' Felix asked.

'We'll see.'

'But there's more . . .' She stopped herself. What about the other bowl? she would be thinking. Her brother was hungry and they should take advantage of this opportunity.

'You know, Dolores,' Felix said, 'modern medicine, drugs, doctors and specialists, they're all groping around in the dark.' His hands grasped the air as he spoke. 'Henry keeps me alive.'

Henry continued watching the ultrasound monitor, mesmerised, as the walls of the heart seemed to melt, then just as suddenly reappear on-screen when the technician's ultrasound wand was lifted away from Felix's chest for a moment, and the pause-and-applause pattern was revealed again. Rest-*lub-dub*. Rest-*lub-dub*. The machine broadcast this bacchic heartbeat into the room, drowning out Felix's heavy breaths. Rest-*lub-dub*. Rest-*lub-dub*. After a while

Henry found himself putting words to the pattern. Re-*noun-cing*. Re-*pen-tance*. En-*dur-ing*. Re-*pen-tance*. Re-*noun-cing*.

The technician turned down the volume (re-*pen-tance* . . . re-pen-tance) and repositioned the wand, still holding it like a dagger, and now they were looking down at the ventricles. The elegant side-view had been replaced by a shot of two bubbling cloacae, the whoosh of blood making them obscene – gushing vaginas, pornographic geysers – and Henry waited for the technician to surprise him again. The heartbeat changed briefly, a catalectic skip, as Felix tried sitting up (*pen-tance* . . . *pen-tance* . . . re-*pen-tance*) and Henry took his brother-in-law's hand in his to comfort him.

It wasn't much fun watching someone glancing about uncertainly while you peeked in their body to admire the . . . the animated offal that Henry knew well, and all the while the specialist was talking himself through the tests still covered by Felix's insurance. Rest-*lub-dub*. The words started again in his mind.

*

'I saw my brother licking the bowl clean,' Dolores said as Henry waited with her in the corridor outside Felix's room. He had just returned from the MRI and ultrasound tests. Inside three nurses were helping Felix to the bathroom. 'Have you changed your soup recipe?'

He shook his head. 'I gave him some soup.'

'I'm worried that you don't care about being a chef any more,' she said. 'That you're still blaming yourself for Chin's accident.'

'I suppose I do worry,' he said.

She hugged him. 'Don't let your passion die. I know we're trying to laugh off the Janique thing, and that's probably the right attitude for us to have, but you can't let your passion die, Henry. This morning we both saw how your cooking affected Felix.' The soup left over from the first round of the competition, she meant. The new soup wasn't the same. 'I remember us going to the markets every morning, I remember you selecting the best produce, I remember us walking from stall to stall while you demanded the ripest, finest ingredients. Only the best. And now I'm worried that you've lost interest. You don't care where you get your ingredients.' She released him from her hug and looked at him. 'You saw Felix's face.'

'You don't think I want to be a chef any more?'

'Do you?'

It took him a while to find the words. 'Perhaps there's more to being a chef than passion.'

'What do you mean?'

The nurses had emerged from Felix's room. 'He's asking for you,' one said to Dolores. 'I'm not sure if anyone's spoken to either of you yet, but the initial results of the scan seem to indicate that his tumours may have recently shrunk, though they do seem to be growing back again.'

They thanked the nurse who then followed her colleagues back to their station. Henry and Dolores spoke about Felix's recovery, and the news appeared to give her even more determination to want to encourage him about Firsts. 'Henry, it's your passion,' she said. 'It matters.'

Dolores, trust me when I tell you that those early mornings at the market were romantic, but no matter how fresh the ingredients or how exotic or how much trouble you go to, it's all really beside the point. That was what he wanted to tell her. He brushed aside the hair that had fallen across her forehead. 'They aren't feeding him properly in here.'

'Don't Bluebeard me,' she said.

'I'm sorry?' What was this? Bluebeard?

'You think you've got some magic, you think you've got some potion, but you don't want me to look behind the locked door in case something terrible happens.'

'Dolores.'

'Who does that remind you of?' She was talking about his father.

'Go in there and speak to your brother. We can talk about this later.' They kissed. 'I'll see you at the restaurant. Oh, and just for the record, I don't have any other wives hidden away in towers.'

'Other women don't worry me,' she said, 'but seeing you losing your faith does. Seeing you suffering and my brother suffering does. We both saw how much he liked your competition soup. You should go back to that recipe.'

*

Henry caught the elevator down to the hospital lobby, walked past the magazines and chocolates for distressed relatives, and out onto the street which was too bright and too humid. He watched the traffic and when he saw a gap he crossed to the only place that looked welcoming, the bar across the street. Two shots of vodka later he saw Dolores walk out of the hospital, clutching the plastic container, and head off in the direction of the station. He soon lost sight of her in the crowd.

'Would it make you happy?' He realised he might have said this out loud because the barman looked over at him. Henry shook his head and the barman moved to the far end of the bar where he served a man dressed in a military uniform. Tough shift? 'Would it make you happy?' he said softly, and there was no one to overhear him.

He reached into his bag to grab his wallet and almost sliced his hand on a knife – *Christ!* As he pulled his hand back he disturbed his drink on the counter. Who put you in there? He eased the blade to one side and felt about for his wallet, wary of other dangers.

The hospital windows were reflecting the reds of the setting sun. Work or the hospital were his only real options, and he knew that she would be waiting for him at the restaurant.

After paying for his drink he went back across the road and into the hospital where he rode the elevator as high as he dared, whizzing past Felix's proletarian floor in the teens. *Bing!* 30th floor.

The hospital was similar to the city's hotels: one could expect a better class of occupant the higher one ventured. On the 30th floor the carpets were thicker, the wallpaper looked hand-painted and just outside the elevator there was a private reception area with its own miniature garden crowded into one corner.

If this floor seemed familiar to him that may have been because his own world shared the same two colours: the ripe pink of just-cooked flesh and the flat grey of decaying matter. The 30th floor had both colours in abundance.

He set off, not wanting to spend too much time thinking about what he might be looking for. The chandeliers above the passage were either too small – flashy barnacles clinging to the smooth ceiling – or too large – whale-sized leviathans looming above the furniture, their lustres spiralling gently in air-conditioned currents. The 30th floor was not so much the epitome of luxury but rather an Idea of Luxury dreamt up by bureaucratic decorators, and it had been designed to appeal to large corporations and the employees of large corporations. If we spend this much on the décor, the 30th was saying, can you imagine how orgasmic our care is?

Patients passed him with floor-length robes like smoking jackets. Some appeared to be not quite there, but their bodies were nonetheless complete, pre-surgery, whole.

In this world the nurses were governesses, porters were butlers, male doctors old colonels and female doctors the society hostesses. He adjusted the bag's strap on his shoulder – the edge of the blade still nicked him as he walked, worrying his skin. At the far end of the corridor he stopped in front of a closed door. He half-expected an efficient matron – or au pair – to come thundering down the passage, her watch thumping against her breast and her papers all aflutter, ready to interrogate him. But no one intervened.

The room was dark and its bed empty. He tried rooms nearby but he found no one. Where were the post-butchery patients, drugged and smiling on their beds, in this chintzy limbo? he wondered. Was it cocktail hour up here?

Back at the elevators he spotted a security camera above a brass plaque (RECEPTION) in an alcove. He held down the Call button. 'I'm trying to find the cosmetic-surgery ward. Facelifts?' He released the button and waited. 'I'm looking for my mother-in-law. She's had her face done.' 'Fortieth floor,' was the response. 'That's cosmetic surgery?' 'They'll be able to help you.'

It was a quick elevator ride to the sumptuous 40s where the air was soft, possibly filtered, giving the ward a faintly subtropical feel. On either side of the passage metal plaques declared each room's occupant: facelifts, boob jobs, lipo, collagen. He ambled down the Vegas corridor. It was clearly the First Class section of the building. He had left behind the squalid economy-class rooms below the 20s and the silvery business-class hangouts of the 30s; here the nurses were stewardesses, the porters stewards, and the surgeons all captains.

The first door he came to opened with a gentle *swssh*, and in he stepped.

A bandaged patient lay on the bed, alone in the room. Every surface was covered with cards and flowers and toys propped up between vases and fruit baskets and hooch. Hampers stocked with entire delicatessen aisles: acetate rainbows of ribbons and paper notes exploded from their lids. The patient's face was greasy yellow like uncooked chicken.

There were four noises. Breathing. Air conditioner. Drip feeding the arm. Television.

The linen on the fortieth floor was pastel: a pink duvet and blue sheet. On the duvet a snooty swan pondered its reflection on a paint-splattered lake; a silhouetted bridge – possibly Japanese, probably industrial – was etched against a simple mountainscape. This pattern was repeated vertically from the patient's chest down to the open inverted commas that were the feet.

He couldn't tell if the person was awake. On the television people were being interviewed about the heat wave.

Henry looked at the patient in the bed. Not a movement from the face, the arms, the fingers, the chest, the flesh. Was the thing alive? he wondered.

The television broadcast an ad for FK&F Agriculture Development: SPLICING THE SEED. Then FK&F Online Marketplace: WHERE YOU BUY OR SELL EVERYTHING! Sunday Magazine: SLOW DOWN, PLEASURE UP!

Back to the competition, Henry thought, and back to Chin's fingers. *Dao mei.*

On-screen there was a shot of a college student rolling herself into a giant Dorito, her face covered with meat and cheese. Then another of a bride pushing wedding cake onto her husband's face. Henry looked back at the patient, still thinking about Chin's magic fingers while he waited for the Hammer-horror moment when the patient's eyes would blink open and a bouncer would escort him from this room. Hesitantly, he approached the bed.

Henry's bladder was full and it took him a while to locate the bathroom door hidden behind the heavy curtains at the far end of the room.

Staring back at him from the mirror, water still dripping from his face, was a Henry First. He studied the face for a long time, the blue tinge to the skin and the blond hair in need of a trim, and he tried hard to remember whether he had allowed the patient to sleep in peace – hands unmutilated – the knife still dry and sharp in his reflection's backpack. *His* backpack? He had been within touching distance of those fingers, within smelling distance of the dry blood that had formed a black halo around the facelift, caking the bandages and the cotton wool.

He saw himself standing beside the bed, just as the reflection staring back at him must have done, perhaps gently prising the little finger away from the others on the patient's hand. Quick and unfussy. The glossy nail. His fingers leaving marks on that glossy nail as he pulled the digit away. Did he squeeze the finger, testing the meat, exposing the knuckle: a tiny ridge of flesh folding back upon itself for a moment as he held it away from the hand, readying it for the chop? Is this what his reflection had done in his world?

Perhaps not. Perhaps.

After drying his face he ran his fingers through his hair and turned away from his reflection – something behind him in the mirror? – feeling dizzy, and then he flipped open the toilet lid once more and retched up a stew of bitter alcohol and peanuts.

Back in the penthouse-sized elevator Henry hesitated for a moment, his finger almost prodding a button in the 50s – the Concorde level – or perhaps the 60s with its promise of Space Shuttle opulence, or way above to the boudoirs reserved for royalty and earthly gods: the space-station Nirvanas at the very top of the building. Instead he pressed a more familiar number and felt the craft plummet to Felix's level where he waited for the doors to open, allowing other commuters into the silvery box, until one of them hit the Ground Floor button.

When he emerged from the rear of the building he found himself thinking about the hospital basement – a quick drop to the mortuary where he'd be free to lop off bits of flesh, hack at stiffened digits without fear of causing pain. He could plop them into the bag, wipe the fluid from his blade and wrap it in cloth like a professional. He was walking in hot rain. Water ran down the surfaces around him and seeped into the paving stones. He negotiated past the pedestrians and headed for the station, and then on to the restaurant.

CHAPTER 9

Maundy Thursday

WHEN GRANT WHANT walked to his local train station the streets were deserted. Around him metal shutters were fastened tight, protecting suburbia, and the empty supermarket was filled with shadows. Distant traffic surging towards the skyscrapers on the horizon. Let's batten down the hatches and sit this one out, he thought. He looked up – no storm clouds yet.

Underground he waited for his train, and after some time watching the indicator board listing the delays, he realised that a man with a shaven head and thick glasses had been speaking to a poster on the opposite wall for about ten minutes.

Grant had come across the word *schizoid* in his dictionary, and it disturbed him. Its definition had nothing to do with madness or multiple personality disorder as he had expected – like *him*, the chattering man standing beside him. Instead it described someone far more benign: someone with emotional aloofness, solitary habits. He read the definition twice. *Schizoid*. Who is madder, he wondered, the man rebuking the poster on my right, or me talking to myself?

The underground carriage was sweat-filled. A woman on his right held up her magazine like a barrier. The man in front of him scratched a mole on his tanned neck. Grant watched him working the mottled-brown stud with his nail, playing with the ragged piece of skin, his finger tracing a circle around the dot, and then his nail probed its wrinkled core, scraping, tearing.

The people not reading magazines were reading books: fictitious states, political treachery, innocent princesses from the generic Orient. Why did authors feel compelled to carve out independent principalities in the third world? he wondered. Why all the mines in humid Bolivintina, the banausic tyrants raping peasants in squalid corners of Tangeria, the tainted equity transfers from the Korasian capital city to Zurich fund managers, and the terrorists killing Americans in the State of Rukwa?

Soon he was asleep and had missed his stop.

When he awoke he was too far south and quickly got off the train – accidentally stepping on undersized feet, crunching young knuckles underfoot – and exited the station to find himself on a bazaar-like street where none of the signs were in English. He headed north towards the distant skyscrapers. After a while he imagined that beggars were sending their children to chase him and soon he was running along the pavement with one hand clasping his bag's zipper to ensure it remained shut.

There were momentary scuffles when he crossed paths or accidentally got in the way of oncoming pedestrians. The further north he moved, the greater the number of au pairs clutching the arms of Ritalined children – angelic, beloved children – hustling them to school, avoiding the mounds of canine negligence and wet liability on the city streets, straining to keep up with the nannies who charged on ahead. The nannies screamed status reports into their phones to unseen secretaries who would pass the reports – hourly précis of these billionaire toddlers' days – to the personal assistants. He could see it all: the personal assistants would then bully the nutritionists, the acupuncturists, the manicurists, the personal trainers – threatening them to stay on message when they gain face-time with the suprawealthy parents.

He had mislaid his building pass the previous evening (a fabulous sauna and steam refresher at his local place) and had to enter the Furness Kindle & Flint Publishing building via its side entrance, also known as the paupers' entrance, which was normally reserved as a punishment for the blue collars.

Inside an intertwined FK&F (the ampersand grouping and separating the letters) was painted on the ceiling. There were no chandeliers – this entrance was understandably less impressive than the domed grandeur of the main foyer. The only decoration was the door-sized portraits of executives that appeared to float on either side of the passage, a few feet away from the custard walls. There was no wiring that he could see and he imagined the cleaning crews were forbidden to approach these levitating masters of industry. The rug felt as though he was walking on tenderised steak.

He was issued with an FK&F pass (the handwriting he reserved for forms did not belong to him – instead it reminded him of his high-school chemistry classes: a child-like code of surprise capitals and numbers that were diminished afterthoughts) and ushered into an elevator.

Grant stepped out of the transparent lift, swiped his new pass-card, and entered the sprawl of desks that made up the Sunday Magazine offices. The place stank of fear, missed deadlines and major disasters.

A sign for FK&F Publishing (pistachio and cream) was stuck to one of the walls like a stupendous thought bubble.

He navigated the grid of desks that extended across that floor. Employees milled about; some leant on cubicle walls; others chatted to colleagues. All of the desks were occupied, some by two or more workers. Some people appeared to be sharing PCs; four hands grappling for the keyboard.

The cubicles appeared to have been covered in blue carpet. Most of the miniature walls had been papered with printouts of emails, presentations, organisation charts, project plans. Phones rang. And at the end of each row squat printers spewed out sheets of paper.

When he reached his row (prime real estate, this: it was next to the window, close to a meeting room, and within sauntering distance of a drinks machine) he passed a new employee – a non-entity slouching in front of four screens, surrounded by a city of paper and trash, somewhat younger than the previous occupant. Grant never knowingly fraternised with other workers.

At his desk he unlocked his workstation, closed the copy he had spent all of yesterday editing (text shuffled to the bottom of the screen), and began reading his emails.

The employees on either side of him would relax by staring out the window for a moment, and when they had had enough of the view they would either speak on the phone or continue typing. He could hear their voices even when they were whispering.

After a few hours he stood up and walked to the thought bubble. The toilets were well-camouflaged, necessitating directions for new employees, but once they'd been pointed out it became clear that all of the desks appeared to have been arranged in an informal amphitheatre with the twin bathroom doors at centre stage. Why did architects make a feature of company lavatories? he wondered. He noticed what seemed to be a security guard standing outside the men's bathroom, and the man occasionally glanced at his watch.

Inside, Grant washed his face and drank some water. It was just before 10 a.m. Then he went to the urinals and relieved himself while a grey-suited man at a basin behind him gave a brief performance from an extraordinarily accomplished hawking repertoire. Grant looked back and saw the man spitting something – enamel? dentine? – into the running water. He appeared to have a serious glandular disorder; his corrugated cheeks and forehead were shiny from heat and scouring.

'Bastards,' he said and then looked up at Grant who felt obliged to nod. 'They took my life.'

When Grant had finished he walked past the man to wash his hands. He noticed a piece of paper lying next to the man's basin. On closer inspection he could see that it was a company letter. Grant leaned forward to grab a paper towel and to get a closer look at the letter, and he saw a single sentence that began with the word *Unfortunately*.

'Bastards,' the man said again. 'No balls, the lot of them. Nothing.' He stared at Grant for a moment before stooping down for another vigorous rinse and gargled splutter.

It amazed Grant how polite business people were. Films misread this all the time, he felt. The bastards with a 'screw you' attitude never made it this far up in the corporations – they got to work in the Accounts Department making phone calls and leaving messages about late payments. They were all locked in a room somewhere and poked with a stick or somehow adrenalised prior to each call. Everyone else – other than this man – appeared normal.

At around 1 p.m. Grant slung his blue knapsack over his shoulder and stepped out for some lunch. Outside, the buildings surrounding Golden Square appeared faint, as if painted onto gauze. He ran across the street, the bag bumping against his back, and then he eased his pace when he was on the path that led to the centre of the square where he found an empty wooden bench; he sat down and propped his feet on an empty flowerpot.

His sandwich was from a vending machine in the FK&F lobby. When he'd finished the unsatisfying snack (dry chicken, soggy bread) he folded the paper container into itself and dropped it in a nearby bin. He had been avoiding Firsts since the WombWell incident, even though they were now busier than ever before. Some of the new patrons thought that Firsts might make them lose some weight, while others wanted to show their solidarity against Janique. Right now the line of people on the eastern side of the square led from Firsts' front door across to the adjoining block where it petered out just beneath the marquee of a disused cinema that commemorated a long-forgotten day:

CRY OF BATTLE

VAN HEFLIN

WAR IS HELL

A few of the benches were occupied with office workers sunning themselves in the uncertain spring weather, the sky a clean blue and the sun's rays white on the cut-out buildings. The Broad Way Building squatted at the eastern side of the square; on his right the sign for FK&F Publishing glowed in the sunlight on top of Obsidian House and around him what looked like discarded needles were glistening on the concrete. Some construction workers stapled plastic ivy onto the graffitied statue in the centre of the park.

He watched a phalanx of skateboarders eroding the iron- and brickwork on the southern side of the square as he dialled Patrice's number and left a message for her. Nearby he could see how the edges in the park had been worked smooth by the skateboarders: handrails showed the shock of old jumps, metal tubing that linked concrete to more concrete was heavily dimpled.

The boarders rattled across the paths, weaving between employees and the unemployed, before they jumped, spun and caught the underside of their boards on concrete benches, clacking when they hit the ground.

One boy wore a black T-shirt with cities and dates printed in yellow on the back. They all wore caps and their shoelaces flapped about when they jumped and fell.

The kid with the black shirt planted his left foot on his board, steadied himself and then thrust with his right – *again, again, again.* He steered up towards the concrete bench just in front of Grant, settling both feet on the board before flinging himself onto the edge of the concrete. He lost his balance, his arms stretching out to protect himself. Grant heard a smack as the kid hit the paving stones. The others continued their jumps and skirted around his body. Eventually the youngster stood up, arms raw and lanky against his oversized clothing, and with a kick he was back on his board and rumbling across the slabs towards his grubby companions.

On the northern side of the square Grant spotted three traceurs flinging themselves off buildings, while another child used his bike to scale a wall.

He closed his eyes and listened to the traffic, the boarders and the non-stop sound of ringing telephones. His life spent making sly observations from the margins.

When he opened his eyes there were fewer employees sitting around him, and it appeared as if the buildings were rising high above him as dark clouds swept across the sky. In the distance a large block – a Notre Dame on the avenue – appeared to be growing bigger: a hulking mass that seemed to be lumbering past the smaller buildings that lay between him and it. The few remaining office workers were preparing to leave.

By now the air was heavy, and the remaining people on the benches didn't appear to be tethered to the corporates – they were either too old or too drunk. One young man lay across a bench, his legs splayed and a bottle of vodka resting on his crotch, looking as though he'd just fought a war.

Grant's phone rang: Patrice's assistant told him that Patrice would see him in her office. He stood up, wiped dust from his trousers, and crossed the road after a lengthy wait for a gap in the traffic, and was soon heading towards his reflection in the glass-clad Obsidian House. As he climbed the steps the city air shuddered around him and it began raining; he was caught in a crush of people who were, for some bizarre reason, shouldering their way out of the building and into the tempest.

(He would need to stop by his desk to drop off his bag, and then go up to Patrice.)

Grant pushed towards the security barriers and as his arm reached for the polished-brass turnstile for a moment he saw two hands – his own and a reflected brass hand – both swiping their cards through the slot. The light flicked green and he elbowed the barrier while his mirrored double pushed past him, its face as heavy and frightened as the employees leaving the building and continuing towards the storm outside.

He stood and stared.

He checked the number above the elevators. It was his floor, sure enough, but what had happened to everything? Everyone? The desks were gone – everything apart from his own in the distance – and he was alone.

He cut across the empty wasteland where desks and chairs had once stood – small rectangular indentations in the carpet were all that remained of the table legs, larger rectangles where computers once lay; it was easy, a straight line.

His belongings had been neatly packed into two plastic crates stacked next to his chair. Stickers on the crates had his name.

The assistant sent him through to Patrice's office, saying, 'Ms Czarny is out.' He remembered that Patrice preferred making entrances.

'You're missing the monsoon outside,' he said. The assistant nodded and continued working. There was no reason he could think of why Patrice would want to fire him in person.

Being alone in Patrice Czarny's office was a pleasure afforded to everyone, from the cleaners to executives from rival corporations – they would all be left to snoop about for opportunities and weaknesses. It was her way of saying that you could be trusted; that you were part of her corporate family. Grant suspected that this wasn't Patrice's real office, that it was no more than a stage set, but even so he shut the door behind him in order to give himself some privacy.

African art hung from two of the walls, while the other two sides of the room were floor-to-ceiling windows. On his left – a good half-marathon away from Patrice's desk – were sofas and wingback chairs grouped around an irregular wooden table that was large enough to be a sequoia's cross-section. You could park the Hindenburg in this place.

He went to the window behind her desk and looked down. Outside, there was water. Buildings flashed off the traffic, the traffic flashed off the buildings, and the sky reflecting it all back again. The traffic lights on the northern side of the park turned from green to amber, and then he watched this wet colour dominoing down the avenue (. . . *green-amber; green-amber* . . .). Cars slowed and waited at the lights. Some time later there was a cascade of greens and the pack of vehicles sped into the storm.

Cyclops printouts covered Patrice's desk along with an unopened diary and a piece of yellow notepaper half-hidden by her keyboard. Three drawers ran up the right-hand side of the desk. He could hear the secretary speaking on the phone in the other room.

From Patrice's office there was a clear view of Firsts and the rows of cars double-parked outside its entrance. He imagined Patrice staring out and wondered what she thought when she saw people queuing outside the restaurant. In this weather?

Close up, the papers on her desk appeared less interesting: printed numbers with handwritten notes running down both margins. There were copies of invoices and a brief letter from the Mumbai Dialysis Centre.

He returned to the window and watched the clouds descend, enjoying their threat. Still no Patrice.

It occurred to Grant that she may have left him a voicemail explaining the reason for this meeting. He went back to her desk, doing his best to ignore the printout, and picked up her phone and dialled his voicemail. As the number rang the phone's LCD display began timing the call.

He transferred the phone to his left hand, and thought for a moment about giving each of the drawers a quick tug. The top two were locked; the bottom glided open and he shut it again as quickly. He glanced at the office door again. Safe? Inside the bottom drawer were some files, a few unopened letters and some forlorn stationery. Unnerved by his own audacity, he slid the drawer shut.

He could no longer hear Patrice's secretary and he stared at the office door while a voice listed options on the call. He dialled 9 and the voice prompted him for his password.

He reached for the handwritten note under the keyboard. The page was filled with doodles and intricate patterns – curls and curves across the page. He was struck by the mess and had almost slipped it back under the keyboard when his focus shifted and he saw that the page was covered with two words almost hidden beneath the arabesque scribbling: a repeated name across the page, defaced by the loops, camouflaged by the paisley swirls:

HENRY I HENRY I HENRY I HENRY I HENRY I
HENRY I HENRY I HENRY I HENRY I HENRY I
HENRY I HENRY I HENRY I HENRY I HENRY I
HENRY I HENRY I HENRY I HENRY I HENRY I
HENRY I HENRY I HENRY I HENRY I HENRY I
HENRY I HENRY I HENRY I HENRY I HENRY I

The door opened and Patrice walked into the room.

She seemed surprised to see Grant standing there, as if he'd dropped by unannounced. His right hand continued its journey up from the paper that he'd slipped back under the keyboard and then he watched it giving her a quick wave, and it was saying Here I am, while trying hard to look innocent.

'Your call isn't time-sensitive?' she asked. He shook his head. 'Do you want to refresh? Coffee? Sure.' She turned away and then glanced back at him and at the desk. Was she about to come over? 'You don't do milk, right?' she asked and he nodded.

As she stepped out of the room to address her assistant he reached down and repositioned the page under the keyboard. He dried his top lip and the Amazonian goddess returned.

'Important call?' she asked. 'Can you reschedule?'

'Checking my messages,' he said. 'Nothing there – yet.' He replaced the receiver. The paper under her keyboard looked untouched.

'Give me a second,' she said and left the room again.

He went across the room and sat on the sofa. The African masks were staring down at him (I see evil; I hear evil; I speak evil; I do evil) when a waiter wheeled in a tray of refreshments, followed by Patrice. She sat alongside him on the sofa while they were being served.

'Congratulations on getting all of your restaurants in the Hot 100,' he said. 'If you don't make the top three I'll be insulted.' He tried hard to appear sincere.

'I *do* have a wonderful team,' she said. The waiter left the room. 'Though one can never be sure about competitions. Will you be at Firsts tomorrow?'

Grant wanted to ask Patrice about the missing Sunday Magazine employees, and wondered if this was the best time to raise this. He nodded.

'Do you think "Henry First" is his real name?' she asked.

'I don't see why not.'

'I'd be very interested to hear an insider's account, *yours*, about what it's like for an underdog to prepare for a competition as large as ours. That would make excellent copy, don't you think?' He nodded again. 'There are obviously things that you'll know as their confidant that will make it more reader-realistic. Not that I intend telling Grant Whant how to write award-winning articles.'

She was waiting for him to speak. He noticed hail tearing at a stunted tree just outside the window. The tree clung to the tower block that blanked out the river.

'Ever get the feeling that you've missed an important email or something?' he said, and then by way of explanation: 'I'm feeling a bit lonely downstairs.'

'You and I were meant to face-off about this last week but the decision was escalated and I was de-empowered from giving you a heads-up. We had to flush that entire floor minus one. The Office of Special Powers apologises for the dysfunctional timing of it all.'

'You had to *flush* the floor?'

'They're well taken care of,' she said, looking concerned. 'I don't expect any blowback from the redundants. And if you haven't already worked it out, you're the minus one.' Patrice had a habit of clasping both hands together, as though she was about to pray, when she wanted to look sincere.

Grant remembered attending a launch party that Patrice had organised in an uptown museum for a miracle drug that was meant to cure arthritis, although sadly it had been hastily withdrawn soon after the event. The Egyptian Hall was filled with dazed octo- and nonagenarians in wheelchairs surrounded by granite columns with palm capitals.

Sarcophagi had been transformed into serving platters; their chalked hieroglyphics looked dull in comparison to the extravagantly inky caviar and delicate patterns of alphabet-shaped sushi. Libation bowls were filled with champagne, bubbles popping, and a feast of baby vegetables had been used to construct a dhow. A shrieking baboon, harnessed to a wheelchair, towed an equally frightened pensioner. The curators had been ordered to unwrap and display a row of snarling mummies. Towards the end of the evening, Patrice Czarny had surrounded the reporters with a troop of liver-spotted geriatrics in cotton rags (looking like dime-store Egyptians), when it transpired that one of the guests, a man in his late nineties, had died of a stupendous myocardial infarction. The dead man's mouth was still full of uneaten caviar. Patrice said, 'Why don't you park *that*' – pointing at the dead body – 'at the far end, over there' – indicating the line of grinning mummies.

Patrice certainly had a way with words: Why don't you park *that*? We had to *flush*.

'Speaking about Henry First,' she said, 'how much do you know about his brother-in-law?'

Grant bit into an aerogel biscuit that was faintly scented, but seemingly without any weight or taste. The smell of Dardic tribesmen dispensing cumin in a crowded souk; smiling slaves forced to collect vanilla pods under the watchful eyes of the bwana's youngest daughter; that sort of thing.

'Not an awful lot, if I'm honest,' he said.

'You know he's dying?' she said. He did. 'Do you know what of?'

'I think he's got cancer,' he said. The masks above his head were watching him.

It was her time to nod. 'That's what I've been told, yes.'

They drank coffee in silence and he looked at the rain running down the windows. He had a second biscuit, this one the aroma of strawberries maturing in a field while colonialists waited for the natives to ransack the farmstead.

'Have either of them ever mentioned to you an accident that happened during the first round of the competition?' she said. They hadn't. 'The authorities have been attempting to trace some of his kitchen staff but they all appear to have vanished into thin air. The emergency services have a record of an ambulance picking someone up from Firsts, but the patient could hardly speak English and Henry paid for the treatment. The patient then drops off the face of the earth. Perhaps Mr First isn't as lily-white as he appears to be.'

'Do you mind me asking what's happening to the magazine?'

'I've had to make you a contractor,' she said. 'It was either that or you having to leave along with the others. But I think there's a way that we can get this to work in both our favours. We've had to relocate everything else. We've moved content provision –'

'Our writers?'

'Yes, the content producers, offshore.' Over the past few years FK&F had gone from freelance, to contractors, to permanent employees, and now they were offshoring. All the journalists downstairs had been 'flushed.' 'Our rivals are outsourcing. Did you get caught in the storm?'

'Very nearly,' he said. The masks were staring out the windows. 'It still looks pretty wild out there.'

'This is Thunderstorm Week according to the news.'

'Yes, that's what I heard. Patrice, do you need me to relocate?'

'Heavens, no' – she laughed – 'you're no use to anyone over there. I need you here for the competition.'

'Why were you asking me about Felix Stoll?'

'I've been alerted to some unusual internet traffic that appears to be coming from our friends across the square. Are you sure that Felix doesn't have a history of kidney or liver problems?'

'Not that I'm aware of, no.'

She thought about this. 'I've released you from the corporation so that you'll have more time on your hands to assist Mr and Mrs First. And if you happen to learn something from your new friends then you may be kind enough to share it with your old friends. In the longer term it will raise your profile within the organisation.'

He was thinking. He was uncertain how wonderful this news really was.

'It's time-sensitive,' she continued, going across to her desk. The masks were avoiding eye contact.

'How sensitive, Patrice?'

'A parcel is due to be delivered to Firsts later tonight. I need someone on top of this, starting today.'

He told her he would do it, but he needed a car. She agreed to arrange one for him.

'Henry First has a lot of independence-potential,' she said, 'so I'll need you to keep your involvement strictly personal. Don't brand any of this FK&F.'

'No more empathic emphasis?' he asked.

She smiled. 'Every now and then the public likes to think that it's getting something unique and non-corporate, and I need to ensure that the public's desires are well catered for. Now I'm sure you'd agree that it would be wonderful if Firsts were to make it into the Top 10?'

By some strange coincidence this would also give Grant more time to embed himself with the Firsts.

CHAPTER 10

The Stock

STOCK IS WHERE it all begins. The chef's primordial soup.

Henry First could feel the kitchen waiting; he could feel it demanding magic. One last trick, please, it said to him.

On the steel table in front of him was the cast of secondary characters: vegetables, raw carcass bones, trimmings and waste. Bit parts awaiting the star.

He wiped the bones – they polished easily as he drew the cloth across the hard white and the soft red. Then, picking them up with both hands, his fingers splayed by their weight and size, he placed them in a large pan on the stove behind him. Now the kitchen had a sound – the *friss* of gentle frying.

He sliced the vegetables on a wooden block, thumping the blade over and across, each time hitting down with the heel of his hand. Behind him the sound of frying was beginning to change tone so he lowered the flame. Back at his station he finished cutting the vegetables. His chopping was coarse and amateur. Some carrots broke free – running away from the action – and he had to reach out in order to thwart their escape. Onions, perhaps too many, were followed by some inexpert hacks at drying celery. What else?

He walked past the cold store, not looking at its Fort Knox door, towards the storeroom where he grabbed herbs both dry and fresh. Back at the pan he pulled at these twigs and leaves, ripping them apart, and folded and then shredded them with a quick twist. Now his hands were fresh with the smell of the Mediterranean as he rubbed them above the pan.

The room was heavy with the aroma of meat. He glanced at the clock, the pan and the stairs. Time enough. He poured some rum into the tall glass that had been biding its time beside the mound of vegetables. The alcohol rose to meet his lips, and after a quick sip he carried the glass with him to the sound of the orchestra in the restaurant upstairs.

Sound all around him. Something classical, something for the night owls and the city outside.

On the road he saw the car parked between the Furness Kindle & Flint Publishing trucks. In another ten, eleven minutes he would need to add the flesh. *Be with you shortly, sir.*

He walked to the glass front doors that spelled Firsts backwards, a cluster of limp keys hanging from the lock, while across the road waited the car. He peered through his own reflection with its rum-scattered colour but couldn't see anyone. Not at this hour, anyway. After a fumble with the keys Henry First stepped into the night. Cool air blew past him into the restaurant and then the door swung shut, silencing the orchestra.

An empty road lay between him and the vehicles. The car was an insipid grey, the colour of nothing. Another gulp of tart rum, followed by a wipe with his free hand at the dribble running down his chin. He heard the *tink* of keys against his leg as his fist swung down and brushed his trouser pocket. Behind the car lay Golden Square and behind that the glowing FK&F Publishing sign perched on top of Obsidian House.

'I'm as tanked as you were,' he said to the car. He looked at the clock on the face of the Broad Way Building behind him. Any time now. He drained his glass and walked across the road. A few paces away from the car he could see his silhouette on its side window. Nothing inside it, he told himself, nothing in there. Engine running.

'I've been giving it some thought,' his father had said. Dad? Henry looked around. Dad? His eyes pricked at the words and this memory. He was only a teenager. His father asking about his college plans, his voice so loud and clear – even tonight. 'I've been giving it some thought,' his father had said. That he certainly had.

He looked at the car, waiting for the memory to play itself out. 'Once you begin studying, your life will be work work work. I've been giving it some thought.' Later the conversation with his mother in the kitchen: 'What did he promise you, Henry?' 'He'll help me with my trip.' 'Did he promise money, Henry?' 'No.' 'No?' It was far simpler. He felt nine but was seventeen. Winter had turned into spring and he handed his father the money.

Nothing in front of him, Henry told himself when he looked at the car. No body in the car. No gun beside it.

Henry turned to the blazing restaurant and felt a blast of air as something fierce gunned past him, full sound, engines roaring. 'Shit!' Entirely real. He leapt back against the car, his glass hitting tarmac, and for a moment everything became the shuddering motorbike that had stopped less than a block away. His heart did something deep and painful in his chest as he leaned against the door.

'You moron,' he shouted. The motorcyclist gave him a wave, kicked the engine into gear and steered over to Henry.

'You Henry First?' the cyclist said. 'Sign here.'

Henry took the red-and-white plastic box and watched the bike speed away from him; leaving him to stand in its limp trail of poison.

'Don't know what I wanted to say to you, anyway,' he told the car. Glancing both ways he crossed the road, pushed open the restaurant doors and was embraced by the warm sound of an orchestra in full swing. He only remembered to lock the front door after he had visited the storeroom. Back upstairs the road looked peaceful when he bolted and then rechecked each lock.

The frying bones needed to be turned. A mystery guest was waiting patiently in the storeroom, eager to make an appearance. Drink, then work, he thought as he poured himself a fresh glass, and then followed this with another.

In the storeroom he picked up the red-and-white cooler box and returned to his station.

Yes, Chef, the meat, Chef.

What you do, he told himself, is open it and take out the meat.

Yes, Chef, the meat, Chef.

He cranked the plastic arm across the top of the box and over to the other side. The lid popped up an inch. He prised it off, and pushed aside the ice bags to reveal a perfect specimen which he then cradled in his fingers like a puppy before laying it on the wooden board in front of him. It gave an *oooh* as it settled on the wood, relaxing, stretching out, took its time and filled the space. You are too perfect to waste, he told it prior to acknowledging the knife.

Behind him the large pan had begun spluttering and popping. (The frying bones should *really* be turned.) The vegetables waited patiently – they were as excited as he was.

As Henry reached for the knife it was as if a cold hand had just settled on his shoulder.

The kidneys of cattle, sheep and pigs are articles of food; the kidneys of man are less so. This organ in front of him was still encased in fat, old style. Kidney suet can be used in crust.

Yes, Chef, the meat, Chef.

He would need it all, fat included. It would set them up for life; making enough stock to dilute for years. It would turn everything into gold.

There was applause upstairs as the orchestra finished with a flourish, and as he heard the crowd rise to its feet with shouts and whoops he picked up the knife and rested the palm of his left hand on the cold meat.

No going back now.

He slit the skin on the rounded side. Again, he thought of cold fingers pressing into his shoulder. No going back now, he told himself once more as he drew the skin towards the core of the kidney, pulling gently to remove as much as possible. As he worked he felt a dark and heavy presence looming over him, monitoring his progress. He dared not look up for fear of seeing . . . what? A tattered cloak covering an unseen head? A hollow shroud which exhaled rotting flesh?

'No going back now,' he said aloud and it was as if nails had bitten into his neck. He cut the skin away and sliced the organ lengthwise, the dark flesh juddering as he sawed through the meat. 'Satisfied?' he asked his unseen observer as he turned over the top half of the kidney and laid it alongside the bottom half. Perfect match. He cleaned out the remainder of the core.

On the fringes of visibility he thought he could see a heavy cloak. Death is my guardian angel while I prepare the sacrifice. Where did that line come from? On the night he was betrayed he took the bread. That one was simple enough.

He sliced the meat hard.

When Henry looked down at the board there was nothing but protein sludge. Like any other meat. He wiped the blade and placed it beside the board.

'I need to turn around now,' he said. 'I can't drop the meat.'

He was alone in the kitchen. The pan spluttered as he added the meat and gave it a quick stir. He flicked up the heat and sautéed the flesh until it had turned a reassuring, even brown.

He reached back to collect the vegetables and once again felt the presence near him. 'You'll need to leave me to it,' he said. The vegetables were in the pan. A new aroma, something sweet, a seductive smell calming everything, allowed him to focus on his task. Soon the vegetables were perfectly coloured.

There is beauty in preparing a meal, the time and care with each ingredient, and the love. In the middle of all of this – the heady smell, the perfect colouring – he was overcome by a need to speak to Dolores. He tried their home number using the downstairs phone, but there was no answer. It was just after midnight according to the clock. Out at this time, Dolores? He began dialling her number but was stranded after a few digits.

He returned to the pan where he scraped in the remaining herbs and peppercorns, and followed them with a jug of water. Henry sauntered up the stairs to consult the phonebook beside the computer. Once he found her number he dialled. The car was still parked across the street and the trucks were still waiting.

She answered and he felt a twinge of self-doubt – perhaps the call wasn't such a good idea after all. 'Dolores?'

'I've been calling but your phone's off,' she said. 'I've left messages at the restaurant.'

He saw a flashing red light beside the phone. 'It's taking longer than I expected.'

'Is everything all right?' she asked.

He tried but failed to be coherent in his answer. *Rene* was his idea: inspired by the Janique's theory of obfuscatory edible nouns.

'I drove by an hour ago,' she said, 'and the lights were on, but I couldn't get in. You'd left the keys in the door.'

'They're out now,' he said, double-checking. 'Did I wake you?'

'Sorry?'

'Did I wake you up?' He heard talking in the background. 'Where are you?'

'I'm at the hospital with Felix. Hold on.' More talking. 'Felix had a bad turn.'

'I'll come and collect you,' he said.

'No, stay there. I'll come down to you and that way I can get something to Felix tonight. Is anything wrong, Henry?'

'Nothing wrong with me,' he said firmly. 'It'll be ready.'

'You've been drinking.'

'No more than usual.'

'They need me to sign something,' she said quickly. 'I have to go.'

'I —' he began, but although his thoughts were willing his mouth was not and his words froze. There were many options for Henry's sentence, from *I want to say* . . . to *I feel like killing myself* . . . He tried again: 'I'll begin making the soup now.'

'Wait for me,' she said.

He said goodbye to the dead phone and placed it on the cradle beside the red light. He felt the keys in his pocket, turned off the radio and went down to the kitchen where he brought the stock to a slow boil. Once it was bubbling and steaming he gave the pan a vigorous stir, lowering the heat, and half-covered it with a lid. He threw away the empty rum bottle and gave his glass a quick rinse at the scullery. It was time to start the soup.

When Dolores arrived his knife and the chopping board had been bagged and binned; his hands and arms were pink from an energetic scrub. She went to him without glancing at the pots and they hugged. The loving wife, the loving husband.

She watched as he ladled vegetable soup into a plastic container. 'The stock will need to reduce and simmer for another five, six hours' – he dipped the ladle into the large pot containing the *rene* stock, taking just a little – 'but this should do the trick. I'll finish long before we need to begin preparing for tomorrow's round of the competition.' She sealed the plastic bowl, kissed him, and then studied his face for some time. 'It's OK,' he said firmly. 'I'm OK. I'm the chef, remember? How is Felix?'

'None of the nurses is looking me in the eye tonight. I think they've reached the limits of their optimism.'

'You've got the silver lining in your hand. I'll stay here and keep an eye on the *rene*.'

'What did Grant have to say for himself?'

Grant? He skimmed the dead bubbles off the stock's surface, trying to remember when last he had spoken to Grant. Key in his pocket. Nothing . . . 'Nothing important,' he said. The large spoon in his hand moved in an anti-clockwise direction. 'Call and let me know how it goes with Felix.'

She took the soup and went out. For a moment there was noise from the waking city but then he heard the door shut and the key turn. The competition comes later, he told himself. For now he had work to do, and as the steam rose above the stove a man, hidden in the shadows at the rear of the kitchen, watched everything.

PART III

A Proposition

CHAPTER 11

Freshening Up

C LINGING TO the consulting-room wall were photographs of the surgeon's Befores who had been successfully transformed into his Afters: the young into much younger, the beautiful into glamorous, the ugly into unremarkable, the bored into intriguing. Smooth angelic faces with the surgeon's trademark nose.

Lucilla Godzinci was detailing the risks associated with each medical procedure – how easily things could go wrong – while Janique and Janique's son Ingmar, a skinny kid with dark eyes, selected a new face from the celebrity line-up. Janique instructed the crew to stop shooting, thanked Lucilla for sharing – 'Enough already with upping the ante, Lucilla' – and they waited while Ingmar's make-up was re-applied.

'We're not using the sound from this shot,' Lucilla said.

'Ingmar can hear you.'

The child has no sense of humour, Lucilla thought. It was common knowledge that the hospital's backup power was always failing. One can never be too young to learn, and besides, it was time this kid fended for himself.

Filming resumed and they went through the selection process again – chin from this model, eyes from that one, brow shaved like that other over there, cheeks from a once-famous idol. Satisfied with his choice Ingmar watched his mother sign the consent form while the surgeon (an enormous cetacean mass; his jaw protruding like a blue whale's; his forehead with a forward slant; his eyes, seemingly independent from each other like a chameleon or a French philosopher, appeared to be focusing on Lucilla and Janique and Ingmar individually and simultaneously) countered Lucilla's risk list.

She sent the production team to prepare the recovery room for Janique's WombWell special: Daddy's Li'l Pumpkin.

'And the nose, Mr Jolly?' Janique said while Ingmar stared at the surgeon. 'He doesn't like how the nose photos.'

'We can see that the nose is a little strong here and here,' the surgeon said, still visibly angered by his discussion with Lucilla, 'but we can correct that. As for the issues you've been talking about' – Mr Jolly addressed Janique directly – 'I'd attribute that to the way the brow falls. If I perform a mini browlift it takes away the stern look. And you, little fella, will soon be a prince.'

The surgeon's success rate was only slightly higher than his peers', although the survival rate of his failures was dramatically lower. Lucilla noticed that the man was more agile than he appeared, especially for someone of his size. He approached narrow spaces side on, surging forward with one hip, and just then he performed this manoeuvre as he thrust himself between Janique and Ingmar like an ocean liner scraping into a narrow port. He was wielding a black felt pen.

'Honey, don't bawl,' Janique said after the surgeon had marked Ingmar's face with ink. 'What about lipo? Could you lipo the flanks to remove the love handles?' The surgeon studied Ingmar's torso and stomach. 'Honey, save your blubbing for the shoot,' she told Ingmar.

'Sure, we could perfect that, but as a rule I don't lipo under the age of sixteen.' He saw the disappointment on Janique's face. 'Number one: that area will gain more fatty tissue as the body matures so any procedure would need to be repeated, and number two: while I understand that it would repair the confidence, I'm always hesitant about correcting nature prior to puberty. Who knows, he could end up with a naturally slim physique, but looking at the maternal genes that he's inherited I have my doubts.'

The cameraman filmed Janique leading her son from the elevator at the very top of the building for the interview. 'You're such a brave prince,' Janique said. That take had to be repeated because of static in the air, and Ingmar was expected to cry again.

After the filming two nurses prepped the boy for surgery, handed him a gown, took away his sweets and injected him with medication to dry his mouth. He was left alone – everyone remained in the room but watched from behind camera – until an orderly collected him and took him down the corridor, the gurney gliding like a dhow on strong currents, through white swing doors leading into the operating theatre. Once inside Ingmar climbed off the gurney and onto the table, meek elbows and knees, and lay back and listened to the anaesthetist.

'Honey, don't frown,' Janique said to her son, and then, direct to camera, 'You're with Janique and this' – her trademark, overlong pause – 'is a WombWell special.'

The anaesthetist was the hospital's worst but one – Lucilla had reviewed his stats – and if panicked he might well become its worst; however if, as now, he was as relaxed as he appeared, then he was merely bad. Perhaps the surgeon had reassured the anaesthetist earlier that day – there were many bottles of red wine at their lunch with Janique and Lucilla – and now the two medics were chatty and chipper.

Theatre nurses were averagely successful, assisting when expected and mindful of the gaffes and slips. They even, on occasion, averted disaster. But their presence was of limited value when tricky procedures were made trickier by the size of the prepubescent child lying on the table.

'Can we run through this again?' Lucilla asked no one in particular. She had been allowed to cup the oxygen mask over Ingmar's mouth and nose, and his skin felt cool to her hand. 'We caught the boom in our tracking shot.'

The anaesthetist looked up. 'He's out cold,' he said.

'Resuscitate him.'

'Ingmar's not dead, Lucilla,' Janique said, 'he's under anaesthetic. You *can* wake him, can't you?' she asked the surgeon.

Lucilla was staring at the anaesthetist. 'Inject adrenalin into his heart. I don't know – you're all the experts here. We need to reshoot.'

'And I'm telling you that he's under. No can do, lady.'

'If you're going to continue filming,' the surgeon announced, 'I'll need silence in this theatre. Appreciate it.'

'We'll use a double for our opening shot,' Lucilla said when she was standing beside Janique. 'Lord knows we should have done something about his legs years ago.'

The electricity supply appeared to be holding out, but then again, the operation hadn't officially begun . . .

Saturdays were statistically the worst for medical procedures. Studies had shown that the day, together with the surgeon's abilities and the anaesthetist's track record, almost always determined the surgery's outcome. Patients who went under the knife on a Thursday fared best, benefiting as they did from the staff's improved morale and alertness, and these patients showed remarkable recovery rates when compared with the short-straw Saturday group.

'Rhinoplasty,' the surgeon was saying as he held up the steel chisel and hammer, 'is derived from the ancient Greek for "big ol' schnoz" combined with "enough money to get rid of."'

'We'll edit his crap out,' Lucilla reassured Janique. 'Give that mallet a good whack,' she instructed him. 'Our viewers love experiencing pain secondhand.'

After he'd finished hacking Ingmar's nose he basted the child's forehead with an iodine solution to sterilize the surface before cutting, inflating, stretching and stapling the skin back onto his skull. Next he fashioned dimples on either side of the mouth with a skewer-like piece of metal. 'Right where the levator anguli oris meets the buccinator,' he said proudly as he touched the cheek. 'Natural dimples are never horizontal' – he stepped back to admire his work – 'but I strive for perfection. Next, we lipo out the puppy fat and transfer it back to where the baby fat is normally carried. Not a permanent solution, you do understand?'

Janique nodded vigorously at the camera.

An opportunity for a repeat special in a few years' time, Lucilla thought. If the ratings were kind to them . . .

*

Janique and Lucilla looked out the recovery room's window at the pregnant storm clouds, waiting for news about Ingmar.

'Three blobs of gum on this glass,' Lucilla said, 'and everything in here would be Semtexed onto the street.'

'Where the hell did that come from?' Janique said.

'If it was winter we'd be frozen solid before we slammed into the road.'

'If this place gets hit by a tornado I'll follow your instructions to the letter, no questions asked. You reckon we'd shatter on impact?'

'We certainly wouldn't bounce, would we?'

'Can we have a bit more empathy?' a voice behind them said.

Janique looked over her shoulder. 'This is, like, the seventh take.'

'I can pick up what you're saying,' the soundwoman said. 'Hold back on the funny stuff. And try and make your shoulders look more pensive. Life-or-death moment, et cetera.'

'*Janique* –' the first voice said once more.

'Yes, we get the picture. We'll shush.'

Down below, in the busy streets, Lucilla could make out a dim alley, filled with angular vegetables and fruit, leading to Chinatown. At its far end was a displaced Mediterranean scene: men wearing black, seated at elegant tables; a flickering television. Back on the main street she saw the Greek butcher with the rabbits hanging in his window that she had walked past earlier that morning. This chorus line of skinned animals wearing their soft furry booties, hung to look as though they were balancing on their dainty feet, had fascinated her.

'Janique' – the voice behind them again – 'do you possibly think you could show a bit more emotion? You might want to hug Lucilla. Or something?'

'He's my child,' Janique said. 'This *is* me feeling emotion.'

'Stasis doesn't play well, honey.'

Lucilla felt obliged to move closer to Janique, hug her, and there were murmurs of approval.

*

'You're with Janique and this . . . is a WombWell special.'

Back in the operating theatre, Ingmar's unwanted remains had already been wiped off most surfaces; his blood was being mopped off the floor.

'For the committed obese, food is Lord,' Janique read off the large cards held to the side of the camera, 'and at the public altar food must be praised and devoured with reverence. However, when unobserved, the true nature of the food god reveals itself, demanding praise before an ivory refrigerator door. On shaking knees, head bowed, these sinners seek sticky-fingered forgiveness over hollowed tubs of ice cream. "Lord, why has thou forsaken me?" they choke before licking their spoons and forcing them down for another scoop. "Why this pain?" as they hover over their chilled offerings. The food god calls them to prayer late at night when other distractions have been silenced by the darkness. And after the feast they are left stricken and empty. Obesity is an epidemic.'

'Pandemic,' Lucilla corrected her. 'The line is "Obesity is a pandemic."'

Janique finished her to-camera and then sent the intern to locate her son. They were ready to film his wake-up. 'What time does the leg double get here, Lucilla?' she asked. 'And do you think obesity is a relevant topic?'

'*Hello!* You convinced the surgeon to lipo Ingmar. Of course it's relevant. If we film you talking in an operating theatre then it's relevant, honey. You could be singing Cole Porter, and so long as you're in an operating theatre, it's relevant. Besides, if we're seen to be addressing obesity then we can't be accused of glorifying plastic surgery for its own sake. It's all about healthy lifestyle choices, yaddah yaddah yaddah.'

The intern came back into the room and went to Janique. Lucilla heard the word 'complications'.

'What do you mean, he's in *another* theatre?' Janique said.

Lucilla motioned to the cameraman who had already started filming – they could reshoot the intern making her entrance later – and he moved up to Janique who, after listening to the intern's hysteria, held her hand over the intern's mouth and said to Lucilla, 'Should I be crying?'

'How urgent is it?' Lucilla asked. The intern shrugged her shoulders. 'If we don't know then you need to be crying, Janique. And honey' – to the intern – 'next time you have some news don't approach the talent, come speak with me first and I'll make a call. As it is, we're going to have to waste time redoing this scene because bad news always plays better when the recipient is sitting down. Now go and find the surgeon and give me a shout. Janique, I want you to de-glam your make-up so that we're prepared for all eventualities. I've got a piece to-camera to write.'

The crew was staking out the theatre entrance and Janique passed the time by interviewing people in the corridor.

'They will *hack* and *hack* and *hack*,' one of the vox pops, a corpulent man, bellowed at her, 'and then *hack* some more. Take it from me: you're better off going into that theatre right now, picking your son off their diseased, thei-thei-their *morbific* table, and going home. Plus it would make better television than these interviews.'

'Thank you,' Janique said to the camera. 'My vigil continues –'

'You know my sister,' the man insisted. 'Dolores First.'

'. . . thank you . . .' Janique kept talking to the camera.

The surgeon thrust the door open and went to Lucilla, asking her to accompany him to a private room large enough to accommodate the crew. They had to speak. Ingmar was on the critical list. Lucilla glanced at her watch: if they rushed they would be in time for the late-night news.

'You're speaking to Janique, or better I speak to her?' she said. 'I can consult her about harvesting. Perhaps I'm being a bit premature but it'll make a fantastic closing scene, don't you think, no matter what the outcome. It would be a clean, beautiful gesture. If we shoot now we'll bring the viewers into our story.'

CHAPTER 12

The Chef's Tasting Menu

G RANT WHANT entered Firsts, and words not so much failed him – which they never did, there being far too many to choose from – but rather presented themselves to him, daring him to select . . .

Diners were licking their plates. When juice slipped from mouths and dribbled down chins, someone – anyone – reached out and swiped it away with a finger that was then sucked clean. They were axe-murdering, serial-killing, spit-roasting, deep-throating, knuckle-popping, back-stabbing, auto-eroticising, sixty-nineing their food. They were freedom-fighting, napalming, pistol-whipping, acid-tripping, mass-murdering, transubstantiating, bush-whacking, spontaneously combusting . . .

He was intruding at this orgy.

And it was at this moment that he realised Henry had already won the competition. Henry was beyond it. And even though Grant knew there was no chance that Henry could ever really win, even though it was impossible, this scene was so . . . so . . . miraculous, perhaps he could win. *Couldn't* he?

Patrice Czarny was staring at Grant from a table of Furness Kindle & Flint execs at the far end of the restaurant, and the look on her face – the look on all of their faces – told him they also knew that Henry First was the winner. He smiled at Patrice, feigning innocence. She pointed at him while conferring with the executives: Grant had become a Name.

So, Patrice, he thought, *this* is winning. This is it.

He walked past the sadists and the masochists, the masters and their slaves, and people eating complicated food that looked like hats designed for the races or weddings or baptisms. Would she dare find fault with her meal and return the dish uneaten, unbeaten, to the kitchen? he wondered.

At the FK&F table everyone was still waiting for their food and they looked nervously at the carnage around them – the bashing, the plugging, the combusting . . . In the centre of their table lay a large green brassiere, a stiffly upholstered thing that looked as though it had been manufactured from pipe cleaners and dried twigs, snuggling against an unopened bottle of vodka and another of water. No one paid the unusual centrepiece much attention.

He was still uncertain about what he would be doing in the corporation – heaven knows what Patrice was expecting of him – and then there was yesterday's meeting with her . . . He was still trying to decipher what, precisely, he had committed to. The mayhem in Firsts reminded him of the African masks in her office: *I see evil; I hear evil; I speak evil.* This restaurant was like the fourth monkey: *We do evil.* Grant hadn't yet spilled the beans or let the cat out of its bag or the kidney out of the stock. He was still trying to find the right time to tell her what he had learnt from Henry's little show the previous evening, and he was aware that time was running out, but what could he say? What on earth does one say?

He took his place at the table and Patrice raised a glass.

*

Hearty Broth with Dito Stock

*

Waiters laden with food ran up the stairs passing exhausted colleagues returning to the kitchen with plates licked clean. Every table was a private gang-bang – genital-heaving, freedom-immolating, acid-murdering – and those diners still waiting for their meals watched the waiters emerge from the kitchen, trying not to panic, attempting to sense whether the offerings were destined for their table. And when the meals eventually arrived the patrons pounced, they shoved aside the waiter's hand as it placed the dish on the table and they began gorging, gang-licking, pre-biting.

A knife dropped from one of the tables and, instead of calling a waiter, the diner threw aside his fork and began clawing at the meat on the plate – ripping at the sinews and stuffing the shreds of beef into his mouth – while the sauce dried on his lips.

Grant spotted Dolores at the far end of the room, struggling past the feeding people. She wore a silky dress, a light greyish blue – saxe – without jewellery, and she look-ed radiant.

Patrice had evidently seen Dolores as well, and she raised her hand and began clicking her fingers. 'Champagne,' she said.

Yes, Grant thought. He could do with a drink, and then he'd tell Patrice. One drink and she'd believe him.

'A very Good Friday to you all,' Dolores said once she was at their table, ignoring Patrice's clicking fingers. 'Have you been good, Patrice? These people are driving me mad, I tell you. Some are on their second main course.' A woman behind Dolores began shouting. 'Yes, in a mo-ment, *madame*, I'll be with you in *one* moment. Janique will tell you that you're sitting at the Punishment Table,' she said to Patrice, and then explained: 'It's next to the loos. Don't say I never warned you, but as you can see we're full. Sorry about that.'

'We need champagne,' Patrice said.

'I'll see what I can do,' Dolores said and before long the steward was there with the booze.

Grant slugged his champagne and poured himself another. He would finish a second, he told himself, and then reveal all to Patrice. A few sips into that drink, he noticed that the woman sitting opposite him was *sans* bra and upper apparel.

'She took it off a few minutes ago,' the executive on Grant's left said, indicating the bra.

Grant nodded. Her large breasts pointed dead ahead. None of the punters at the other tables was paying them the slightest bit of attention – instead they were rubbing, there was frottage, they were slithering. The naked woman looked unimpressed. He recognised her: Janique.

'You're in television,' he said when she caught him staring. 'I watched Daddy's Li'l Pumpkin.' He found it difficult keeping his eyes away from her two prominences. She ran an appreciative hand across the skin above the two objects, but still no one – . . . bush, freedom, pistol, spit . . . – took any notice. 'How is your son?'

'*Enchanté*,' Janique said, still stroking her neck. 'Ingmar's hanging in there. He's a real little trooper. He could do with some of Henry's food to perk him up, let me tell you.'

'Patrice . . .' Grant said, but when he turned to her he saw that she was otherwise engaged with an executive. He tried attracting her attention but she continued talking. It occurred to him that she might be deliberately ignoring him, punishing him, for not contacting her earlier that day. He would have to bear this humiliation.

'I've ordered tasting menus for the table,' Janique told him.

Just then the fattest man in the world joined their table. Grant recognised him from a sauna.

'My husband, Armondo,' Janique introduced the man to Grant. 'And this is my life coach, Lucilla.' Armondo leaned across the table, grabbed Grant's right cheek between his thumb and forefinger, gave it a good shake, and then he kissed his own hand. '*Such* a European!' Janique said. Later, Grant would notice that Armando flinched whenever toilets were flushed in the nearby rest-rooms. (In Grant's dictionary *latria* came before *latrine*.)

'Honey,' Lucilla said to Armando, 'look at Janique when she's talking about you.' Now Lucilla was kissing Grant's neck.

'It's a bit Hieronymus Bosch in here,' Grant said, but they evidently didn't hear him. There weren't looking at the murdering, the killing, the roasting, the throating, and the penetrating going on around them. It was as if the people sitting at his table were in a different restaurant: none of them paid the slightest attention to the mayhem. These two women looked successfully made-over and Janique's obese husband appeared jovial enough. Armondo was one of those men who preferred shaving off their hair instead of allowing his sign of weakness, male pattern baldness, to make an appearance.

Grant picked up a menu discarded in the centre of the table. Armondo reached for the bottle of vodka alongside the bra and filled everyone's champagne glasses.

'What do you do?' he asked Grant.

'Armando,' Janique shrieked, 'Grant works for the Sunday Magazine. He's a writer. Honestly, you never listen –'

'Technically I'm a food critic,' Grant said, 'although I won't quibble. And I no longer work for the magazine.' He realised that Patrice was looking at him.

'I was expecting your call today,' Patrice said.

'I needed to speak to you in person,' he said softly. He'd spent the early hours of the morning asleep on the car's back seat.

She looked at him as if to say, *Well?*

'I made progress last night,' he said, keeping his voice low so that just Patrice could hear him. 'He uses –' he stopped. What good would it do telling her the truth? Perhaps he should keep this to himself? 'It's in the preparation.'

Patrice looked puzzled.

'I can show you,' he said.

'You can show me?'

He nodded. 'It's the way he prepares the food,' he said with conviction, and then he forced himself to pick up the menu and begin scanning the dishes. Hmm, the one he was looking for wasn't there. He'd wanted to taste the broth the judges had been served in the first round of the competition, but never mind.

'And how does he prepare the food?' Patrice asked.

A phone rang in the distance, somewhere in the storm around them.

Grant swigged back his vodka. Armando scanned the room, his eyes never settling on anything for long. His eyebrows were well plucked and his lips looked plump and moist.

'I'd need to show you,' Grant said to Patrice.

Lucilla was still talking. 'This is really apropos of nothing at all,' she said, 'but even though I'm allergic to shellfish, I've heard the fish here is to die for. I met my husband when he was chartering boats for deep-sea fishermen, but that's another story. Not the best of matches, honey.' Then she ordered another bottle of vodka; clear, fiery stuff that was soon finished.

'I said I *thought* I smelled it.' Janique was arguing with her husband. 'You smelled it too. Let's put it this way, when I met Henry earlier I remember thinking to myself that his kitchen must have its very own liquor licence.'

'I think I'd probably also be nervous,' Armondo said.

'Nervous? The man reeked of alcohol. Either that or he'd been gargling aviation fuel.'

'It doesn't appear to have had an adverse effect on his food,' Grant observed, 'judging by what's going on around us.'

'Let's hope it keeps him airborne for the entire evening. Some artists –'

The sound of applause: the judges had arrived.

They stood up to get a better view. On the street side of the restaurant the judges and a battalion of journalists and photographers and cameramen were making their way to a table in the centre of Firsts, bright arcs of light swinging across the crowd.

Two waiters arrived at Grant's table; the one deposited plates in front of them, while the second stood to one side with a saucepan of gravy into which he proceeded to twist a large ladle, and as he scooped out the warm liquid with a flourish, he noticed that Janique was almost naked and, for a moment, it appeared as if he might slop the gravy onto her. She was delighted.

*

Lampreys with Rene

*

They were staring. Patrice, Janique, Lucilla, Armondo, Grant. Zombies. Armondo was punch-drunk. Other diners screamed and gnawed their meals, but this table was silent.

Patrice, together with the FK&F executives, was staring. Every chair was occupied. Grant's lips, his cheeks and tongue tingled – self-heaving, genital-immolating, pistol-whacking, wet-murdering, bareback-dreaming. They had stopped talking after the first mouthful.

Janique held out a box of cigarettes with a shaking hand. They accepted. Her lighter was covered with rhinestones or diamonds or both.

Grant hadn't smoked since his teens but now he felt that nicotine was necessary – something to dull his senses after the onslaught.

'I could eat that all again,' Lucilla said.

'So could I,' Patrice said.

They inhaled; they nodded.

'Should we?' the exec on his left said, and then they looked at Grant as if awaiting his permission.

'Again,' was all he could manage. He stubbed out his cigarette. 'That was *it.*' His lips, cheeks, mouth, arms, the soles of his feet, they all tingled.

'Waiter!'

*

Namibian Lamb with Dito Stock

*

Grant's early-morning dreams had been truly shocking, coming right after the dinner at Firsts. And now he thought he'd woken up, but he couldn't be sure. Did he? Had he?

In the distance he could hear the whistling of a low-flying aeroplane. Close up, everything was too bright.

He lay on his back, his eyes still shut. Later, when he eventually opened them, he could make out a shifting in the whiteness. Something flapping. He shielded his face with his left hand and squinted at the movement. Petals in the breeze, he thought, but it was a curtain.

He got out of bed when he heard bottles rattling as a street sweeper picked his way up the street.

There were no clocks in the unfamiliar bedroom and the bathroom wasn't quite where he expected to find it – a short detour; he stood listening to himself urinate. When he washed his hands he caught himself staring back from a strange mirror. Whose place was this? he wondered. And who was he, this mirrorman staring back at him? No clocks in that world either.

He returned to the bedroom where he sat on the edge of the bed, inhaling a new scent.

There was a note on the Louis-Philippe tilt-top table at the far end of the room: *Here's a key.* And sure enough, lying beside the note, there one was.

He put on the flannel bathrobe that was slung over the side of a wingback chair and walked out the bedroom past a small sitting room and continued down the passage where one door led to the main dressing room and its two adjoining bathrooms; he turned left past three smaller bedrooms (one on his right and two on his left) and the staff rooms and continued until he found the kitchen. He sat at the table, its wooden surface scoured clean, and wondered where he was. These empty glasses from the previous evening, perhaps? What happened last night would need to wait until this morning had eased into the afternoon, he decided.

According to his watch he was late for work, but then he remembered that this ought to be Saturday . . . or perhaps *that* was Saturday – the day just past? And then he recalled that he was no longer officially employed.

He located a bottle of something at the back of the butler's pantry and decanted a healthy amount into a glass, stepping into the dining room by mistake, before finding his way back into the kitchen. The taste was sharply medicinal and for a moment he was pretty damn close to being sick, but he pulled back on the nausea, shutting down that reflex. Easy does it. After a second mouthful he refilled the glass and went into the entrance hall – cutting through the too-bright drawing room – to the media room, where he lay on the sofa in order to appreciate the punky oil painting hanging above the fireplace. He swallowed, draining the glass, and lay on his side. He was in love, and he thought about the blond man who might come walking into this room, the rich and powerful man with whom he would spend the rest of his life.

After a nap he almost felt like his old self and things around him appeared less scratchy. There you are, Mr Whant! Welcome back.

The door in the northern wall of the room led, via a wet bar, into a library. After scanning the spines and looking about for photographs of his mysterious host (the desk drawers were all locked) he returned to the leather sofa and focused his attention on the painting. 'Child's play,' he said after deciphering the curved arcs on the gesso, and then he toasted the image. To his good luck.

Ringing. He floated through the gallery past the bed-rooms, one two three four five all there, up towards the ringing, but then reconsidered and veered right into a small floral sitting room that had sprung out of nowhere and then stumbled into a mirror before locating the bathroom where, after an aggressive shower where he found his groin tender to the touch, he ate a tube of toothpaste. He clawed at his gums with the bristles of a strange tooth-brush, rinsed, gargled and wrapped himself in a towel the size of a billboard. He had a vague memory of having sex with someone in the stranger's bedroom, and from the look of his knob that person had ravaged him.

He heard a noise: someone else, possibly in a nearby bathroom. He waited; the high-pitched ringing in his ears growing louder as he listened. Anxious about his mystery host Grant wiped the condensation off the mirror and wished himself more presentable, virile and taut.

A voice called out from the other side of the door: 'Honey?' it said. It couldn't be Henry, could it? Grant felt his face growing warm and flushed. Had Henry done this to him, he wondered. What a tiger! Surely not. If only he could remember more about last night. And if only the delicious Henry First knew how often Grant had murmur-ed his name . . .

Grant turned to the bathroom door, the towel slung nonchalantly over his shoulder, ready for his dreams to be fulfilled.

'Henry?' the voice called out again – or was it 'Honey'? – as the door swung open.

They stared at each other, not moving, and then Grant grabbed his towel and quickly tied it around his waist.

'Patrice,' he said, his mouth dry.

She continued staring at him. Had they? he thought. *Had they?*

'I was just leaving,' he said.

He had to step around her in order to get back into her bedroom. The force of her slap took him by surprise, and he felt a muscle in his neck giving an angry pull as his head swung to the right. If it hadn't been for the explosion now detonating in his left ear he may have been able to pretend that nothing had happened. He'd slept with *Patrice*?

He dressed quickly without glancing back, and then, uncertain what to do with the towel, he placed it on the wingback chair's left arm.

'Did you spend the night?' she said.

He shook his head without looking at her. 'I don't think so.'

'Yes, I don't think so either.'

Once dressed he stumbled across to the elevator where he punched the call button again and again and again and again until the lift arrived – apologising with a *ping!* – and he caught it to the lobby where the doorman could ease him into a cab. Only when it was halfway down the avenue did he realise that he'd somehow taken her apartment key.

Sometimes the best decision is not making a decision, he thought. His left cheek felt hot and thick. Stand out of the way and let the decision make itself, that sort of thing. His memory of the look on Patrice's face when she had seen him in the bathroom made him laugh out loud, and this sudden movement hurt his neck again. What had they *done*? he wondered.

So he was not making any decisions but he was nodding gingerly. She would forget this, he thought. That violent slap would make her feel better; it put her back in control, and she would forget all about whatever may have happened. Sitting there nodding. Christ, he knew that she could never forget, slap or no slap.

'Where to?' the driver asked when they reached the first intersection. But there would be no decisions, just nodding; the nods were eminently preferable to deciding.

Patrice Czarny had screamed when he was trying to exit her apartment. And she had thrown something expensive and rare against something hard.

CHAPTER 13

Dao Mei

'A FTER ALL,' Patrice Czarny said on the other end of the line, 'it's called the Restaurant of the Year competition, not the meal of the year. *Restaurant.* It's refresh time for your place, honey, for your brand – the Henry First brand. He's the story. Make sense?' Dolores knew better than to interrupt Patrice's rant. Things were about to 'ramp up', everyone needed to prepare for the 'publicity onslaught', there would be 'discretionary bonuses' for whoever met certain 'key performance indicators'. 'We must all look like winners. The top ten chefs are facing off over here. Where is he? Can you communicate?'

'Do you want to speak to Henry?' Dolores asked, unsure about Patrice's questions. She looked at her husband who was sitting next to her in the restaurant.

'What?' Patrice said.

'Will Henry represent us both at the meeting?'

'*If* you don't mind,' Patrice said. 'Dolores, I need you to review our design proposals for Firsts. We're super-keen to have your buy-in. If I was in your position – and now I'm talking as a friend and not as a competitor – I would be *inclined* to analyse and answer a.s.a.p. I'm going to assume that you'll get your wheels turning?' And Patrice hung up.

Dolores considered the restaurant, the empty tables and her décor. The small room at the back of Firsts had just been converted into an office with space for assistants to handle bookings and enquiries. She had been trying to rewrite the menu for some time – the sum total of their planned changes.

The phone rang again; Patrice's calls had postscripts.

'I want to talk you through the designs, Dolores.'

Dolores opened the parcel that had arrived earlier that morning. The first sketch was of a French bistro.

'*Very* continental,' Patrice said. 'The details are in the pack.'

The next two pictures were more contemporary. Then a drawing of what appeared to be a whorehouse with an ostentatious chandelier, ferns and stuffed animals. The final picture was of a country-and-western-style restaurant: cowboy paradise.

'Fabulous, no?' Patrice said.

'To be honest, I can't envisage them working for Firsts. In fact none of them quite captures what we're about, if that makes any sense. Could I propose a design of my own?' No response. 'When do you plan on upgrading our restaurant? I'm guessing not until after the competition?'

'I'll confirm timeframes with your husband.' Patrice ended the call.

Dolores and Henry were at their favourite table in Firsts from where they could see Patrice Czarny's office across Golden Square; they were waiting for the cleaners to finish. Henry tilted a glass of icy water away from him, wiping the condensation with his thumb.

'That was a teensy bit mad,' Dolores said. She was worried, she was spent, she was a bit happy; she had a secret she needed to tell him. 'Patrice is waiting for you in her office.'

'Let her wait.'

'*Henry.*'

'Chinese curse,' he said.

Dao mei. The two words surfaced unexpectedly and she felt sick. 'Getting what you wished for?' she asked.

'Sure, we get what we wish for.'

'If we *ever* – and I mean it, *ever* – talk one another into entering a competition again, we both need to be taken out and shot.'

'No,' he said, 'because then Felix would be left running things. If we agree to one of these things again, *you'll* cook and *I'll* do front of house.' He emptied his glass.

'The word on the street is that my husband is a genius.'

He shook his head. 'This is from Felix who's been bed-ridden for a year?'

'The whole city knows it,' she said, ignoring his comment. 'Felix is merely repeating what he's heard.'

'Then why aren't you celebrating with me?' he asked, holding up his glass. 'We should be out ingesting stimulants with the beautiful people, don't you think?'

'After last night I need a full-body transplant.'

'Well the good news is that we could probably afford one. Wait here.' She watched him go down the stairs. The head cleaner had been waiting for this moment, and came across to the table.

'Finished?' Dolores asked.

The cleaner nodded. She thanked him and locked the restaurant doors once his crew had departed with their equipment. Down below she could hear Henry cursing in the kitchen and she went to help.

She was unable to see him in the half-light. 'Henry, Patrice is waiting.'

He was ignoring her. The storeroom door was ajar. She stepped inside, into the sweet smell of wine and spirits, and she saw him at the far end of the room, his back turned to her, staring at the bottles.

'Need assistance?' she asked. 'Tough choice for 11 a.m.?' She got close to him and placed an arm around his waist. 'You've done really well,' she said. He turned, his face wet with perspiration or tears. 'It was one hell of an evening,' she spoke into his chest. 'We should go home and sleep.'

'Have the cleaners gone?' he asked.

She nodded. 'I've locked the door.' She kissed him, and he was still crying so she held him tight. This was the man she had married; the man she had first loved. They embraced in the storeroom, his body, her body, the aroma of food and the liquor tang.

'Let's go home,' she said.

'I came down here for a reason,' he said. 'We need to celebrate.'

'Vodka's a bit too gangsta-chic, don't you think? This room gives me a headache.'

He grabbed some champagne and followed her into the kitchen where he found a knife and lopped off the bottle's neck with a single thrust. Liquid erupted over the sharp edge and dropped onto the floor. He filled two glasses. 'To my wife,' he said.

'*And* my genius husband.'

He downed his drink.

'Come on, drink up,' he said as he poured another round. 'And after this, another bottle.'

The alcohol was good, it was pleasing, and she felt herself grow drowsy.

'One might be enough.'

He lifted Dolores into his arms and carried her up the stairs. She clung to his shoulders and tried not to think about them tumbling back down again . . . the bottle smashing . . . the glass . . .

'I'm plastered,' she announced once he had settled her into a chair. 'And so are you, Mr First.'

'I propose a toast to Patrice Czarny,' he said holding his glass toward the Furness Kindle & Flint building. 'I'm going to mash her. I'm going to knead her.'

'I thought you weren't competitive.'

'Of course I am,' he said, repeating the toast, 'and I like her less than I like competitions.'

'Talking about kneading,' Dolores said, wiping some alcohol off his cheek, 'I think she wouldn't mind kneading you.'

'Patrice Czarny? Sex with me?'

'The one and only.' She raised her eyebrows inquisitorially.

Henry looked at the floor, perhaps trying to remember the previous evening. 'We should go home.'

'Yes,' she said quickly, 'let's spend twenty-four hours in bed.' And then she could tell him her secret.

'Are you sure you don't want to open today?' he said. 'A Saturday and we're booked solid. And the staff are all up there.' He meant the roof.

She looked at her watch.

'What are you thinking, Dolores?'

'That we'll have to open even though neither of us wants to. And I should visit my brother. And Patrice wants you for lunch. And you're a genius.'

'The last bit isn't true.'

'You are a thoroughly modest man, Mr First. You cook, you gave last night's diners an indecently sensual experience – quite frankly it's left me with a few memories I could have done without.'

She finished her drink and turned the glass upside down.

He winked at her. 'I think we should sneak across the square and paint our secret onto their building,' he said. 'Can you imagine their faces?'

She felt cold. How did he know? She wanted to say, 'What secret?' but she watched him finish his drink instead.

'Can you imagine Patrice's face?' he laughed.

It would be better to sit this one out, she thought, instead of frightening him. He held her gaze and went to the restroom with the purposeful gait of a morning drinker. When he returned his face was wet and there were pieces of paper stuck to his chin. She wiped them away.

'I'll fetch the staff,' she said, 'while you make your appearance at Patrice's.'

*

Dolores walked through the Broad Way Building's tiled lobby, forgetting to greet the concierge, and caught one of the creaking elevators to the top. How could he know she was pregnant? And why didn't she just tell him straight? The utility door was open and through it, the roof.

It was a normal day. In every way it was a normal day.

Up here she had a clear view of the no man's land of buildings that had been shunted together in this part of the city. In the distance the financial centre appeared to grow higher as she watched. She sat on a small box at the base of the large wooden Y that helped spell BROAD WAY and shielded her eyes from the morning sun. The kitchen staff were on the opposite side of the flat roof, smoking and talking, all of them seated on the small brick lip that ran around the building's edge. They were silhouetted against the morning sun; she could feel them watching her.

Over there was Golden Square. A grid of televisions in the window of a pawn shop on its south side was flashing white and red, and it looked as if the store was on the move – zigging and zagging as an advert shuddered across the screens. Dolores saw that it was *the* advert: their advert. The letters R O T Y slid from right to left across the televisions, moving over images of food and hysterical people. The Restaurant of the Year competition – *The HOT 100!* Images of food and more text scrolled across: THE ANGUISH! She hadn't seen this ad. Then there was a close-up of Henry. THE STRESS! A picture of Dolores with her head in her hands. THE COMPETITION TO END ALL COMPETITIONS!

How dare they! She watched, fuming. Where did they get those shots? And then the screens were filled with her picture again – distorted and discoloured like silkscreen replicas – each head looking earnestly into the camera.

Up on the roof with her Akhilesh, Ishwar and Chandresh were laughing with Ramanuja, Vasudev, Yogendra and Swapnil. They couldn't have seen the advert, could they? To their right were Dhananjay, Devadutt, Kavi,

Martand, Prahlad and Ambar. Then Shankar and Shreyas and Sharad and Yudhisthir and Prasanna. It was impossible for them to hear her (the traffic's ocean noise) so she walked across and asked for a cigarette.

When she returned to the small box at the base of the Y she drew reluctantly on the cigarette, feeling queasy . . . Look what smoking had done to Felix. Dolores closed her eyes.

Her brother's first brush with cancer was when he'd just turned 30. Their parents had reacted to his illness as though it was nothing more than a damaged toe, a missing finger or a worn tooth. Perhaps they thought if they fussed it would become real.

She was already married to Henry and the two of them would drive Felix to his hospital appointments. The trip home was always slower; she sat in the passenger seat with Felix curled up in the back and watched her brother's reflection in the vanity mirror. She'd spend her journey looking at him; his eyes opening whenever the car slowed.

Late one afternoon, after a lengthy bout of chemotherapy, the setting sun caught Felix on the back seat and she could see that he was burning up. His sweat made the inside of the car humid. She looked at Henry and, aware of her distress, he turned off the main road and headed in a new direction. It took an hour to reach the sea. Fenced-off fields replaced the buildings and then the car's wheels were kicking up gravel, slowing further, until Henry parked on the top of a hill overlooking the ocean.

'Up for a walk?' he asked Felix. The three of them climbed into the strong wind. In the distance the sun touched the horizon; winter spray blew into their faces. Henry led her brother down a grass track to the shore. When they reached the sea there was no longer any sign of the sun and they stood squinting into the cold blast. Three people standing on the beach, she remembered, watching the storm. Felix burning.

Henry had said, 'Come on then,' and began undressing his brother-in-law. They stripped naked in the cold air and walked into the surf. The water hurt when it struck her legs. They waded in further until they were up to their waists, and when at last a wave hit they went under.

With the swells that followed Dolores allowed herself to sink beneath the surface, and by the time she returned for air she had lost her brother. Far ahead she heard Henry shouting. Pleasure or pain? She saw him, chest deep, preparing to dive into the ocean, and she waved her hands, trying to attract his attention. Still no Felix. They could die out here. Henry lifted his head out of the water and she was about to call her brother's name when she saw Felix swimming face down on her left, his arms pulling himself forward. He looked up and blew a raspberry.

'Who knew it could get this cold?' she remembered shouting. It was warmer under the water. Was he OK? Did he want to go back out? The gale meant she couldn't hear herself either so she pointed towards the land.

'I'm feeling human,' Felix had said when he reached her. Henry called out in the distance. 'Your husband's mad. Let's stay a bit longer.'

The night was bitter and dark when they drove away with the car's heater working hard against the storm.

Welcome back into our lives, Captain Cancer. A final tour of duty?

She dropped the cigarette on the roof. How long had she been sitting there? No smoking in her condition. And Felix's condition?

In the time it took her to grind the cigarette dead the staff had begun walking towards the utility door. The morning had passed without warning. Dolores motioned to the second group; a man came forward and she thanked him, Ramanuja, for the cigarette. He stood in front of her and she waited for Yash and Swapnil and Dhananjay and Maheepati to go out the doorway.

He watched her, perhaps nervous about being alone on the roof with her, although he appeared to be at ease. 'My brother,' was all she could think of saying. Her phone rang: Henry ranting. She asked Ramanuja to wait and went across to the west side of the roof that overlooked the square.

'We're being refreshed,' Henry said.

'Is this about the redecoration?' she asked.

'Apparently Patrice is here to help us.'

'I see.'

'Which means they're closing the restaurant.'

'They can't do that,' she said. She should have said something to him before he left for Patrice's meeting. It was all going wrong.

'Well, it seems that they can. They're offering to re-decorate our place, which effectively shuts us down for the remainder of the competition.'

She had wanted to tell him that she was pregnant. *I wanted to tell you this morning but Patrice called . . .*

'I'm on my way back,' he said. 'And Dolores, call Grant Whant – he'll know what to do about Patrice.'

She ended the call and apologised to the sun, walking back across the roof, and then once more to the man's shadow falling alongside her. It was a normal day . . .

'Is your brother fully recovered?' Ramanuja asked. 'Did the kidney help him?'

She guessed that he was in his mid-thirties. 'He's dying,' she said finally. The truth. 'And yes, thank you for the contact details – the kidney helped.'

Dolores asked about Ramanuja's family. A wife back home. A daughter. She asked about the town where they lived. Where had he learnt to cook? She found herself thinking about Felix's winter swim all those years ago, and then she thought about her baby, but tried to stop because she was worried that everything around her might just start unravelling. She asked Ramanuja about his child again. He answered patiently, ending with, 'I'll be seeing you downstairs after your contemplation.' He seemed keen to get their informal exchange over with. She nodded. Downstairs.

He waited. She moved closer to him, his shadow now covering her knees. 'Thank you for your help.'

She embarrassed them both by shaking his hand. What to do? He went to the door and stepped into the darkness. Her palms were wet. She had been in the sun for too long.

A warm updraft caught her hair as she walked through the giant letters and peered over the edge of the building, looking down at Golden Square. The queue for their lunchtime sitting snaked around the block. Full again. From brunch until late, six days a week. The competition ate into their time, and now it would eat them.

She had come up here to get away from the madness in the restaurant and not to think about her brother. 'How does this end?' she said out loud to the buildings and the line of restless people waiting below.

She returned to Firsts where she left a message on Grant's phone before opening the doors to the lunchtime crowd, followed by the late-afternoon crowd and a call telling her that her brother was thinking of checking out of hospital, then the early-evening crowd with the news that Grant would be there later, then the dinner crowd and the late sitting. Felix was up. She had to speak to Felix.

*

Dolores, Henry and Grant sat in the empty restaurant kitchen.

'Just because something bad happens doesn't mean we should wait for something good to happen,' Grant said. 'Life doesn't work like that.'

'We're jinxed,' Henry said.

'You're not jinxed,' Grant said.

'I'm being realistic. You'd have to be pretty damn naïve to believe that we're not scrapped. Patrice will pay us the restaurant's average weekly takings prior to the competition for however long her renovations take.'

'We're not doomed, Henry,' Dolores said.

'We're all doomed, Dolores,' he replied. 'At least we will be once she's bled us dry.'

She ignored him. 'What you're doing, what you've already achieved, is due to your genius, your hard work, your determination. It's art.' She noticed Grant looking at her husband intently. 'There must be a way out of this. Felix can recommend a good lawyer.'

'By which time the competition will be over,' Henry said. 'It's like Midas getting what he asked for, don't you think? There's always a catch. The good news is that whatever you touch turns to gold. The bad news is that whatever you touch turns to gold.'

'I think the Midas story is helpful to a certain degree,' Grant said.

'To an outsider it looks great.' Henry stood up. 'To an outsider Patrice is doing us a massive favour, and any objections we raise will look churlish, and if the building work overruns then that's simply down to bad luck.'

'You're afraid of the consequences of your success,' Dolores said. 'There has to be a way for us to beat Patrice at her own game.' She noticed that Grant's hands were shaking. Every now and then she caught glimpses of his fingers. She couldn't remember seeing him gnawing away at his nails like that, but there was the evidence.

'Success can be harder to deal with than failure,' Grant said, and Henry laughed.

'I reckon we should go with our anger,' Dolores said.

'I want to cook in the final round of the competition just to see the look on her face,' Henry said. 'I'll think of something.'

'My stomach' – Dolores clenched her right hand into a tight fist – 'feels like that when I think of her. I want to rip out her jugular.'

'Is this what's called an "intervention" on your self-help workshops?' Henry said. Dolores punched him on the shoulder. 'So what do you reckon, Mr Whant?'

'Patrice will quarantine your place first thing to-morrow.' Henry nodded. 'You should plan for that. Take what's important' – again, Dolores saw Grant giving Henry a look – 'and prepare for the worst. I'd suggest you put what's useful in storage and leave everything else here so that it doesn't look too obvious that you were alerted. That way you'll have a bit more ammunition when it comes to fighting back.'

They began working.

CHAPTER 14

The Clean-Up – I

Grant Whant went into the kitchen to double-check that the stoves and the electrical appliances were unplugged before switching off the lights. As he was about to walk up the stairs he saw a sliver of light coming from the cold store. He went back into the kitchen without turning on the lights – he could remember its layout and there was enough of a glow filtering down the stairs to guide him past the hard edges – and across to the cold store.

He pulled open the door, half-expecting to find some-one trapped inside the room, but everything appeared orderly and quiet. At the far end of the store he saw a row of saucepans. He stepped back out, about to close its heavy door, but then decided it was worth another look.

Up close the pans were battered and dirty. He con-tinued searching.

CHAPTER 15

The Clean-Up – II

HENRY FIRST congratulated himself on being able to recognise who his friends were. He may not particularly like Whant, but he respected the man. They had an understanding.

During the clean-up, Henry had gone up to the roof to have some time by himself; his eyes burning from the acid wind blowing across the river, and he thought about Firsts – the possibilities within reach. He'd had some of his best ideas up there. That moment of creation counted the most: that unexpected spark. It didn't matter whether he acted on the impulses or simply watched them float by, what mattered was that he could still create. And even though there was nothing left to prove now that he could turn lead into gold, water into wine, blood into wine – now that he was able to Midas any meal he wanted – part of him still needed to create dishes that no one else had thought of. Midas. He knew how he felt. Henry First was in the big league now. Felix was right. Henry First caught the whispers: *There he goes. There goes the chef.*

Back in the kitchen he tried to remember what else would need to be packed up. Apart from the obvious, of course. How would he explain to Dolores that he wanted to take the stock with him?

Everything was quiet down here; the metal shelves undisturbed, patiently awaiting the morning shift.

A fine strip of light outlined the storeroom door; its glow fell on the work areas and the silver equipment. Midnight. No, the shaft of light was illuminating a scale's face with its hand at zero. Someone had left the light on. He walked over to the storeroom and peered through the crack of light; waited for his eyes to adjust to the bright interior.

Something was moving about inside, and now he felt the throb in his chest and his ears . . . re-*pen-tance* . . . re-*pen-tance* . . . His eyes were useless. Something in that room. Someone searching the shelves, pulling away containers, prising them open, pushing bags to one side and feeling around. The person stopped and turned to the door, and Henry recognised him. What was Grant doing? Grant waited a moment before continuing his search until he found the large pot. He lifted the lid.

Henry stepped back and looked around the kitchen, knowing that Grant knew; and as his eyes tried adjusting to the darkness it occurred to him that there was a human animal in the storeroom, and it would provide Henry with the meat that he needed.

Without turning, Grant said out loud, 'I have a proposition for you, Henry. Something that Patrice can't resist. Your meal ticket.'

PART IV

Easter

CHAPTER 16

Living to Eat

THERE IS NOTHING worse than an empty restaurant, Patrice Czarny thought. The dead space that had once been Firsts was what she had been so eager to achieve.

Henry was where she wanted him, she was sure of it. The kitchen equipment, dulled by a fine layer of dust, reflected a thousand Patrices, each distorted and distorting, as she peered into nooks and spaces. Down here reminded her of up there: each kitchen workstation a city block, each path an arterial road – its layout was the city in miniature. She'd spent a good deal of the morning searching the storerooms before she would allow the FK&F Construction builders down the stairs. And even though it appeared as if everything was still in place, all unpacked and eager for a day's shift to start (Where *was* everyone? the kitchen demanded), something was missing. Yes, this scene had already been interfered with, despite her protestations that this dawn raid was not a dawn raid. 'Honey,' she had said to Henry in a voice that assumed shrugged shoulders and eyes raised to heaven with a what-can-a-girl-do kooky smile, 'the building team are super-keen to get started.' She'd invited him to a meeting, all in the same voice, later that afternoon. Someone had tipped him off.

She heard the main door upstairs open, and the sound of men's voices. The builders had arrived.

She took out her phone and dialled. 'Whant,' she said when he answered, 'where is it? Where is it? I'm at Firsts and I need to know what I'm looking for.'

'You're doing what?'

She hung up, swore, and dialled again.

'Hello, Patrice,' Grant said.

'Hello, Whant. Did you have a pleasant sleep? You're awake now, which is good.'

'Where are you, Patrice?'

'In the kitchen, of course. Firsts. We had to get started with the refurbishment. So tell me – what am I looking for?'

'What do you mean?'

She asked the question once more, and again he refused to give her the answer.

Patrice dialled his number a third time.

'Patrice?'

'Are you having an enjoyable time, Whant?' she said. She closed her eyes, counted to ten, and opened them again. She waited; Grant waited.

A labourer came out of the storeroom carrying a red-and-white cooler box. She motioned for him to come over and she took the box from him.

'I'm bound to have fun today,' she said. 'I think I might have found something.'

'Oh?' Grant said without emphasis.

She opened it. Empty. Smelled clean. She ended the call and then dialled his number again.

'Patrice,' he said.

'What's the weather like in the suburbs?'

'Identical to the city, I'd imagine,' he said. He was sitting in bed, alone, with a light on.

'Where is it, Whant? What am I looking for?'

'Patrice, I honestly don't know –'

'Where where where where *where*?'

'Patrice –' But she'd already ended the call.

She picked up the cooler box and, almost as an afterthought, she threw it at the ceiling where it thundered against the metal pipes. The lid flew free and the box hit the tiled flooring, narrowly missing her. She grabbed the box and flung it again, in the direction of the storerooms; the labourers watched it spin above the workstations until it bounced off the wall.

She called to one of the men. 'Don't just stand there. Pick it up. And take these pots upstairs.' Her phone rang: Grant Whant. She accepted the call without saying a word.

'He suspected something,' Grant said. 'I denied it, but he suspected something was going to happen this morning.'

'What are their plans?'

She could hear him breathing as he decided how to answer. 'He wants to sell.'

'Loser. That is the first thing you've said that I believe. Dolores will think she has a plan. Even if she hasn't thought of it yet she'll come up with something. I need you to focus on achieving your milestones. No interference.' Grant was answering her – something subservient – and she cut him short: 'We all have strengths; we all have weaknesses. You and I must talk. I need you to stop by my place, at your earliest convenience, to discuss next steps. Shall I send a driver?'

'Yes, let's do that. Discuss next steps.'

She let his snide echo pass unchallenged. This kitchen would be mothballed. Onward towards her future . . . Henry's future . . . their future?

CHAPTER 17

The Flight

GRANT WHANT sat in front of his television, content for the morning to be divided into half-hourly chunks and non-news bulletins, waiting for the driver's call. Two hours had passed since his conversation with Patrice.

He knew how she would respond to Henry's, and in turn his own, proposal. She would only go for it if pushed. Never one to close doors unless she absolutely had to, she would string Henry along while trying hard to unearth the real reason behind his sales pitch. The psychologists were right all along, she had once explained to Grant. The reasons behind our actions are never what we say or even think they are: our true motivation is always our basest motivation. If Henry wanted her to give up a part of herself then that would mean he wanted to eat her, which meant, in turn, that he wanted her dead. In ordinary circumstances Henry's waffle about her legacy could be ignored if it was merely about wealth or success. However, Grant knew that an offer of immortality would appeal to her narcissism. Reinforce her place in the grand scheme of things. She would be hesitant about closing this door – she had, after all, witnessed the effects of Henry's cooking. That could be you, Patrice. It might be you.

His phone had yet to ring. The television channels were undergoing their gentle shift from morning tat to afternoon hysteria intercut with bulletins featuring deadly meteorological symbols on maps.

If she detected Grant's hand in Henry's offer she would only mention it obliquely. It was all too much fun for her to be limited by straight talking and direct questions. She would play along.

When eventually his phone did ring he listened to the driver's instructions, and then Grant stood up, dressed for the strange city with its brutal architecture and brash workers, ready for his plunge into darkness.

When the car door shut with a hefty sigh Grant felt himself sucked back into the leather upholstery as the driver pulled away from his apartment, past an idling removal van outside Henry's and Dolores's apartment, and he considered how best to get his previous evening's dalliances with Patrice out of the way. There was a chocolate egg on the seat beside him. Ahead in the city was Firsts, now empty and dark, with its rich stock safely out of the storeroom. Her key was in his pocket. She might be playing music when he arrived. Yes, the elevator door would slide open and she would be playing the blues and he would simply begin talking to her: *I don't want to hurt you, but. I've been thinking about this, and. You and I, we're just so. Patrice, this is difficult for me to say, but we really should.*

At one point of his journey they must have swung a sharp left down the ramp into the underground garage – he missed this deft move – and when he blinked awake they were parked at the far end of a row of limousines. He stepped out the car, leant against its cold metal, and reviewed his options . . . her soft music, the scent of gardenia in the bedroom, the restaurant with a pot of gold, the death on his hands.

He was her wildcard, and he knew that once played he would be discarded. For a moment he almost asked the driver to take him to Henry's apartment in order for him to fetch the stock and deliver it to Patrice. Or perhaps he should just call her – that way he could keep what he had to say about their passionate evening to a neat paragraph:

beginning, middle, end. He ran through his conversation again. Without question she would crush him.

He was aware of the driver shutting the car door behind him as Grant lurched over to the basement elevator where he thumped the button. Inside, he took the key from his pocket, inserted it into the keyhole at the bottom of the panel, pressed the top number and dropped a tiny ball of chocolaty foil onto the red carpet.

'Is it proceeding?' she asked. Grant had ventured alone down her hallway, passing the many rooms, and pushed open her bedroom door to see her lying on her bed: her way of defusing any sexual hysteria. 'Plan-wise?'

He answered.

She continued, 'The ingredient, the special ingredient . . .'

'The *rene*,' he offered.

'The *rene*. What has Henry said about it? I couldn't find any in the restaurant so I assume he's taken it with him.' He started his answer – was there time for his rehearsed speech? – but she cut him off. 'It's as we expected?' she said.

'Henry's using the kidney,' he said. 'Patrice, I should say something about us –' *I don't want to hurt you, but.*

'There is no "us".'

'I was referring to last night,' he said.

'So was I,' she said, getting up. 'We only have a relationship inasmuch as I look after you while you do what I tell you to. I've closed the restaurant.'

'I warned him,' he said.

'You *what?*'

'I need him to trust me.'

She got up and walked out the room – he listened to her marching down the corridor, stop, mutter to herself – then she returned. 'Whose side are you on?' she demanded.

'Patrice, it stands to reason that if I'm close to you – as everyone knows – then it isn't very believable if you do something momentous like shut down his restaurant without me letting anything slip.'

She patted the back of her hair with her right hand. 'Have you even asked him about the kidney? No. Well, why are you so sure about it? What did he say when you told him about my plans for Firsts?'

'That he'll beat you at your own game. He's going ahead with his final entry, and he doesn't want you to be there.'

'There's no way he's getting access to that restaurant,' she said.

'He has another plan. I'm on my way to his apartment tonight to learn more.'

'Don't bother. I've invited him around here to toast his success – he's made it into the final round, after all. I'm hoping we'll find a way out of our little disagreement, and I'd be interested to hear any offers he has to make. And you can relay that to him beforehand, if you want.'

'You should know that he's inviting FK&F's competitors to his final entry. He's told me that he's going to sell, no matter what.'

'Did he really? And when were you planning on giving me this information?'

'I'll be here for your meeting with him,' he said.

She ignored him. 'You don't happen to know what he's asking for?'

'I'll find out tonight.'

'Forget it,' she said. She needed time to consider her options. 'I'm not sure about your kidney theory. Personally, I think it's a cover: he's doing nothing more glamorous than spiking his meals with dope. I've got the sniffer dogs in there at the moment.' She led Grant to her study where she handed him a black file. 'But if Henry's doing what you think he's doing with the *rene* – and let's be honest, my theory is more plausible than yours – then I need to ensure that, for the sake of the corporation's survival, we stay ahead of the game. Either way, I'm productionising things, and I've redefined your role. You leave tonight. Read the file on the plane – your ticket's inside. I have your buy-in re this?'

Once reassured, she held out her right hand and he heard her say, '*Monsieur.*' He took her hand and shook it. She kept it extended. *Of course*, he realised, and cupped her warm hand in his again and kissed it, grateful for the peace offering.

This was his moment: 'Patrice, I don't want to hurt you, but I've given it some thought – a lot of thought, in fact – and you and I . . . we're just . . . well, this is difficult for me to say, but regarding what happened between us last night, we really should . . .' The look on her face was not what he'd hoped for. He quickly released her hand.

She enunciated, 'I said "my *key*". Give me the key.'

He dug into his pocket, retrieved her key and placed it on her outstretched palm.

He stood outside her building, thinking. Should he call Henry? He should call Henry. The tower blocks around him bristled: they were growing thorns and spines for protection. Her curt farewell would have to do. Was that it?

The city was still his, barely. Behind him was the politburo haunt that housed Patrice's apartment, with its row upon row of square windows, no larger than a human head, extending up into the gloom. This city held possibilities for his future. Henry would sell and they would use the cash to set up a restaurant together. There was just the pesky issue of Patrice's task that he had to get out of the way first . . .

He'd almost walked to the end of the block when an empty cab slowed. Once he was on board it swung into the oncoming traffic, missing a bus filled with ageing matrons (they leaned in unison as their vehicle took remedial action) and then the cabbie swore all the way back to the suburbs before parking a block from Grant's flat. Grant enlisted the doorman to help with his bags while he searched for his passport.

*

Grant was dumped in the international arrivals' terminal parking lot as the cab driver sped off bitching about the low tip, his guidebook still on the back seat, and after screaming at a belligerent salesperson Grant caught a bus to the correct terminal where there was too little time at the check-in desk to renegotiate his reservation.

Patrice had evidently made a mistake.

He was shooed down the tilting corridor towards the plane where he saw the pilot glance out of the cockpit's triangular window and salute him. A steward grabbed Grant's elbow and propelled him inside, pulling the door shut behind them, towards a seat in the rear. He had never flown this far back, ever.

Had Patrice made a mistake?

'Sir?' was all the steward said when he complained. Grant explained his predicament while the man smiled aggressively (Grant made a note to speak to the airline about empathy training), slamming overhead lockers. 'Sir, I *understand*, sir,' he said before chastising a choking infant in the last row.

'I always travel first class,' Grant said. 'Get me the purser.'

'I'm sorry, sir, but we don't have a purser on this flight, sir,' the man said over his shoulder as he strapped an obese pre-teen into her seat. 'The Sunday flight is always full, sir, so may I suggest sir sits back quietly and *enjoys*, sir. This isn't something we're able to resolve for sir at the moment. Sir.' He walked away.

A stewardess strode down the aisle, turned, and began miming the emergency procedures, evidently a long-running gag between herself and her colleagues who obviously had no regard for their own lives. Who on earth chose a career where a bad day at the office meant a terrifying, plummeting, scream-inducing spin as baby waste and vomit and aviation fuel laced the soil of a peaceful field before incinerating everything in a whooshing fireball?

Grant looked at the passengers. Cattle class. The seat chafed his back. The plane's sing-song whine changed tone as it began taxiing down one of the airport country lanes that would eventually lead to the runway.

The security demonstration continued. Soon he'd be thrust back into the ribbed seats as they rumbled down the tarmac – a hippo dashing back to water – dislodging luggage and kitsch; overhead compartments falling open as passengers cowered in their seats, waiting for something – a skid? an explosion? Perhaps his life would be cut short by a minor wiring mishap that caused this craft to swerve hysterically off course, a tumbling roly-poly of horror, before they were returned to earth coffined in steel? Or an unannounced flash as the stewardess handed out food – the fireball surprising and then sautéing them during their meal, incinerating the piles of diaphanous trash?

Out the window he saw another monster straining at the end of the runway, its engines shuddering, and behind that plane were buildings and clouds.

Still they waited.

The pensioner on Grant's left was engrossed in a book: *Great Aviation Disasters for Beginners: Terror at 30,000 Ft.* He glanced at her well-thumbed copy, uncertain whether he should be reassured to discover that he was no less paranoid than this fellow adventurer, and noticed that its chapter headings were listed on the back cover ('Hydraulics Don't Work', 'Where to Sit if You Must', 'Battling for Survival Against Your Fellow Passengers', 'Weathering the Storm'), each giving him too much to think about.

The craft's engines stuttered and increased pitch – they were moments away from the pilot battling gravity and wind and mechanics and God – and then one of the engines coughed. Grant looked for the stewardess, hoping to be able to tell from her face whether the bronchial engine was unusual, and he eventually saw her strapped into the jump seat just behind him, the belts pulling against her roadhouse-diner outfit, and on her face a beatific, if non-committal, smile.

Again the jarring noise, and this time he felt his guts thunder and then lurch forward in a take-off of their own. Christ! Perhaps those sips of stock in the restaurant store-room hadn't been such a good idea after all. He clenched his stomach. Something you ate, sir? The pain was intense. Thinking about what had passed his lips nauseated him. It'll all be over shortly, he consoled his gut . . . in a flash.

All he could think about was the joy of clambering into the plastic latrine just behind him, sitting inside that well-lit and unventilated box, as a flood of relief engulfed the bowl. The tingle in his bowels – he was certain of this – had been replaced by what felt like a trickle. Had it morph-ed into a trickle? He clenched his thighs.

The wait continued. *For what?* Jesus Christ. A gap in air traffic? Time for the serial-killer pilot to take a quick gamble on that shuddering left engine? His fingers tugged at his watch. *I. Need. To. Evacuate.*

The plane thundered down the runway and as it surged into the air Grant threw open the metal buckle in his lap, pushed his way past the pensioner sitting between him and the aisle, and, ignoring the crew's shouts he staggered in the direction of that heavenly, that beautifully cramped, toilet. After falling down the aisle he struggled with the concertina door (the latch not quite locking at the 45-degree incline) and with each attempt to shut it the fluorescent light above his head flickered on and then off again, just like the drama of resistance and release in his bowels.

A familiar face stared back from the mirror as he felt his blood pressure plummet with relief. Valhalla! He adored Henry! He felt the endorphin high. How he adored Henry! Why are we drawn to the creators? What is it about their endless hard work that makes us so satisfied? The bliss!

'Your deliverable,' Patrice had said in her study earlier that day, 'is an exchange programme. The eastern bloc knew how to build prisons and FK&F has identified an opportunity.' Punishment dressed up as responsibility, he suspected, but she would reward his loyalty. This flight, however, was her way of chastising him for the sex. 'Have you ever been to the Baltic states?' He'd listened while she explained her plans for converting foreign molesters and murderers into meat.

He washed his hands, wiping the basin with a fistful of tissues, before stepping into the plane's artificial happiness. As a rule he avoided aeroplane lavatories for anything other than a quick urination or an even quicker hand wash. Their clammy metal levers and soggy paper with the distressing undertone of something ripe . . . all best avoided. But at this stage of the journey his experience had been perfection. He was the room's first, and possibly its last, occupant for this particular flight.

His pensioner-disaster-expert neighbour stared at him as he squeezed into his seat. He held her gaze, ready for confrontation ('What!') or gracious banter ('Why yes, I am the writer.') but she returned to her book without a word.

Grant bumped awake when the steward nudged his elbow with a supper tray. Around him people unwrapped meals as sunlight flooded the cabin. Excited passengers in the rows ahead were peering over their seats to see what was being served. The dismal food, standard airline fare, was as bad as expected. (*Monstrance* was followed by *monstrosity* in his dictionary.) Each mouthful was death.

CHAPTER 18

Positive

DOLORES FIRST watched him watching her: Henry's body appeared to have been folded double into the bed. In this half-light he looked far older, far sicker, than the man she had been celebrating with the previous evening. Patrice had woken them with a call that morning.

'It makes me sick,' he said.

She held him close to her; he was wet with perspiration. He would be thinking about his father. 'Did you have a dream last night?' There was only one dream, it was always *the* dream, but she used the indefinite article to spare him. What had Henry's father done to him? They never spoke about him but he was always there, hanging around, getting in their way and colouring Henry's thoughts. 'Felix thinks we should expand Firsts,' she said. 'You're hot property now. I think we must sell up, clear our debts and leave the city.' It wasn't much of a life if it meant living as they did. 'Come on, let's clean you up.'

She led him to the bathroom where she took off his wet shirt. Henry pulled away from her and threw up into the loo. She wiped his mouth and neck. He closed the toilet lid and sat on it.

'I can't take this headache for much longer,' he said. Their bathroom smelled acid: wine, champagne, vodka.

'I'm not surprised.'

He opened the medicine cupboard and swallowed four of his headache tablets along with an equal number of her homeopathic capsules and then washed his face.

Dolores took his shirt to the pile of dirty laundry in the kitchen and brought him a fresh one from the bedroom. She would have to change their linen: he'd saturated their bed with sweat.

'I'm still drunk,' he said, 'and we should be sleeping.'

'Let's get you into a warm bath,' she said, and ran the water for him. Once the tub was full she took his hand and helped him into the hot water.

Dolores went to the bedroom where she removed the bedsheets and pillowcases, returned to the kitchen where she folded them with his shirt, pressed the bundle into the washing machine along with two detergent cubes, and set it working. She could see that he had just been in the kitchen – his wet footprints were on the floor – yet nothing appeared out of place.

She poured orange juice and, back in the bathroom, she sat on the edge of the tub, watching him feel ill.

She gave him time to choose his words, to think about what he wanted to say. He spoke as though he'd been damned.

'I believe we all go to a good place,' she said when he had finished, feeling the water with her hand.

'Do you ever think of Chin?' he asked softly. 'The accident?'

This conversation was too big for her – she wasn't fit to handle it, not now. She remained quiet, hoping to end the discussion. Yet he spoke about Chin's injury. She listened to his sentences, afraid to interrupt him but wanting him to stop, remembering everything.

'It doesn't seem real, does it?' he said.

After the accident their Chinese staff had resigned because they said Henry was jinxed. *Dao mei*, she could hear their words now: bad luck.

'It was just an accident,' she said. 'Is that what you were dreaming about?'

'Is there anything you want to ask me?' he said. 'You've seen it work.' She didn't answer: they all had. 'The price of fame or success isn't just the cost of losing.' Now came memories of when he'd taken Chin to the Emergency Room, and how he'd waited for her at the hospital.

'Felix lit up like a Christmas tree when I fed him the stuff,' he said. 'I spent my time waiting to hear if the judges had got food poisoning. Back then we were struggling . . .'

Dao mei.

'Your cooking got us into the next round,' she said.

'And I became the genius chef.'

'You *are* the genius chef,' she said firmly. 'You always have been –'

'Dolores, it doesn't matter,' he said. Now she found herself keen to continue the conversation. His eyes were red. 'I'm just some guy who found a Holy Grail,' he said, 'but it's all over.' She helped him out of the bath and dried him. 'If it's any consolation, I'm not drunk any more.'

'We need to talk about what we do next,' she said. Perhaps Felix was right: they needed to expand. She took the wet towel and handed him a fresh one from the cupboard. 'Dry yourself and then let's go back to bed.'

She left him in the bathroom and went to the kitchen where she stood, waiting, and after some time she returned to collect his glass, still half-filled with juice. He was pulling on a clean T-shirt. She sniffed the glass. Now she understood what he'd been doing in the kitchen when she was changing the bedroom linen. She poured the alcohol down the toilet and left it without flushing so that he could see that she knew.

*

Dolores had to place the large empty suitcase on the wet pavement outside their apartment because her phone was ringing. It was the hospital. Felix's insurance company had just contacted them to report signs of remarkable improvement in his recent tests. Congratulations! They would naturally be downgrading his level of care in light of these fantastic results. Congratulations! And yes, they had agreed that Mr Stoll could check himself out. Thank you!

She ducked under an awning, kicking the suitcase to one side as her back pressed against the shop window. 'What do you mean by "downgrading" my brother?' she said. 'He's not to leave the hospital.'

She heard muffled voices – the sound of a phone slung over a shoulder? – and then the man said, 'This was simply a courtesy call, ma'am.' As Dolores repeated her question an ache spread across her brow. 'You need to take that up with Mr Stoll's corporate insurance, ma'am.' Drop the attitude, missy, was the subtext.

'Please don't release my brother.'

'Ms First, I have no control over that' – the man's sentence was sing-songy from frequent repetition. 'And besides, he's already checked himself out. We're a care facility.'

He ended the call, and Dolores tried to decide who she should, or who she could, call. Henry's phone was off. God knows where Felix was heading. She tried Felix's number but it rang with no answer. This was Felix wanting to be young and single all over again. He might be waiting for her at the apartment. Yes! She snatched up the case and ran through the rain. He was single and free but with Death looming over one shoulder. She'd do the same in his position. A pedestrian bumped the case, throwing her off balance, and as Dolores stepped away her shoulder grazed the wet brick wall. She stopped, ready to throw the suitcase away, but her clothes were getting wet.

She dialled Felix's number again, and he answered. 'Felix,' she said firmly, 'I need you to listen. You have to meet me at the hospital. I need your help with this, Felix.' She was against the wall, her eyes prickling in the heat.

'Surprise!' he said. 'I'm on my way over to your place to celebrate Easter with you, Dolores.' The line went dead. When she called him again there was no answer.

Felix phoned after Dolores had finished her bath and was putting wet towels into the tumble drier. He was lost and this time he refused to hang up, insisting that she give him street-by-street directions to the apartment. It sounded like he was grappling with a large map.

'Are you *driving*, Felix? Tell me you're not driving in this weather. You won't be able to see a thing.'

'Directions, Dolores.'

A stilted conversation followed – 'North?' 'Turn north, Felix.' 'North *where*?' – until he located her street and then circled the block, punching the horn, until she assured him that she could hear the racket. There was just enough time for her to tie back her hair before he began working the downstairs buzzer with violent jabs. His large squinting face – distorted by its proximity to the lens – appeared on the security monitor. Dolores touched the Entry button and soon he was banging on the front door, which she managed to pull open before a second volley of knocks.

He walked into the apartment, passing close to her body, and then dropped his luggage, a gammon and a frozen turkey and hugged her, refusing to answer any questions. After peering into the lounge he selected the sofa he was prepared to settle into. She offered him a drink and she went into the noisy kitchen – cursing him – to pour a double rum and orange for him, plain orange juice for herself. When she returned he had opened a window and was peering outside.

'They're bums,' Felix said, taking the drink from her. 'Look at me. Do I look as though I'm about to pop my clogs?' Without waiting for her to respond he waved his hands about for a moment, motioning to the apartment. 'Are you moving?'

'Is everything OK outside?' she asked. In other circumstances it would have been good to see him.

'Look at my beautiful car. We need to talk shop.' He went over to his suitcase, unzipped it, took out a folder that he opened with great care and began laying drawings and papers on the coffee table.

'Where did you get the car from?' she said. It was a low-slung sports model, metallic blue with swirling red flames painted on its bonnet.

'I bought it.'

'You bought it?'

He nodded. Once he was happy with the arrangement of his documents he returned to the sofa by way of a quick lean out the window to admire his car.

'What I was trying to say on the phone,' Dolores said, 'is that you've only just entered remission' – he began talking so she had to raise her voice – 'yes, *no one is an expert*, Felix, but you've just entered remission and you need to be with people who are qualified to take care of you. The fact that *you* don't regard them as experts is another matter.'

'They're a bunch of bums. You said so yourself.'

'I did not say that.'

'Well then, Henry did.'

'It wasn't me.'

'I don't need to stay here tonight,' he said. 'And any case, it's a teaching hospital. A seat of learning. About as unprofessional an outfit as you could hope to be incarcerated in.'

She told him that, despite his protests, he *would* be staying the night. 'I'm taking you back to the hospital tomorrow.'

'We'll see,' he said.

She looked at the papers. 'And these are . . . ?' she peered at the images: Felix's crude drawings.

'They're the plans for our next restaurant. Suggestions. We need to expand pronto, little sister.' He glanced out the window again.

'It might help if we included Henry in this discussion,' she said.

He nodded. Of course. 'Where is the chef?'

'He's meeting Patrice Czarny.' Felix lifted an eyebrow dramatically. 'Shut up, Felix. Give me a hand with your bed.'

There was something different about the smaller bedroom and something different about Felix. The room was almost empty; he appeared rested. Watching him as he fetched linen from the closet she wondered if she had ever really slept alongside this bed years ago when he was delirious with fever, shortly before he was admitted to hospital? She thought then that they would lose him – lose this relatively healthy-looking man . . . He was uneasy in the room: bad memories, no doubt.

She touched his forehead. 'You're flushed. Do you want me to open the window?'

'Perhaps a little,' he said. He placed his wallet on the bedside table, and this reminded her of the hospital.

'Have you eaten?' she asked.

'That's another reason for me leaving the hospital. They wanted me force-fed. All because they resented Henry.'

'Felix, I'm sure the hospital only wanted to get you to eat. I'll make you something later, but it's not going to be that turkey. Are you feeling tired?'

'I'm fine,' he said. 'I'm not going to feel bad because I checked myself out of the hospital. I'm happy to see my baby sister.' He rubbed a hand across his chest and his stomach. 'The stuff about your restaurant: is it true what I hear?'

'Patrice has shut us down, yes.'

'Patrice Czarny is a vampire. The woman doesn't just want to shut you down, and she won't be content with just putting you out of business: she wants to slaughter you. She wants to rip off your skin. She wants to dance on your graves. And don't think that if she wins the competition she'll leave you alone. She's a great white shark in a dolphin suit. I know her type. When she tastes blood she's

205

only just started. Because, you see, she *knows*. She knows that unless she sterilises you both she'll have two distractions that can make things difficult for her in the future. Unless she eliminates you there will always be mutterings about how she never won the competition fairly.'

'We're not expecting to win.'

'It's too late, Dolores. You entered it. You're a challenge, and now she's focusing all her attention on killing you both. She has to: it's in her DNA. What are you going to do about it?'

Her head was starting to hurt again. She worried about Felix. A strong drink might help her relax.

'You'll never beat her at her own game, Dolores. Forget the competition. You've got to expand. It's possible that she might want to buy the Firsts brand, but don't sell it to her. She'll insist that Henry works for her, and that way she'll steal him from you.'

Dolores was finding it difficult concentrating. 'He's making Patrice an offer.'

'You're both crazy,' he said, 'and I can't watch you let this chance slip through your fingers.'

'It's up to Henry.'

'Henry *can't* sell,' he insisted. 'Not the Henry First that I know. Sure, he's wounded, but he knows that he needs to grow. *Now* is your chance to expand aggressively, while you're still in with a chance. Get the Firsts brand out there. In a few weeks' time the hype will die down, no one will even remember who was in the top ten, and you'll have lost your opportunity. Good luck expanding *later*, is all I have to say on the subject.'

It was too late for this. Her eyes felt dry and the bed was floating in a haze of dots.

'We all know this competition is rigged,' he said. 'This is my final bit of advice, but God willing your restaurant is refurbished in time for the next round of the competition, we know what the outcome will be. The only way you can really win this thing is by expanding.'

'You need to focus on getting better,' she said.

'I *am* better.' He fiddled with the spare change in his pocket. After a prolonged, but ultimately abortive, attempt at heaving the mattress up and over, he said, 'I've saved some money you can use. You must advertise.'

'Felix, there's no need –'

'Listen to me. I've got savings. If you need money then use it, my celebrity sister. It's the only thing I can eat.' She wasn't sure what he was talking about. 'Your food, your award-winning food. It's the only thing I can eat. I'm doing this purely out of my own self-interest.'

'No more worrying,' she said, and she kissed her brother's cheek. 'And no more talk about expanding. We can only cope with one existential crisis per family and I've already booked a place on that ride. I need a drink, and then you can talk me through your plans.'

They walked into the kitchen, the washing machine and the drier churning loudly, when the force of the explosion stung her eyes and made her ears pop. *What was that?*

It took a while for Dolores to recover and she thought she could see Felix standing in the middle of the darkened kitchen, a glass in each hand. He appeared to be sniffing the air, like an animal. She reached for the light switch. Off and then on again, but the room remained dark. He said something that she couldn't quite hear because of the noise in her head. What had just happened?

'I'm sorry,' she called out. If she went past him to turn off the machines they would both be in the dark. But the machines are already off, she realised. What was that noise?

'Did the bulb just fuse?'

'Didn't you just see it?' he shouted. 'Lightning. It's blown out most of the city. I didn't want to break your beautiful glasses,' he said as she cleared space on the countertop as best as she could. Her phone was ringing. 'God, that gave me a fright. I should put the turkey and the gammon into the fridge.'

'Sure,' she said, 'but if this power failure continues for much longer we'll have to chuck all the food away.' She noticed him sniffing the air again as if trying to find a scent.

The sound of the telephone was driving her crazy.

'That's Henry calling,' she said. 'The oven uses gas and not electricity. I'll come back and heat something up for you. Candles are in the bottom drawer over there.'

Dolores negotiated her way back down the passage and answered her phone. Henry had just left Patrice's – something about him having a piece of her, that he had her in the bag; the static on the line made him difficult to understand – and she promised to return his call.

Back in the kitchen she couldn't find her brother. The empty glasses were on the countertop.

She called Felix's name but there was no response; she walked to the rear of the kitchen, and as she passed the fridge she must have tripped or bumped into him as he crouched in front of the freezer. She felt something – a hand? – grab her leg. She half-turned, half-apologised. 'What are you doing down there?' His hand gripped tighter. 'Felix, you're hurting,' she said and pulled free. There was a noise like an animal feeding. 'Felix?' she said softly. 'Felix, are you OK?'

'Positive.'

The word must have been a good word once, but not now. The figure in the darkness knelt in front of the fridge, the freezer compartment open, sucking and gnawing. He had found the frozen stock. She watched him reach up and open the fridge door, and now Dolores wished that she couldn't see him. He took a bite of something and spat it out. Then he crouched again and began nosing through the frozen bags, ripping them open and licking, clawing, gnawing the icy chunks. An animal feeding in the half-light.

He turned and looked at her, his face a blank shadow.

She felt Felix grasp her leg again and again she pulled free. He rose and his hand half-grabbed, half-cupped, her throat and she ducked under it but found herself trapped by his other hand that held on to her, that pulled her towards him. She shouted and swung out, attempting to push him back, and when she felt his grip loosen she ducked free from his grasp and ran without looking behind her. She pushed open the bedroom door, closed it, locked it.

The bedroom was dark. For a moment she thought someone was lying in the bed and she almost reopened the door in fright. Her breathing was loud and sharp.

'Henry?' she said. Outside the room Felix was talking to himself in the passage. There was blood on her hand.

'Dolores' – Felix outside the door – 'are you there?'

'Please give me a moment,' she said. 'I've cut my hand.' And then to the figure in the bed, 'Henry, is that you?' No response: the bed was empty.

Her brother remained outside the room, calling her name. Please would she tell him why she was so upset? What had happened that made her so upset?

CHAPTER 19

Eden

THE ROOF GARDEN was primed for seduction. It felt larger than it could possibly have been, taking up more space than this standard apartment building's footprint in this standard city block in this, the most standards-aware city zone . . .

A sublime field of salvias covered its surface – a bruised river pooling around islands of blond savannah grass – and it appeared to extend out to, if not far beyond, the building's perimeter. In a distant part of the garden, a good day's walk north from where Henry First stood watching Patrice, were anxious large-headed purple flowers suspended in mid-air; in front were thick wagging red fingers belonging to plants fidgeting in the breeze like chastised children. Along the building's edge was a line of eager-to-please cherry trees, stooped with blossoms and shimmering white. Shades of fading memories of almost-forgotten summers. Beyond the garden were geometric buildings and beyond those hung the sun, trapped in the sky.

Patrice had positioned herself beside an overwhelmingly successful, if desperately overachieving, red valerian. Its outstretched limbs reaching in front of and behind her.

The scene may have been exactly as she had hoped and planned, and, if Henry hadn't been near haemorrhaging violent sneezes into a handkerchief, it might well have been perfection.

'Do you have any idea what set you off?' she'd had to repeat her question.

'Back there' – he jerked his thumb towards her apartment – 'it's *too* flor–.' He'd begun sneezing the moment he arrived. She greeted him at her private elevator ready to guide him into the living room for champagne and a chat.

'Too floral?'

His nod was cut short by another sneeze. 'Synthetic. Cheap.'

Despite this unfortunate start she'd managed to lead him to her 'outside room' – a wooden balcony running around the entire floor – and then up to the roof.

Now he was coughing.

'There's something I'd like to show you,' she said as she rubbed his arm somewhat ineffectually. She took his right hand, giving him time to transfer the drenched handkerchief to the other, and walked him to the very lip of the building's western side, stopping between two trees, until there was nothing but air between them and the setting sun. They were less than a foot away from the drop. He held her tight.

'Isn't it beautiful and relaxing?' she said. 'Come closer.' The breeze cooled the sun's glare from the city's many windows. She moved closer to this furnace, pulling him with her. 'It's so calming up here. Let me know if you feel a bit faint after all that sneezing – I wouldn't want you taking me over with you.' She smiled an open smile – one of her best, he was certain. 'It's perfectly safe, Henry.'

He'd stopped sneezing and there were no more coughs.

'Your friend was just here,' she said, gazing at the city. 'Mr Whant. He's recently had a lot to say about all this, hasn't he?'

'I don't know him that well.'

'Of course not. There's no reason for you to know him well, is there? But we're all friends and the competition has brought us even closer. I've been thinking about his place in the organisation – his place in all of this – because for a while I've suspected that he might have a hare-brained scheme to open his own business. The only problem is that he needs capital. Trust me, I know what he's paid. But, thankfully, he won't have to worry about this any more because I've placed him slap bang in the centre of things.

'You don't have much of a head for heights, do you? My balcony extends beyond the edge of the building. If we jumped we'd land on it.'

'In another life, Patrice.'

'Let's just *be*, Henry. Let's just be in the moment.'

By now his heart was making valiant attempts to attract his attention. *Repentance, repentance, repentance*, was its message in the flood behind his ears.

Her grip was firm but nothing like the one he wanted to give the tree on his left – if he allowed himself to grab that tree she would have to drag him away from it, crying hysterically – anything to get away from the brink of her madness. The reflected light made it too bright for him to see the drop clearly, but he could sense that it was just in front of him. The void was just there . . .

'What am I looking at, Patrice?'

Shadow began extinguishing the suns. She waited.

He had been rehearsing what he would say to her all morning and he wished that he'd been able to blurt it out the moment he arrived. 'Patrice, I have a proposition for you,' was how it began, but he felt uneasy up here and his words sought the safety of confined spaces.

She pointed into the canyon between this building and the one opposite. At street level, running the entire length of the opposite block, was a glass-fronted restaurant. A large sign lit the windows: HENRY I.

'You can't be serious, Patrice.'

'Don't say anything, Henry. Just take it all in.'

Immediately. Suddenly. Spontaneously. Adverbs that never happened to anyone he knew, yet here they were. In a flash. He knew that he had to sell, but he felt an urge to retain this part of his life that he . . . loved? And now this offer of a new restaurant?

He could never join her. He would fight her. He would *never* join her. Even if she tried to squash him, aided by Furness Kindle & Flint bullies, he could triumph. He'd welcome back the stresses that had ruled his life. He was ready to hand back control to the thing that, until now, he thought he hated the most. He wanted Firsts to take charge again; he wanted Firsts to be his; he wanted his life to be ruled by Firsts again. And yet . . .

Had Grant known about this new restaurant that Patrice would offer him? Grant must be in on Patrice's game. He was beginning to question Grant's motives. Hell, he questioned his own motives: why did he care so much about Firsts? This last-minute infatuation with the place, his sudden remorse of conscience, had certainly crept up on him. All the hatred, the venom, the stress . . . and now he felt ill because he was about to sell.

Another sneeze. How could he even consider taking back that horror? It ranked among the worst ideas he'd ever had, possibly the very worst. Why was he fighting himself and not her? He knew he couldn't take Firsts back, not if there was an opportunity to sell it. Selling restaurants never happened in the real world. *Never* happened. After all, what was there to sell? A name? Possibly, but that was only true for top city establishments and he wasn't in their league. He'd seen it before – chefs growing old while desperately trying to get someone interested in buying them out of their misery. Grant was right: he'd be forgotten by the time the competition was over. He had to sell. The trick was in presenting Firsts – which no one else had offered to buy – as the deal of the century to Patrice.

And yet . . . And yet, he would tell her to forget it, lay off her theatrics in this ridiculous garden and take him back to terra firma so that he could return to Firsts. He'd have it open in a week: relaunched, repackaged and ready to wow. It had almost been fun. He'd turn down her offer of this new place – the look on her face would be worth it – and he'd announce that he was ready to take her on, ready to battle the mighty FK&F and its competitors. There was space for them all, he'd tell her. His public would support him, he'd tell her. After all, he was becoming a household name – *that* went unsaid. He remembered the joy he'd experienced when they opened Firsts. Was he crying? Surely not: it was the wind. After all those years of working for others he eventually had his own place. It had been, and still was, horrifically thrilling.

It was too late for his sales pitch, with her, anyway. Patrice had snookered him with a few tins of paint and stepladders and Firsts was out of bounds. You're offering me *what*? she'd say. You want me to *buy* that dump? Look at the place *I'm* offering you, buddy!

If only he hadn't drawn attention to himself in the competition. He should have allowed Firsts to exit gracefully so that he could make a solid living by quietly adding a splash of *rene* to a few of his signature dishes. He might have been able to open more restaurants – nothing too flashy or threatening – and he would have enjoyed a moderately prosperous life. Why had he allowed the stock to draw attention to itself? He was about to push his chips into the centre of the table. He could control this thing, surely? As someone who'd spent his life avoiding the slightest gamble he now found himself with little choice but to bet the farm.

The garden moved in time with his thoughts: swaying back and forth, vacillating, changing direction, and beyond it lay the void.

'We need to talk,' he said after gulping down a glass of water once they were safely back in the living room and, without waiting for her to respond, he made his pitch. Word perfect. Named his price. As rehearsed. She listened without interruption. And when he had finished he waited.

'Henry, I don't bargain. It's never so much a question of what someone's offering me, but what I'm willing to take.'

'Do you have a cigarette?' he said. He needed to slow the conversation.

'Doesn't nicotine destroy your taste buds?' she said fetching a pack and a box of matches from the cupboard in the passage. He lit, inhaled. She picked a cigarette for herself. 'If I was crazy enough to consider your proposal, you don't have that much to offer me, do you? The refurbishment work is unlikely to finish any time soon.'

'I don't need access to Firsts to sell it,' he countered.

'No?'

'Carry on with your plan.'

'I don't have a plan, Henry.'

'Of course not, Patrice,' he said, faux naïve, 'stick to your plan, nevertheless. I've invited all sorts of interesting guests to my final entry. The only thing our artist friends love more than underdogs are underdogs fighting corporations.'

He let her think about this.

'You really should attend my last submission,' he continued. 'I'm *very* topical at the moment. And don't worry about the restaurant remaining shut; you should be delighted to attend the next round of the competition. So delighted that you invite all of the FK&F brass along to see just how magnanimous you are with your rivals. And, of course, when you eventually win the competition everyone will know that you won fairly. Is it really your fault that the builders are dilly-dallying when they're meant to be refurbishing Firsts? Buy it from me, Patrice,' he said softly, pleading. 'I'll have nothing but praise for your success. I'm happy to sell my name to someone as deserving as Patrice Czarny. This one's going to be my last.'

'Restaurant or cigarette?'

'Both. I need enough money to leave the city and I don't plan on returning. Dolores and I want to start a family.'

The air was pink, and down on the street, centuries away, were the sounds of traffic and everyday life.

'The number of healthy marriages I've seen break up because of stress simply astounds me,' she said. 'Incidentally, how are things between you two? I hope your plan to sell works out. Only it won't be to me. I promise not to tell: I don't do conversations with my people.' She went back to the balcony.

Tan nimbus clouds grew on the horizon – meringues in the oven with seconds to spare – and extended up towards the sky. The neighbourhood buildings resembled matt appliances – kitchen gadgets for an emerging super-race. She stood between him and what looked like an oversized whisk; on her right were phalanxes of knives while on her left was an extraordinarily cumbersome egg timer.

'Take me up on my offer, Henry.' She held his gaze. 'Join me.' He was aware that his opportunity was slipping away. And yet . . . He could offer her immortality.

'I need to launch a new division and I want you to be my key chef,' she said. 'Otherwise you've lost, haven't you?' He didn't respond. He had sufficient cigarettes to keep him occupied for a few hours. Evidently tiring at the prospect of waiting for him to accept her offer she came back inside.

'Patrice, I'm offering you a sublime taste that will live beyond this competition,' he said. This was good stuff. 'Nectar of the gods. Something that will be spoken about, written about, dreamt of and sung about well beyond your four-score years and ten.' This was not part of Grant's script. Grant had told him to wait it out. He'd made Henry promise to give Patrice time to talk her way back to him, but Henry could see that she was losing interest.

'How very biblical,' she said. 'Mine is more prosaic: I'll make your name in this city. You've seen the prime location I'm giving you. I'm even prepared to let you win the competition.'

He took her hand, her soft skin against his, and placed the back of it against his cheek. 'You were there on Friday night, Patrice.' His voice was quiet. 'You've tasted what I can do.' In another diversion from Grant's chaste script: the tip of his tongue touched her skin, his warm breath on her flesh, and he let it circle a small point on the back of her hand. 'Remember the taste?' Despite herself, he could see her allowing the memory to return. 'I'm selling.'

'You flatter yourself,' she said, withdrawing her hand. 'A bunch of socialites getting their rocks off, going out of their minds, during a *meal*? Is that it? You've got to be kidding. They're on the lookout for their next fix. Even you aren't egotistical enough to believe that they remembered you afterwards. Join my corporation and you'll never have to worry again. I'll make the announcement at the final round of the competition.'

Yet . . . She *had* to buy Firsts, he knew. Someone had to. It was the only way. Would he ever work again? Was the amount he'd agreed with Grant sufficient? He'd lived long enough to realise that once money was spent it was spent. In a few years he'd be incapable of taking a young man's chances. He felt uncertainty drain his resolve. It was as if his skin had been sensitised by the wind and made vulnerable from exposure to the sun. He felt the steady pull of unemployment. Was this it? Is this how it ends? Was this *really* it?

'You remember my meal, don't you?' He took a fresh cigarette. 'I'm in the mood to overindulge. What I'm offering requires a bit more imagination, Patrice. Let me tell you what I've learnt. Even a blue-collar chef like me knows this about life: everything is bull. The corporations will be around for a while longer, I'm sure. They'll merge and de-merge or whatever you call it, but this will pass. If I joined it would only be for as long as I was a novelty. But when I run dry . . . that's when you'd cut me loose. On the other hand I'm offering you a shot at immortality.

'Listen. You get the big names in literature and poetry and music and painting and sculpture to attend my final entry in the competition, my very last performance in this particular medium, and we'll tell them that they've experienced *you*. We'll announce that they're tasting *you*. You'll be their first, Patrice. They'll immortalise you.'

'You're insane.'

'It won't shock them to find out that they're eating you,' he said. 'The public is unshockable. You're formulating plans to cut into this market. This way *you* get to be the first. You'll beat FK&F. No one will ever take that away from you.'

'You really are insane.'

'I'll sell my restaurant,' he continued, 'and my name, to the highest bidder.'

'You're paying too much attention to Whant's delusions, Henry. The man's infatuated with you. When I mention your name he's like a bloody geisha. You need to think about your future.'

'But that's precisely what I'm doing. *You* need to think about *your* future, Patrice. How safe are you, really? Even with the help of the *rene* you still need a good chef to make it into something extraordinary when it's launched. I'm your man. This way we get to do both: you launch your new division to guaranteed success and you go down in history as the first . . . "contributor", shall we say, to the meat, while I get bought out. Your competitors are none the wiser. I don't want to spend the rest of my life in a kitchen.

'You know the corporate game, Patrice: they'll dump you, eventually. We know how corporate stories end. You've had to drive the knife in deep just to succeed in their environment and now I'm offering you an opportunity to transcend the people you need to please. When I've finished the competition *everyone* will want to taste you

– hell, everyone will be clamouring to buy Firsts, but it will be yours for the taking. With my help we'll blast the name Patrice Czarny stratospheric. They won't be able to touch it.

'I know about your plans to productionise the meat. Grant called on his way to the airport. I'm giving you the chance to launch that division with a little personal sacrifice of your own. When people hear what I've done, what *you've* done, what *you've* given, then they'll want a piece of the pie. FK&F will salivate when they see how much money you've made them. You'll be their hottest *überfrau*, your own notoriety and immortality in the bag.'

There was the question of the final meal that he needed to prepare. He'd stopped at an industrial estate on his way to the city and spent most of the afternoon in Johnny B's Restaurant City (FK&F Catering), searching through the warehouse's furniture, cutlery and crockery before placing an order with lengthy delivery instructions. He'd charged it all to Patrice Czarny.

'You're walking away?' she said.

'I get my life back. I get enough money to be independent.'

'And if this backfires?'

'You control the media. Invite enough of your journalists to my final entry and they'll ensure it's a success. Their presence guarantees it. Your public is ready for the next big thing: *you*.'

'If I allow Firsts to open again –'

'Keep it closed. I need to marginalise you. Correction: I need to be seen to be marginalising you.' He took her hand. 'If FK&F isn't interested then I'll approach another large corporate fish in this pond and you'll be screwed. My original suggestion is so much nicer for both of us, don't you think? Win-win.'

He led her to the kitchen, the gardenia's scent still permeating the apartment, and she sat on a blue Shaker-style chair while he searched for some cloths. The clean ones were in the top drawer beside the stove.

He reached into his bag and withdrew his knife; the blade reflecting a flash when the clouds revealed a perfect bolt of lightning. It was followed by a bottle of spirits.

'Interesting luggage,' she said.

'One sip.' He held the liquor out to her. 'What's the joke?'

'I was wondering if there was any more of the sales pitch, Henry Jekyll. I was thinking of something along the lines of this, for instance . . .' She reached for his shirt collar and pulled him towards her so that he could smell her skin. She kissed him on the lips; now he could taste her. 'Or perhaps . . .' She stood up, her cheek against his. Her mouth was soft on his ear. 'Join forces with me, Henry. I'm open to suggestions.'

'You know what I need from you, Patrice.'

'My kidney?' Her laugh was soft.

'Why would I want your kidney?'

'I thought it had to be the kidney,' she said. She was kissing him on his mouth again, her hands cradling his neck while her fingers played with his soft blond hair. She stopped. 'Well?'

'Who knows? Anything seems to work provided I call it *rene*.'

'Cute.' She began unbuttoning his shirt. 'You can have my finest cuts, Chef.' She kissed his right nipple, leaving lipstick smudges on his skin, and then she took the bottle, unscrewed the cap, and swallowed. 'What do I do with a cold fish like you, Henry First? How does a girl like me get a boy like you to join her club?'

Back to the knife. 'I think we should get on with it,' he said.

She stepped away. 'In here?'

He looked around the kitchen. 'We'd mess up your bedroom.'

Her laugh was real this time. 'You naughty boy. And such a big strong knife. Remind me why you're doing this.'

'It's us against them, Patrice. That much you know.'

She drank some more and then held up the bottle like a connoisseur. 'Here's to eternity,' she said. 'My offer won't last for ever.'

'Suitable vintage?' he asked. She swallowed again. 'Sit down. I don't want you passing out on me. Take it easy while we break new ground.'

'You're pretty sure about me, aren't you?' She was on the chair, kicking off her shoes, allowing him to caress her calves, lifting her right leg to reveal terrifically smooth skin. 'Join forces with me.'

Patrice leant back and Henry stroked the delicate arch of her foot. He held it. She closed her eyes. 'I could sense that you were a good chef,' she said, 'when we first met. I bet you never even noticed me at the launch party.' He massaged her toes. 'What part of me are you focusing on now, I wonder.' The laugh again. 'Other than, say, my toes? Yes, let's pretend it's my toes. A small one?'

'Not much flesh there,' he said. 'But it'll do. Are you sure about this?'

'And if I wasn't?'

'I met Grant Whant at that same party.'

'Don't talk to me about Whant. All he ever says is, "Don't tell Henry I told you. He doesn't want you to know." Sound familiar?'

'Relax, Patrice. Are you sure you're sure about this?'

She closed her eyes. 'I *knew* you were a good chef. You're going to take me up on my offer, aren't you? Are you sure we wouldn't be more comfortable in my room?'

He brought down the knife, cutting off her toe.

Lightning and thunder cut short her yelp and with it the city lights.

'I can't believe you did that,' she said. The sight of her foot in the early-evening shadow transfixed them both. 'Oh Jesus, *blood*!' Despite Henry's protests she skipped over to the fridge like an injured frog. 'Fuck! Fuck, fuck, fuck, *fuck*. Christ, Henry. You and your preposterous stories about what you can do for me. Why the hell did you do *that* to me?'

'I thought we had an understanding,' he said, surprised. 'Immortality. You were up for it. Does this building have a generator?'

'You piece of shit,' she said. 'I thought you were joking. I was talking about the restaurant I'm offering you.' She dug for ice. 'I can't believe you cut off my toe, Henry. *Henry!* We need to get some light. *Jesus.* Everyone's a surgeon.'

'Patrice, I thought –'

'I heard you the first time. An understanding? *You* thought we had an understanding? I was coming on to you, Henry. Jesus Christ, talk about miscommunication. Why can't you think with your cock like a normal man? *Fuck*, it hurts. Don't just stand there, help me find some ice in this bloody' – she slammed the door shut, ripping its rubber seal and it swung open again; she gave it another wallop and this time it bounced back and smacked her on the arm – '*refrigerator!*'

She was in shock – he'd seen it before – standing there rubbing her arm.

'I've made you immortal,' he said.

'Get me an ambulance.'

'You've made yourself immortal, Patrice.'

'Get me an ambulance. I was flirting with you.'

'But I thought you were a lesbian. You said –'

'You thought I was a lesbian? You thought I was a *lesbian? Why?* Oh, don't bother. Get more ice. Damn, this stings. I need an ambulance. Get me an ambulance.'

He found ice, put it in a cloth, and pressed it hard against the red stub on her foot. 'You were flirting with me?'

She wasn't talking to him any longer. 'Get me an ambulance.' He had outstayed his welcome.

There was too much blood. 'Patrice, look outside – there's no way an ambulance will get here in this storm. Where are your staff?'

'I'm Patrice Czarny, Henry. What the hell did you do that for? I am not the *amuse bouche*. I'm *Patrice Czarny*.'

'I thought you understood. About the competition.' He began shouting for her staff. No response.

'I sent them away for the night,' she said. 'You're a psycho. Dolores is welcome to you. You're a psycho. I was planning on outsourcing this part of the deal, Henry. That's what I've got Whant doing. I'm Patrice Czarny – I'm not buyable-edible-disposable. *I'm Patrice Czarny!*'

'Here' – he handed her the bottle – 'finish it.'

They both saw the toe on the tiles. He reached for it, picked it up and half-handed it to her but she pulled away. Yes, perhaps he should put this piece of Patrice Czarny into his bag.

'Get out.'

CHAPTER 20

Harvesting

IN THE FIVE DAYS that passed, the muscles in Patrice Czarny's neck seized up. Her sudden jerk . . . after Henry's sudden hack . . . had frozen her neck, and now she was having to move the phone to her right ear, and back to her left, and back again, to make herself comfortable. There had been no recent bowel movement either – Henry's meal had seen to that. She sat on the edge of her bed, scowling at the carpet, and transferred the handset back to her left ear.

She was on hold. Lucilla had phoned the Friday-morning edition of FK&F News Live to break the story about Janique's son, and now Patrice, along with every other nut in the city, was attempting to contact Janique. 'Patrice Czarny,' she repeated. 'This is Patrice Czarny.' (She had to wait.)

She needed to control Henry – scarce resources meant difficult decisions, and the scarcer the resources, the more difficult the decision – and if he went ahead with his final entry the following evening, in the presence of her competitors, she would have lost control. If she went against him it might even undermine her in her own corporation's eyes.

Plus she had to protect her resources – the meat – to keep FK&F's profit margins high. If she could quarantine the magic ingredient, keep it away from her competitors, then she would have moved from competitive capitalism to a world of maximised profit – a kind of cannibalistic capitalism – for so long as this advantage was retained. If

Henry refused to join FK&F there was a chance that he would be bought out by a competitor . . . too painful for her to contemplate. She would have to string him along, if only for tomorrow night.

A notepad on her desk:

- *Clear the purchase – Firsts. Part of FK&F's strategic transition into new marketplace.*
- ~~*Invite Board.*~~
- *Unveil purchase to Board at Henry's final entry.*
- *Alert up-and-coming young artists along with bankable names. <u>Expected</u> <u>to</u> <u>attend</u> <u>meal.</u>*
- *Unveil details of the prisoner exchange programme – cross live to Whant at the Eastern European relaxation pools.*

Her Plan B was the new restaurant, no longer branded HENRY I, which was on standby if, for whatever reason, he failed to pull it off. She would use the opportunity to show just how supportive she had been prior to shipping the Board and the talent away from Firsts.

After a good half hour of transferring the phone back and forth she managed to reach Lucilla. 'Let me say how truly sorry I am for Janique, honey, and how I'm pledging to do everything in my power to preserve the memory of little Ingmar.'

'Janique would want me to tell you how much she appreciates your call, Patrice.' The television on the far wall looped footage of Janique embracing Ingmar. 'It was very peaceful,' Lucilla continued. 'We shot Ingmar's last moments in the operating theatre. Something for us all to treasure.'

'You did *not*,' Patrice said, congratulating Lucilla.

Long pause. 'We recreated it yesterday.'

'Tell me' – Patrice shut her eyes, the nurturing sound of her voice comforting even herself – 'as you're close to Janique, do you know if she had any plans for the passing ceremony?' Lucilla didn't. 'I've thought of a way to make it more artistic.' Patrice knew all about the lure of Art and it surprised her just how useful something so obviously useless could be. FK&F had its own corporate style – foreign artefacts – and she had used these objects to project an image to others. Here was a different opportunity. 'But I'm getting ahead of myself. Is Janique there?'

'She's interviewing body doubles for Ingmar.'

'That woman is a true professional,' Patrice said.

'We all grieve in our own way.'

'Amen.'

She sat on the end of the bed and looked at her feet; she pulled the smallest toe on her left foot away from the others, holding it at an angle . . . Was it too early to get him to cut off this one as well? Beauty makes sufferers of us all. Toes were disposable, almost irrelevant. The loss of a second small one would be an inconvenience, nothing that a good surgeon couldn't fix. If she lopped this one off it would realign her. The bad news was that she had to wear orthopaedic shoes until she healed; the good news was that once the swelling went down she'd be wearing slimmer, daintier, more fabulous shoes.

'If you get Janique's agreement this morning that Ingmar's organs can be harvested to improve the lives of others then no, there's nothing more that society expects of you. She retains the rights to the story, naturally.' Patrice Czarny recognised contributions to humanity.

CHAPTER 21

Father

I T WAS A NORMAL DAY. In every way it was a normal day. Thunder of water in the bathroom. Dolores First had woken to the sound of radio, closed her eyes, and listened to the city news before getting up. She had news of her own.

There was a whoop of flame and she set the kettle on the gas stove. She sat, waiting for the whistle and the steam. After her coffee she went back into the bathroom, testing the water with her hand, and then she heard her own breath as she climbed into the bath.

Henry came running down the corridor, stepping first into the hot empty kitchen before finding her in the bath. He explained later that he dreamt she'd fallen unconscious in the water, her skin soft and dead, and beside her foot was a . . .

It was a normal day. In every way it was a normal day.

She dried herself and returned him to bed where she lay beside him. He explained that he'd been convinced that she'd hacked off a toe. After that early-morning muddle he was on his best behaviour.

She watched him shower. Would there ever be a right time to tell him?

'Do we need to talk?' he said. 'Dolores?'

She waited. Before he said another word she could guess at what he was about to say. Dolores, he'd begin, I'm sorry. Dolores, I'm truly *truly* sorry. Or perhaps he'd say, Dolores, about tonight. Dolores, I've been thinking and I realise that I'm *not* my father, that I'm not cursed. Dolores, everything I touch needn't turn to crap or gold. Dolores, about your brother . . . Dolores, can you remember when we first . . . Dolores, why so worried? Dolores, I've been thinking about us. Dolores, have you *tasted* it? Have you seen what it does to them? What does it taste like to you?

It was a normal day. In every way it was a normal day.

She waited.

He stepped out of the shower; she saw him glance down for a moment, perhaps checking to see whether she'd gnawed off a toe. Where there's a will . . . Where there's a dying brother . . .

'Henry, we can still back out,' she said.

He dried himself. 'I'll see you at the restaurant tonight.'

'Prepare something extraordinary,' she said. It was time for her to go to Golden Square – she had things to do.

'Do we need to talk?' he said.

'Leave it to me. I'm ready.' She had things to do.

'Dolores . . .' he began.

She waited. Dolores, I'm sorry. She waited. What does it taste like to you?

'I should leave,' she said; she could smell the alcohol on his breath but she had things to do.

CHAPTER 22

The Last Supper

FOR HENRY FIRST success, almost certainly, meant he would be remembered when he was dead. It was a human disease: this desire for something – *anything* – to remain behind. To linger on Earth when everyone else had faded.

Almost everyone gets forgotten when they're gone, he told himself. And because of this he knew that his offer to Patrice was too good for her to pass up.

He worked in a different kitchen now: his apartment's excuse for a kitchen, which was nothing like the restaurant workshop, his studio, in which he'd grown accustomed to spending his days. It was quiet and bare in here.

Henry had been watching the stock reduce over a low heat since midday – his was a profession where reduction made stronger. Patrice's deliveries had arrived late that morning – she hadn't skimped when it came to the raw material, rarer than U-235 – and the bathroom reeked like an abattoir. Surprisingly, the pot on the stove had been most accommodating and less than a quarter of the organs, and fewer memories, remained. Everything else had already joined the illegal kidney and Patrice's own modest digit.

A quick peek into the pot revealed an oil slick on the liquid's surface reflecting his face. He worked like an apprentice who had been set a task: no tastes allowed of this final meal; wait for the boss to decide.

There was nothing for him to do but wait, ignoring the smell, until the syrup clinging to the inside of the pot made space for more. Reduce and make stronger: as prescribed by the world's great religions. Take away, and it will be provided to you.

His father would have balked at these odds – sure, the old man would have played anyway, but not before a healthy round of self-medication. Life starts tonight, Henry told himself. My worst meal is the one I get remembered for. That's life. A lesson in there somewhere.

The phone rang: Dolores. Patrice had not transferred any money.

The meal itself was of less concern to Henry than the stock. Last Sunday in the catering superstore he had purchased a gross of frozen meat pies, still encased by their increasingly soggy packaging, all neatly stacked against the refrigerator. He'd promised Patrice a gourmet meal – five courses or more – but the only thing tonight's diners would eat were these pasty pastries filled with meat and lard. It was his final meal for profit, he realised; a final act before freedom. He checked and the viscous liquid was ready for more.

Henry collected the remaining herbs and vegetables from the fridge and dumped them on the countertop. Here were three-inch nails that were greying French beans, Brussels sprouts as hard as metal offcuts, sliced carrot like unpunched rusty washers and the weighty remains of a bean and pea salad mixed with ball-bearing peppercorns. He dropped them whole into the pot and followed with the remaining flesh.

His creation was illegal: something to be posted to the Web and tracked by clandestine organisations. He armed the mixture with a handful of incendiary chillies before finishing with a blast of salt. As he raised the heat it re-leased a strong benzene smell: the distant memory of aviation fuel and jellied gasoline that makes napalm.

Now all that remained was to stir the thickening solu-tion. His actions were a compromise to his profession.

They were the work of an ingenious novice preparing a very different dish (timer, flax, heat, explosion).

The liquid began to boil – the lid shifted uneasily as the pressure increased and the elements fused – and he lowered the flame so that the stock could settle and allow its weaker components an escape. Unnecessary water steamed off.

His was a life of physical activity, a life of necessity – we must all eat – with no time for much else. And yet he was selling Patrice this potion. The feelings of dread he had experienced during his first encounter with the kidney had evaporated. Instead of that unseen horror lurking behind him – outside his body – now it lay within him. Moving about inside. He could sense it directing his hand to stir the pot and then pause before deciding which ingredients should join the fun. It lifted the lid to expose the liquid horror and he saw the black: not a good colour for stock, he was sure. He certainly had never seen anything like this colour in a kitchen before – caviar is tinged yellow and olives are dark purple and treacle is brown. Nothing should be as dead as this.

He dipped a spoon into the liquid void and it disappeared, ceasing to exist. His hands burnt through the plastic washing-up gloves, his eyes red with tears. Henry First was dying – he was sure of it – the antimatter in the stock-pot would be his end. The thick crud forming on the bottom of the pot caught the spoon and the mossy scum floating on the surface of the liquid tarnished the metal handle. He tried scraping the cruddy fallout off the inside surface – it reminded him of crystallised sugar, but only if the sugar had been dug out of a sewer or a plague pit – but he gave up hacking when the dark crystals refused to break off. After throwing away the spoon he opened a window to allow the chaos to escape the kitchen, to negate the suburbs.

What he hadn't expected was Patrice's call: 'I'm not happy about this, Henry. I'm not happy at all.'

'I won't mention your contribution to the meal until you give me the go-ahead. Have you arranged my down payment?'

'I've got a bad feeling about it.'

'Patrice, I can't talk. I'm preparing the meal. Tonight will be subversive and anti-corporate and . . . I don't know, *astonishing*. Ground-breaking. *You'll* be ground-breaking. Leave it to the food to do the hard work. Remember: *you're* the next phase of cuisine.'

'And then you leave?'

'That's the plan. I'm going to need you to transfer the money.'

'We can talk about that when I see you. Just tell me: you're not going to stage this in the centre of that God-awful square, are you?'

'That wouldn't buy me much street cred with your artists, would it? I've got a special place where we'll hit them with your contribution.'

'Talk me through the menu again.'

'Forget the menu, Patrice. This meal takes you beyond the competition. Enjoy your last day of obscurity. This time tomorrow you'll be *the* Patrice Czarny, and then we'll both have what we're after. We need to talk money.'

There was a long pause. 'I'll get to it, Henry. Will keep you in the loop.'

'We have a deal, Patrice.'

'Have you added my contribution? My foot isn't heal-ing. I think it's infected.'

'All in.'

'There's one more thing,' she said after he had reassured her that his *meshuga* plan was still on track, that there was no way that her reputation would be tarnished and that he understood that his future – his financial future – was at stake; only then did she ask what he sus-pected she had been wanting to ask all along. 'What do I taste like?'

*

Once the pies were defrosted Henry flipped off their pastry lids, infiltrated the centre of each with the heavy liquid and lay them on trays awaiting transportation.

It reminded him of the first time he had made stock at Firsts, his delight as sublime flavours blossomed in the food, but back then there were no paying customers to appreciate his hard work – one of the many disappointments that had led him to this fleshy mass he slopped into each limpet.

Money or no money, he would finish this himself.

CHAPTER 23

Protein Sludge

A S INSTRUCTED, Grant Whant handed his passport to the apparatchik who exchanged it for a pair of swimming goggles. Grant followed his hosts into the changing room where, once undressed, he bundled his clothes into a linen hamper and walked behind his naked comrades into the wet area.

Prisoner exchange negotiations were to be conducted in a Slavic pool – an honour of almost unheard of proportions. 'Symptomatic of our new openness,' his translator explained less than an hour after the sirened motorcade had rushed Grant here from his hotel. 'We do not normally bring our guests here.'

'Did Patrice request this?' Grant said.

'Exactly: at her request.'

A babushka, who appeared to have been holed up in the Urals, dispensed towels. Grant twisted his around his waist. He caught his escorts smiling at each other ('These Westerners!') as their own towels were draped casually over their shoulders.

The translator had particularly large and painful-looking testicles. Sensing Grant's interest the man stopped and proceeded to hold up his testes for group examination.

'Remains of haemorrhage of the gonads,' he said while the leader of the group, a burly Russian with metal teeth, prodded the translator's scrotum and nodded vigorously.

Feeling loose and vulnerable Grant entered the pool area where he saw a lifeguard with red trunks pulled taut across his waist and crotch. For a moment Grant won-

234

dered whether anyone else was nude, or whether this was another honour reserved for the foreigner and his escorts, and he felt somewhat reassured to see naked men easing themselves into the water while others were having a quick rinse under the poolside showers where the cameras were being positioned and the lighting rig erected.

Grant's group stopped to discuss the live broadcast before selecting a semicircle of metal chairs from which to hang their towels. It was decided by this committee that a shower was required prior to swimming.

Grant stepped under the closest nozzle and, gasping in the freezing water, he gave his body a quick wipe (along with a few inconspicuous tugs as he attempted to counter the effects of the cold water). Just then the television director introduced himself to Grant, kissing both cheeks, and the man spent fifteen minutes detailing his vision for the broadcast.

The pool was warmer than expected. Grant's comrades stood with him in the shallow end, splashing their chests, and occasionally wiping away hairy rivulets running down their stomachs to their bobbing cocks.

There was an English sign on the nearby wall:

GUARD NOTICE
NO RUNNING, DIVING, ANGER OR HORSEPLAY
THANK YOU

The translator touched Grant's shoulder. 'We have permission to send you our most hardened criminals,' the man said briskly.

'What state are the bodies in?' Grant asked.

'Dead,' the translator confirmed. 'Murderers and rapists and the pathologically insane, all dead.' A triumphant smile.

'Yes, I know they'll be dead,' Grant said, 'that's the whole point of this exercise. I was asking about the body parts themselves. Will you be able to freeze and package individual organs, or are you wanting to transport entire bodies, shaved or flayed or whatever?'

For an additional cost the organs and major muscle groups could be vacuum-packed and frozen. 'Now we swim before your broadcast,' the translator announced.

Grant knocked the water from his goggles and pulled them over his head so that each lens's foamy seal grasped the tender skin around his eyes. Blinking, he readjusted the hard plastic cups and plunged underwater, kicking against the wall.

He surged behind the others, enjoying the feeling of freedom after a week cooped up in the hotel. With a few strokes he allowed himself to drift alone in the shallows while bubbles escaped his ears. In the distance a pair of legs danced over the blue depth; tiny kicks keeping their owner floating in the mirrored surface. Grant drifted past those legs. Everything was slower down here, somehow safer. He resurfaced, saw the translator at the deep end of the pool, and paddled across, breathing hard.

There were more swimmers than he had expected. Almost everyone was tattooed. In the lanes on his right a few musclemen swam lengths. Grant's colleagues floated about, submerging and slipping their heads out of the water, like baffled seals. Everyone wore the regulation goggles: all the better to see you with, my dear.

He enjoyed the feeling of the water against his skin, and despite the weight he'd gained in the past week he felt confident that he still cut a decent figure in the pool. From somewhere came the occasional squeal of ecstasy.

The deep end was more adventurous than the prissy shallows – more given to straying hands and accidental brushing against naked bodies. All very proper and heterosexual above the surface, of course, but with more erotic pull than anything he had experienced in the depths. He glided along, held on to the wall and rested his left elbow on the brick edge. As the swimmers powered past he dipped his head underwater for an excited glimpse of these mermen. Some acknowledged him as they passed, smiling and heading for the shallows.

'Are you having fun?' the translator asked. 'We were wondering, apropos of our earlier discussion, what FK&F's maximum capacity might be?'

Grant considered the question, taking a moment to dip his head under the water to follow the progress of a lithe Henry First-type churning past with his own version of the Australian crawl. 'How many bodies?' Grant clarified.

'Yes, how much meat?'

Of course. Meat. 'How much can you send us?'

'We have an almost limitless supply of recidivists,' the translator said proudly. Hysterical shouting somewhere in the distance. 'Even if we were to focus on the psychotic members of that particular sub-section of re-offenders, the aggressive paedophiles, the multiple murderers, the serial serial-killing machines, those behemoths – how does your Milton put it? – condemned to dwell in adamantine chains and penal fire. Even if we were to limit ourselves to that pool, or, indeed, *this* pool' – he dismissed the room with a swish of his hand – 'we estimate tonnes of raw material each month.'

'I'm sorry' – Grant dropped his voice – 'but are you saying that the men in here are prisoners?'

'Of course. Where else did you think we were taking you?' His comrades laughed. These Westerners! 'We're allowing these inmates to clean up prior to their transformations.'

Grant spotted a gang of huddled men plotting at the far end of the pool. 'Isn't it dangerous, us being here?' No more thoughts of a summer holiday camp.

'Let us worry about that.'

His sense of freedom had slipped away. He wanted to jump out of the water and streak to the exit, but from the clock on the wall he had another thirty minutes before the broadcast was due to begin.

The wire-toothed Russian touched his back and Grant almost leapt out of the water with surprise. He tried hard to convert his shock into a nonchalant gesture.

'Hello,' the man said, 'you've got a nice back. Very good muscle definition.'

Despite the laughable line Grant was compelled to lower himself into the water, his hands hovering in the liquid space between his groin and the surface in order to protect his modesty. A painful shout in the distance was followed by nervous giggles from the swimmers. They looked at him knowingly. He *must* relax. Patrice would never forgive him if he flubbed the broadcast.

'Do *you* work out?' the man said.

'I wasn't aware that you spoke English.'

'We all speak a little English with varying degrees of hit and misses. For sure we all speak. You should work out. You've got a body that would bulk up. Do you like our Citizen Health Spa? This area used to be a farmyard.' He stopped himself, evidently embarrassed by his unguarded reference to something as unpretentious as a farm.

Grant assured him that the Citizen Health Spa met with his approval. 'Everyone seems to know each other,' Grant added.

'In the past this place was only ever open to Party bigwigs.' Again, the forced familiarity with English: bigwigs, indeed.

'And some things never change?'

The man smiled. 'Fat cats. Party pigs.'

Lambs to the slaughter. Grant looked at the man's arms and chest, keen to be seen to be looking. 'Do *you* work out?'

'A little. Hard muscle isn't good for your purposes, though, am I right?'

'No, I would imagine that, for the corporation, hard muscle might be deemed to be rather unpleasant. As for the prisoners . . .' The Russian was older than Grant had first assumed – late forties, perhaps even early fifties. Grant was having a hard time focusing on the conversation without reverting to his stock questions. You don't know anyone else here? Obviously, yes. Are you involved? A yes, again. Are you on the market? A yes to that, too. 'You worked on the farm, didn't you? Livestock?'

The Russian nodded. Beneath the vaulted green roof, lurid with thick cast-iron fronds, were a series of metal palm trees.

They chatted a while longer before rehearsing their questions and answers about the prisoner exchange programme for the broadcast – 'We exchange our old prisoners for empty cells.' – and their voices were soon lost in the echoing hall once intended for upstanding socialist families.

But now the director was shouting for a Mr Whant.

PART V

Temenos

CHAPTER 24

Jump

A HUNDRED YEARS AGO an ailing Russian princess's almost-forgotten descendants threatened to fling themselves off the Broad Way Building's roof and onto the street.

One of the oldest daughters clasped a worn leather case, no longer heavy with diamonds and gold, as her father and uncles conducted muffled negotiations with a neo-Malthusian who planned to convert the building into a refuge for 'wayward girls' (the encyclopaedia's coy phrase). Jump they did not, and because tears and hysteria are no substitute for money it may well be that the daughter was forced to perform certain last-minute labiolingual favours in order to save her family, though if she inherited her ancestor's dental equipment (as evidenced by the princess's miniature, housed in the city museum – a surly little troll whose closed lips appear to hide tusks and fangs) it was onto the streets with the lot of them. The landlord's plans for his cathouse were scuppered by rumours of war, and he made a hasty sale to a local adventurer who used the rooms for storing God-knows-what (loot from petty thefts?). Nothing much is recorded about this adventurer, although it is commonly assumed that he too disappeared, leaving his creditors to haul in the sheriff to force open doors while they clutched their court order. They found empty boxes, discarded bottles and the lingering smell of alcohol.

There are no further references to the building until the end of that century, though a boarding house (sunken beds, paupers' furniture) seems a likely option. Bit by bit the premises became available for rent as its occupants defaulted, disappeared or were found dead.

At the start of the past century the Broad Way was home to a Polish soup kitchen and the city's poor formed lines that zigged across the park and zagged through the freckled glass doors up to the wooden counters and the sweaty Poles. One floor was occupied by five Lithuanian brothers – fired up by Wilbur and Orville's maiden voyage – who had the bad luck to find themselves at the epicentre of a minor quake where they were crushed by falling masonry while negotiating the price of a spruce-wood propeller.

The Broad Way was condemned, boarded up and forgotten in the depression and many wars that followed. Years passed until, in a summer of love, evangelical hippies ripped away the wood from its windows and doors. The hippies later vacated the derelict rooms to take their place in the head-offices of the corporations run by their parents in the northern half of the city, and the indigent, the down-and-out and the drug pushers and takers quickly replaced them. In recent years these disenchanted drug addicts have been bribed out of the high-rise warren and relocated further south by an excited developer.

Recently it appeared that Golden Square would revive: building innards were siphoned into trucks and removed for crushing; trendy restaurants appeared; the markets boomed and peaked – then peaked again; frenzied teenagers became captains of industry with more clout than large Asian economies; and, a few weeks before an almost global financial meltdown, acting upon the generous advice of his petit-bourgeois broker and attorney customers, Henry and Dolores First purchased a prime cut of this real estate. They celebrated their acquisition with a party on the Friday after the sale, and by the time money was spent redecorating the restaurant and equipping the kitchen, Firsts opened to strangely downbeat financial reports and an empty lunchtime sitting. The funds earmarked by the developers for the renaissance in the lower regions of the city were quickly transferred to holding companies on sunny islands, and once again this became an area of possibility. Nothing but possibility. *Almost* successful, *almost* the heart of the business district, *almost* there . . .

Removal vans began edging down alleyways. Mothers assisted their tweenie entrepreneurs with packing boxes and closing their businesses. New projects failed to ignite the required levels of hysteria among the junky rich; all building work around the square ceased, doors were shut and a few conglomerates bought up the empty buildings for a bargain – Furness Kindle & Flint snapped up Obsidian House, that nasty brute on the western side of the square, for their Publishing division – as the financial nuclear winter took hold.

That was how it started. And now for its ending.

*

Summer twilight, a creamy sky, bathed Golden Square and the guests waiting outside the construction site, once a restaurant, in this yolky glow. A cool breeze carried an ocean smell.

The socialites, small and vulnerable, were chatting ('You look lovely,' meaning *You look thin*; 'You look good,' meaning *You look healthy* meaning *You look fat* meaning *You're past your prime* meaning *You're old*); each paying close attention to the competition's potentially embarrassing final round in order to recount it later – their teeth wet with excitement when they explained how they had witnessed Henry First's eventual downfall.

Eyes were drawn to the restaurant's glum, if somewhat chaotic, interior. In *there*, do you think? It was clear that the renovation – DANGER, NO ENTRY, PROHIBITED – was dragging on a bit. A life of its own. Rome not built in a day. But would the show go on?

Felix Stoll sheltered under the Broad Way's awning, which extended over the pavement. He sported a pair of gold-plated Dior sunglasses, covering most of his forehead and cheeks like a large butterfly, and a dusky chinchilla coat draped over his shoulders, a lush breathing beast of a garment, which revealed its white miniver lining when he swung it loose to hang over his arm. His mauve plus fours sported a matching miniver trim, as did the blue sunhat tethered to a leather strap around his neck. There was evidence of hair transplants on his scalp. Surprisingly, there were no tassels on his cuffs and no pom-poms on his socks. A sign, perhaps, of tremendous restraint, or last-minute remorse, on the part of the couturier who had flogged him the outfit.

Felix took off his glasses and began chewing one of the golden arms. Despite the sweat-drenched cashmere under-coat, despite his gloves and scarf, it was clear that he had lost weight. Skin hung from his body. The top part of his face was gaunt – his eyes and cheeks hollowed and bruised – while the bottom half retained its familiar plump appearance, not because the skin was still taut with fat but rather because it now hung from his face and draped his expressions like a heavy burka.

He glanced down at his body, sensitive to the crowd's inspection, and then clasped his arms to his chest, hugging himself, possibly afraid of adding to his bulk. He pulled his belt, making himself comfortable, and keen observers noticed the rows of newly gouged eyelets on either side of the buckle.

The limo carrying Patrice Czarny and the judges had been parked in front of Firsts for ten minutes when Patrice saw Dolores approach the vehicle. Patrice would wait a reasonable period of time – she stuck to the rules – but if no food was served then Firsts would be withdrawn from the competition.

Henry had left Patrice a voicemail asking when he should announce the Furness Kindle & Flint acquisition. She studied the restaurant. Not in there, surely? 'The renovations are taking much longer than expected,' she told the judges as they left the confines of the limo and waited in that pearly glow, that subtle ocean breeze. 'A great pity.'

'Our guests of honour,' Dolores said, taking Patrice's hand – look everyone, the *best* of friends! – and the judges followed with the rest behind them. Patrice allowed herself to be led through the Broad Way Building's narrow lobby, past the waiters on either side of the elevators, and, after an unglamorous ride, followed by an awkward scramble up the metal fire escape, they were on the roof.

Laid out on this weathered surface was a grid of tables with hard white tablecloths silhouetted against the evening sky. Waiters in white; violinists playing soft music; Henry First and his staff at the northern end, waiting alongside a small marquee.

The city's traffic looked carefree from up here: long roads of vanilla light alternating with raspberry. A cool breeze fresh with salt; gulls calling in the distance above the rush hour. If someone stood at the roof's lip, their sight no longer blurred by the candles burning on each table, they might choose to glance across the square at the Publishing building with its diminutive occupants.

Here it is: the summery twilight bathing Golden Square; the creamy evening sky; the cool breeze carrying the scent of surf; waiters in white . . . Simply disastrous.

Drawn on the bathhouse's walls were fading beach scenes. Grant Whant would have preferred to spend more time looking at his Russian companion's arms and chest but the director's chat about their broadcast had brought with it a spinsterish modesty, and, even though he was still temped to focus on the man's large hands playing in the water, Grant's eyes were drawn to the waiting cameras.

The windows were pitted with rain. The director had noticed the wet glass and shouted at his assistants to get the dismal weather out of shot. 'We need to prepare you,' he told Grant. 'Patrice thinks that a bathrobe will create a sophisticated tone.'

Grant had enjoyed his shower and had happily dressed in the flannel get-up. Further away he could hear the sounds of bathers enjoying their lives. He smiled.

'Five minutes,' the director said, pointing to a metal door at the end of the shower chamber. 'I need you to stand over there. Don't go in that room.'

On the small monitor to one side of the camera Grant could see grainy images of Henry's final meal at Firsts.

Felix Stoll clambered up the metal stairs onto the roof and found Henry overseeing work in the marquee.

'You're not selling out, Chef?' Felix said, sniffing the air. He was wanting something numinous to occur because, like a junkie, each hit wasn't carrying the punch he craved. He gnawed the inside of his cheek: chewing and scraping.

'Don't you look smart,' Henry said. 'I'm selling, not selling out.' A pie on a plate, a pie on a plate, a pie on a plate . . .

'A Freudian slip, forgive me.' Felix's front teeth were smaller than Henry remembered, his shiny red gums like an impressive sunset. His nails had been bitten until they bled.

'I can feel Death here,' Felix continued, 'just behind my eyes, watching. The doctors can't find disease but I can feel it waiting inside me. It's like I'm burning up, Chef, and one day I'll die mid-step. You know autolysis, Chef? The body eats itself. The cells digest themselves. I'm not in control of this crapped-out body any more. I wake up with an erection as hard as anything I remember from my teens but elsewhere my blood pressure is as weak as piss.' There were severe nosebleeds, yet despite the migraines that followed, they left Felix feeling at ease and nourished. He sniffed a pie.

'I've prepared you a special meal for this evening, Felix,' Henry said, 'but that comes later. These pies are for the pigs out there.' Pie plate pig, pie plate pig, pie plate pig . . .

'Do you need help convincing Patrice to buy the restaurant, Chef?' Felix said, wiping his face. 'I still think you should open more restaurants, but if you need me to entice her just say the word.'

'I made her an offer she couldn't refuse,' was Henry's only response.

The air was sharp. Patrice Czarny's foot throbbed despite the tranquilisers and painkillers, the breeze played havoc with her hair, and Janique had just told her that it was not bright enough to film without lights. Henry waited at the far end of the roof – he'd sauntered over to welcome her and the executives – and now he awaited her signal to serve the meal. She would speak; his food would be a disaster; everyone would leave. All he wanted to talk about was the money.

When the music stopped Patrice Czarny would stand and welcome the crowd.

Grant Whant had been watching proceedings on the monitor for half an hour. Patrice was speaking about her achievements and the sacrifices she had made. Next, Janique shared about Ingmar. Patrice, hugging Janique tight, dedicated Henry's meal to her and to Ingmar's memory, and then, without warning, she handed over to Grant.

'I am standing in a state-of-the-art supply facility managed by FK&F Offshore Partners,' Grant announced to the camera. 'Behind me are the Roman-style baths where guests can relax and enjoy luxurious pampering. I've just experienced one of the treatments and, let me tell you, it was fabulous. I emerged stress-free and wholly cleansed.' The camera panned over the bathers.

'Each participant in today's event has been individually selected according to rigorously defined criteria. I spoke with some of the lucky ones earlier and they are all confident that they can deliver the high standards expected of them. Only after each nominee has passed a series of medical exams will they be considered for this prestigious journey. Join me in taking a moment, ladies and gentlemen, to welcome and thank these talented people.'

Applause and endorsement from the First World.

Patrice was talking again. 'And now, Grant,' she said, 'show our guests the rest of the facility.'

The door at the end of the shower room had opened to reveal an L-shaped room: a concrete pen. Inside that pumice chamber lay his destiny, Grant was sure of it. Inside was the meaning of life. He was prepared to die for love.

'Promise me one thing,' Grant Whant said softly to the director, 'promise that Henry gets me.' The director looked at him blankly. Grant tried to find his Russian friend, but the man had gone. 'Tell Patrice that Henry gets me. She owes me.'

'Grant, we're waiting . . .' Patrice said.

Dolores had choreographed the ballet: the corps swept past the tables, depositing plates, and when the waiters had finished they proceeded towards the metal steps that led down from the roof. As the final meals were laid in front of the guests, Henry and Dolores followed their staff down to the elevator. Henry had served his concentrated dose – his successful failure – and left the diners to their fate.

Patrice Czarny sat down as the people around her began eating. There would be no sale. All eyes were on the large screen showing live images of Grant Whant entering a room.

Grant watched the proceedings at Firsts on the monitor: the squeals of delight as the respectfully attired diners bounded across tables, sunk their teeth into nearby flesh or flung themselves into Golden Square.

He stood in the cold room. Patrice's plans for immortality were now his own. On-screen there was a battle between man and gravity. On-screen the wounded rejoiced as they put themselves up for adoption by the Czarny cause. On-screen they watched him.

The metal door shut in front of him and cut off the images. Inside this chamber the corporation would adenine, thymine, cytosine and guanine him. The door lay flush with the wall: no handles, no hinges, No Exit.

A white biohazard suit, like a piping cone thick with icing, walked into the enclosure. The being in the suit wiped its gloves on the pink apron hanging from its waist, and took Grant's arm. The reflective mask showed a distorted, but calm Grant Whant staring back at himself. He allowed himself to be led by the man. His passivity in unfamiliar environments had prepared Grant well.

The delirious squeals coming down the corridor were now almost as loud as those being broadcast from Firsts' rooftop. The shouts grew louder. Just over there. Just beyond the corner at the far end of the room.

The iron hook was a surprise, coming from behind, and it pierced an intervertebral disk in his neck before slicing his epiglottis. And so his contribution had begun . . .

Stunning an animal changes its flavour, he knew, and he appreciated being left to watch his limbs hang meekly by his side as the machinery hoisted him above the concrete floor and allowed him to take flight. There followed the blade's wet burn across his throat and gut, and the accidental *whoops!* as his innards fell out of his liberated body – his invagination almost complete.

His steady journey down this conveyor, bloodless head to one side, continued in silence until his anoxic form was bathed by superheated steam that allowed his skin to be peeled with ease.

Soon he would be ready for the stock-pot.

THE END

READ MORE IN PELTA

Poetry

Aurora Leigh Vol. 1 Elizabeth Barrett Browning (B00JDWEA2K)
Books I – IV exploring women's role in society.

Aurora Leigh Vol. 2 Elizabeth Barrett Browning (B00JWXAC22)
Books V – IX describing Aurora's fate.

Childe Harold's Pilgrimage Lord Byron (B00BE2U3R8)
Byron's epic poem about a melancholic and defiant outcast.

In Memoriam Alfred Lord Tennyson (B00HUCSOPY)
Tennyson's poetic expression of grief.

Odes John Keats (B00L5THQ16)
Keats's awe-inspiring poems.

Ovid's Banquet of Sense George Chapman (B00K02JU86)
A burlesque masterpiece.

The Prelude William Wordsworth (B00I279YDW)
The autobiographical poem dealing with the poet's infancy, schooling
and his trips to the Alps and revolutionary France.

The Rape of the Lock Alexander Pope (B00L1NL8C4)
The great mock-heroic poem.

Rime of the Ancient Mariner Samuel Taylor Coleridge (B00L47A37S)
Sin, retribution and the nightmare voyage.

The Seasons James Thomson (B00KZ17P98)
Thomson's contemplation of the seasons' influence.

Songs of Innocence & Experience William Blake (B00L2CNSS6)
From innocence through experience to enlightened innocence.

Sonnets William Shakespeare (B00IKUDMN4)
Shakespeare's love poems.

The Task William Cowper (B00J35EA9U)
Cowper's meditation on nature, country life and faith.

www.peltabooks.com